DAUGHTER OF THE TAROT

CLARE MARCHANT

Boldwood

First published in Great Britain in 2025 by Boldwood Books Ltd.

Cover Design by JD Smith Design Ltd.

Cover Images: Shutterstock

A CIP catalogue record for this book is available from the British Library.

Paperback ISBN 978-1-83603-057-7

Large Print ISBN 978-1-83603-058-4

Hardback ISBN 978-1-83603-056-0

Ebook ISBN 978-1-83603-059-1

Kindle ISBN 978-1-83603-060-7

Audio CD ISBN 978-1-83603-051-5

MP3 CD ISBN 978-1-83603-052-2

Digital audio download ISBN 978-1-83603-054-6

This book is printed on certified sustainable paper. Boldwood Books is dedicated to putting sustainability at the heart of our business. For more information please visit https://www.boldwoodbooks.com/about-us/sustainability/

Boldwood Books Ltd, 23 Bowerdean Street, London, SW6 3TN

www.boldwoodbooks.com

For my fellow Fivers. My thanks always for your friendship, support, laughter and love.

For my fellow Fivers. My thanks always for your friendship, support, laughter and love.

PROLOGUE
1629, MILAN

The thick, palpable, metallic aroma of blood is mixed with that of sour, stale perspiration and wood smoke, filling the dark chamber. Now, the once tall golden beeswax candles are burned low, guttering and swaying in the draught from an open window and the only sounds in the empty void are the cracks and snapping from a log recently thrown on the fire. Flames throw dancing orange forms to rear up the walls in ghostly taunts.

A sharp rap at the door causes Portia to turn her head, wondering who dares to venture near a chamber in which hovers the angel of death, looking for the chance to swoop, to claim.

For hours she has been listening to the sound of carts in the courtyard below being laden with belongings and furniture, as Lorenzo prepares to leave for his villa in the hills where the air is clean. They have now left, and she suspects he will not be far behind them. Milan is rife with the plague, barely any houses left untouched, and she knows he is afraid to wait a moment longer. Her teeth are gritted so hard, it is as though they are welded together, and she may never open her mouth again. He cares for no one but himself.

It is no surprise that he, together with his brother Niccolo, are preparing to flee. Will he wait for the babe to be born? She prays that he does not, because she knows he'll take the child, leaving the women behind to live or die. He cares for nothing other than himself and ensuring his family bloodline continues.

Soon the plague doctor in his black cloak and terrifying beaked mask, a dark malevolent bird, will be at the door instructing it to be daubed with the red paint of the damned, before being nailed shut to prevent the disease from spreading. Many of their neighbours have already succumbed and lie dying, or already dead, within their homes. No amount of riches and grand marble palaces can stop the illness from occupying any house it chooses. And it has chosen theirs. Now it is a matter of fate as to whether they survive or perish.

The door opens a little, although the visitor remains in relative safety on the other side.

'The master sends me,' comes the voice of Lorenzo's steward. 'He wishes to know if the baby has yet come. If it has, he will take it to the hills, to safety.'

'Tell him it has not,' Portia calls from behind the closed bed drapes. 'Has he said if we may travel with him, will he wait?'

'No, it is too dangerous. For the present you must wait here with the servants he is leaving behind, those he does not need to accompany him.' Lorenzo is behaving just as she'd guessed he would, as the cards had shown her earlier that day. The Three of Swords told of a betrayal and that heartbreak was imminent. The Tower spoke of upheaval, an ending, and the opportunity for a new start. 'He says that God willing, he will see everyone, including his child, on his return.'

With that, the sound of running footsteps disappear into the distance along the white marble corridors which lead towards the enormous entrance hall sitting in splendour beneath a dome exquisitely painted to recreate the beautiful washed indigo skies of Milan.

Portia's mind is racing. She must leave, there is not a moment to lose, or they'll be imprisoned forever. The moment she hears Lorenzo and Niccolo's horses receding into the distance she will be gone, disappearing as a shadow when the sun is veiled by clouds. Running before her lies are discovered, for she is now in grave danger. As the tiny newborn baby girl on the bed pushes its fist into its mouth Portia is already placing jewellery she has snatched from a coffer, hiding it between layers of clothes whilst making a mental list of everything she needs to gather together, she has but minutes to do what she must. The Tower has foretold the truth.

1

2025, LONDON

Beatrice peered into the open box and sighed. Folding the top back over, she stood up and stretched her back, putting her hands on her hips as she looked around her. Although she was standing in a small oasis of clear floor, the rest of the room was piled high with her belongings, and she was now running out of places to search.

Somewhere was a box containing her kettle and teabags. She'd deliberately packed them together, thinking they'd be easy to find once she arrived but now, they were nowhere to be seen. And she was becoming increasingly desperate for a hot drink. For a moment she thought about ringing her father to ask if he could remember which box they were in, but he'd still be driving back to Nottingham. Which reminded her, she patted her empty pockets optimistically, she also now had no idea where she'd put her phone. Another thing to look for.

Climbing over two large blue bags containing flat-packed storage, she gave a little cheer as she spotted a box she'd previously missed and reaching in, she took out her prized kettle and a tin of teabags.

'Yay, well done, Bea,' she congratulated herself as she made her way to the small kitchen off the living room. Her words echoed in the empty space, a stark reminder that she was there on her own. It was the first time she'd lived somewhere that wasn't home, somewhere that wasn't filled with the sound of other people's voices.

The fridge already contained milk and a few food essentials she'd bought the night before in her home village. Even walking around the local supermarket had felt poignant, the last time she'd be there after so many years of popping in to pick bits up. Having only visited her new flat once, and that was primarily to view the shop downstairs, she had no idea where the nearest food shops were. And, she reminded herself, her precious Mini was still sitting on the drive at home so she would have to walk or catch a bus.

She paused for a moment. That small village close to Nottingham was no longer home, she reminded herself. The house had been sold, and Dad would be leaving within days – he'd moved on. Of course, she still loved him and always would, but right now she was so angry with him she needed to get away, to be on her own. She'd been barely able to get more than a few words out on the journey down.

Carrying a steaming cup of tea, she clambered around the boxes and bags scattered across the room and went into her bedroom where a new duvet and bedding had been thrown on the bed. Suddenly she felt exhausted and putting her tea on the bedside table, she sat down.

Now she was still, she could hear the constant hum of traffic on the main road. Even though her shop and flat were down a traffic-free mews, the sound travelled. She'd have to get used to it, this was her life now and she needed to make a success of it. To prove herself, and to do her mum proud.

Picking up a framed photo sitting beside the bed, she smiled at the image, her parents on their silver wedding anniversary. Her mother's head thrown back in laughter, with her hair – still so dark – pouring down her back like molten tar, whilst Beatrice's father looked at her, the love in his eyes shining. Back then was a different era, it felt like a different country and that now they were living in a new world, one she felt lost in. She kissed her fingers and held them to her mother's face before replacing the photo and closing the curtains on the scary new life waiting beyond the window.

2

1644, LONDON

Walking along Soper Lane towards Cheapside, Portia watched her feet, mindful of where she trod. The cobbles had a channel along the middle for water and effluence to run down towards the river, and nobody wanted to accidentally step in it. At the dark edges damp slippery moss covered the stone and she was placing her feet gingerly, whilst holding on tightly to the young girl who walked beside her.

The narrow lane was bustling with people going about their business. Tall, overhanging buildings, their jettied upper floors stealing the light before it reached the ground below, left them in a semi-permanent darkness. It was no bother for Portia, but for fifteen-year-old Vittoria, her eyesight slowly deteriorating year on year, it made seeing where she was going more difficult. With her arm safely tucked through Portia's they navigated past the people milling around who were either stopping to chat or to view wares laid out on the stalls which spilled over from the main thoroughfare and busy market place ahead of them.

Small boys, those running errands and others who'd been ousted from beneath their mother's feet, darted between the adults. One of them almost knocked Vittoria flying and Portia gripped her even closer, hurling a few ribald insults at the children as they disappeared into the distance. She always slipped back into her native Italian when she was enraged, and she reminded herself that thankfully the boys wouldn't understand what she had just cursed them with.

As they stepped out into the brighter sunshine of Cheapside, Portia took a deep lungful of the cleaner air here. The alleyways and narrow streets always held an aroma of food, both that which was being cooked, and that which was no longer edible and had been left on the street. Rats brazenly scurried between people's feet as they searched for their next meal. It was all unpleasant and yet was a part of normal city life. She paused for a moment as a brigade of armed militia marched past. With the country in the grips of a civil war, the recently built forts and trenches on the edge of the city housed many soldiers, and already she barely noticed them.

'Where shall we go first?' Portia asked. 'We need to buy bread, and we must visit Old Fish Street as it is Friday.' Her Catholic roots from Italy had never left her despite England now being for the most part Puritan. In order to blend in with her neighbours she prayed alongside them at St Pancras, their local parish church.

'Might we visit the haberdasher whilst we are here?' Vittoria asked, her face alight. She may not be able to sew as proficiently these days, but she could see the colours of the ribbons with which Portia decorated her dresses and wove through her deep auburn hair which flowed down her back, its myriad of golden hues dancing amongst the deeper red. Together with her hazel eyes, it was unusual colouring for an Italian. It was, however, identical to that of her father, whose ancestors had travelled from England to Italy in the Crusades. Portia quickly put her memories of him out of her mind and smiled instead at Vittoria who radiated her delight and excitement at the thought of new ribbons.

She was the most beautiful person to walk the earth, and Portia knew it wasn't just she who believed so; she'd seen the number of men who looked the girl up and down as they passed by. With Vittoria unaware of the attraction she generated, Portia tried not to utter more of her oaths, because she could see what the girl could not. She might be of marriageable age but Portia felt a fierce burn of protection in her chest – there was no possibility she would allow any man to court her.

'Come then, let us go there first,' she suggested, 'and then purchase our food afterwards.'

They made their way to their favourite stall, where the owner and his wife made a fuss of Vittoria. They knew her well and insisted on holding up various trimmings for her to choose from. Some of her hair had slipped from the front of the kerchief on her head and it caught the sunlight like burnished copper. She held up a length of deep green velvet against it.

'What about this, Mama?' she asked, the dimples deep in her cheeks as she smiled and raised her eyebrows. Portia returned her smile and nodded. It didn't matter what was suggested, she would agree. Never had she imagined just how much she could love someone – nay, worship them – so much. She would lay down her own life in an instant for the child. Sometimes she woke at night and lay on her back listening to the soft inhale and exhale beside her, the two of them sharing the bigger bed. Often it was accompanied by the sound of Maria snoring from the other side of the room, the one bedroom they all shared above their living space, reached by some uneven wooden stairs. Although Maria was a servant, having originally come from Italy with them as Vittoria's wet nurse, Portia now thought of her as so much more. They were friends, equals.

She was about to ask the price of the items Vittoria had chosen when a woman, keeping her head lowered, approached Portia.

'Excuse me, mistress, I am told you are the Italian who can read people's future in the tarot cards?' The voice was husky as though it hurt to open her mouth and from the limited parts of her face Portia could see, it appeared the woman had a large bruise on her forehead, the purple now fading at the edges to a dirty yellow.

'That is I,' Portia agreed. 'Although I cannot tell you the way your life may unfold, my cards will, however, offer you possible solutions to questions. Do you want a reading? It will cost you sixpence.'

'Please, I would like that very much. I know where you live, may I call by this afternoon? After the church bells have chimed three of the hour?' Still the woman had not lifted her face and Portia had a suspicion what sort of reading this would be. Sometimes these women came to her, and she had no prior notion of what would take place, but she would bet a gold noble she knew what would be requested today. Though if it did, then it would cost more than the sixpence she'd just asked for. Except, in truth, she'd do it for nothing if that was all the woman could afford.

'I will see you then,' she confirmed and without another word she walked over to the stall holder and paid him for the ribbons Vittoria was holding. Arm in arm, they moved on to the other parts of the market they needed to visit, purchasing carrots, cabbage and leeks before going on to buy barley, and then the fish for dinner. They'd need to eat early so Maria and Vittoria could be gone from their home when her customer arrived.

* * *

By three o'clock the earlier sun was now hidden behind heavy grey clouds, the air prickling with damp as though the clouds were leaking because they were so full, the rain seeping out regardless. Maria decided she and Vittoria would visit their next-door neighbour, who, with five young children at her skirts, was always at home. It was a noisy and hectic house, but the small ones loved Vittoria, and she them. She'd happily play games and amuse them for hours, which was greatly appreciated by their mother. Maria had made small buns with the remains of some honey and dried fruit and they took those with them.

'Back when the clocks chime five?' she asked. Portia agreed, hugging Vittoria goodbye before the two women departed. Every time she held the young girl and breathed in the sweetness of her soft skin, Portia didn't want to let go. Precious, she was so precious, but she could never know what Portia had gone through for her to be there. That was her secret, something so dangerous she could never speak of it. If the truth were to come out then she would lose Vittoria forever, and she'd do anything, lay down her life if needed, to prevent that.

3

1644

The knock at the door was hesitant and quiet, so quiet in fact that at first Portia was unsure if she'd heard anything. Opening it a little way, she saw a woman waiting, and stepping back, she ushered her visitor in.

Their home was small, downstairs consisting of a single room with the timber frame of the building visible, the wooden struts standing upright along the walls with pale plastered panels in between. The heavy beams which ran across the ceiling made it low, and the room dark.

In the middle of the space stood a long table, its rough surface marked with decades of scratches and gouges. Against the walls, a tall oak press and two deep, carved wooden trunks filled most of the room. Three chairs sat at the table, whilst two more together with a settle were positioned near the fireplace.

In one corner, a doorway led to a scullery, and from there to the yard beyond. Over the lively flickering flames in the fireplace a pot of water simmered, wisps of steam drifting up from it. The wall above was blackened with a column of accumulated soot from years of the chimney not drawing properly.

'Take your cloak off,' Portia suggested. It was glistening with tiny droplets of water now suspended in the swirling mist outside. 'I can dry it in front of the fire for you,' she added, 'so it will be warm on your journey home.'

The woman, who had introduced herself as Mary, paused for a moment as if weighing up what to do but then she undid the ties at her neck and, dropping the hood back, she swung the garment from her shoulders. At that point she had no option but to lift her head and push back her hair, the colour of burnished oak, to display that which Portia had earlier guessed she'd been attempting to hide. A now partially faded bruise stretched across the entire width of her forehead and disappeared into her hairline. Her nose had a bump on the top, a sure sign it had been broken at some point, and now she was closer, Portia could see Mary was also holding one of her arms at an odd angle. Her washed blue eyes had deep grey circles, beneath which spoke of fatigue and a life broken.

'Take a seat.' Portia spoke gently, pointing to a stool at the table as she retrieved her cards from a cupboard built into the wall. Mary had her purse in her hand and upending it, she tipped the contents onto the table. Several coins rolled off the edge and onto the floor and bending down, Portia picked up three groats, placing them back with the rest of the money. 'I only require sixpence for a reading,' she said as she picked up the small silver coin and held it up.

'In truth I did not come for a reading.' Mary's voice came out in a whisper. 'I need to disappear. Forever. I am told you can do this for me.'

Portia didn't reply as she took her cards from their wrapping and placed the piece of silk to one side before shuffling them. The woman in front of her was one of many who had come to her over the years with this request. Rumours spread, whispers behind hands, stealthy words by candlelight to those who needed to do what she, fifteen years before, had also done. To escape, flee a dangerous life and start again elsewhere. To find safety.

At first it had only been the occasional appeal for her help, but they were coming all too frequently now. Twice in the past three months, and now another one. How could she refuse? She needed to be vigilant though, she must have no doubts the entreaty was coming from someone who truly required it, because what she undertook carried great risk. Questions were now being asked on the streets, she'd read the pamphlets herself.

'I am not sure I understand,' she replied, with a bland expression on her face as she moved the coins still on the table to one side with the edge of her hand and carried on shuffling the pack. 'To what are you referring?'

'You can see my face.' Mary's voice wavered and then grew stronger, her eyes filling with tears. 'He will take my life unless I go, but I have nowhere to run where he cannot seek me out. My family are all dead and he will find me if I hide at a neighbour's home. I must flee somewhere far, somewhere he will not know to look. Please tell me you are able do as I ask, indeed as I have been assured you can, to help women escape their tormented lives.'

Without speaking, Portia dealt three cards out, face down, and placed the rest of the pack on the table. She studied the battered face in front of her. It was guileless, and as her customer placed her shaking hands in her lap, she knew she must help. It would be done so discreetly, The Devil card introduced by a sleight of hand so swift it would be impossible to detect, and the card would be dealt.

'The Eight of Swords,' she began as the first card turned

showed a young woman wearing a blindfold and bound to a post. 'This card denotes confinement, restriction. Sometimes in our life, even though it may not be physically, we are stopped by others from being who we wish to be.' She glanced up through her eyelashes, but the woman's face was blank as though she hadn't heard what was being said. However, the rubbing of her hands together in her lap, as though she were continuously washing them, told a different story.

Portia turned the next card. 'And now we see The Magician.' The card displayed a young man dressed in a red cape. 'He is telling you that although you feel you are in a situation with no way of escape, if you believe in yourself you will be able to turn your intentions into the truth. And finally...' She flipped over the third card. 'The Devil. He asks of us what is true, and what is an illusion.' At the sight of Satan, with his horns and fiery tail dancing with a wicked maniacal grin on his face, Mary recoiled and pulled away. Portia placed a hand over the woman's own, now gripping the edge of the table.

'This is not a terrible card,' she reassured. 'It tells of a new life. What is the truth in your world, and what is shown to others, the illusion. Listen carefully to what I tell you. When you leave here you will take a copy of this Devil card, and you must be prepared to flee in two nights' time. At Venours Wharf there will be a boat waiting. One that shall take you to those who can help you escape to a new life in a city far away. You must understand you can never return, and neither may you speak of this to anyone, not even those you believe you can trust. Those women who have reputedly been snatched from their beds and murdered in this city, they are all women now living new, free lives elsewhere. Is this truly what you desire?'

Mary let her breath out in a long shaky stream as she sat up straighter and pulled her shoulders back.

'It is,' she confirmed with a decisive nod. 'I have nothing here now. I was carrying his babe and he punched me so hard it came early and did not survive, and yet he shows no remorse. Rather, he blames me for riling him and is now intent on making me pregnant once again. I simply cannot bring a child into this life. Please help me, I beg you. I will go anywhere to escape him.'

Portia removed a crown together with a half-noble from the pile of coins on the table and slipped them into the pocket on the front of her kirtle. Going to the cupboard from where she had taken her cards, she returned with an additional one. It looked all but identical to The Devil card she'd just turned.

'Take this,' she said. 'Remember, be at the wharf in two days' time, on Thursday night when the clocks chime ten; it will be dark then. My friend John, the boatman, will be waiting to take you to Teddington, and from there women will assist your journey to Winchester where you will be safe. There is danger in being on the streets at night on your own, but it is a risk you must take if you wish to go ahead with this.'

'I promise I will be there.' Mary nodded as she slipped the card into her pocket. 'And I thank you with all my heart for what you are doing. Words are not enough to express all that I feel.'

Collecting her cloak, she put it back on and pulled the hood up to obscure her face once more. Portia gave her an encouraging hug, trying to imbue the girl with the strength she'd need, and she was gone.

Waiting until she was on her own again, Portia slowly packed the cards away. She would go to the river later to find John and tell him another defeated woman needed to escape her life, to start again anew, elsewhere. From the cupboard she removed four small pots of paint, together with a fine brush and a piece of card she'd made by gluing together three offcuts of parchment. Now she needed to make another replica of The Devil card to replace the one she'd just handed over. She'd made so many over the years she was proficient at copying it, starting on the back with the black sword and then gold, red and blue flowers flowing from the brush. It was incumbent on her once again to help a woman depart, just as she herself once had, when she had taken the two most precious things in the world: Vittoria, and her cards. They were all she now had of the family she'd left behind, but she'd fled with her life, hers and Vittoria's, and she was thankful every day for that. No longer was she someone's possession to be treated however they wished. Finally, she was safe.

* * *

The evening air was balmy, summer finally beginning to show her face. For the present it was just shy glances, but she offered the promise of her full glory expected in the months to come. The church bells chimed seven o'clock as the last rays of sun filtered between the tall buildings to reflect off small panes of glass, throwing long shadows along the ground. Soon it would be dark and unsafe to be out in the alleyways and back lanes, the night watchmen looking for those who were out. Portia needed to be careful, but she was used to it and knew what she was doing.

Hurrying down the narrow streets, she reached the river where steps led down into the water. She couldn't guarantee John would be there, sometimes he was found along the river at Hey Wharf, but somehow she could always find him when she needed to. He was dependable and she was grateful beyond words for that, he brought a level of comfort to her life and not just because of what he helped her do.

She'd met him when Maria had innocently told her of a man

whose sister had been brutally murdered by her husband, and how he'd been denied revenge because the perpetrator fell into the Thames and drowned. She'd guessed – rightly – that he would want to exact the vengeance he had been deprived of another way.

It had taken her a long while to find John and to watch him from afar before deciding that she could trust him. He was unmarried and didn't spend long in the taverns drinking. She couldn't depend on someone who might get drunk and loose-tongued. Eventually she'd approached him and, hoping her instincts about him were correct, told him what she wanted. In turn, he had admitted to her that his late brother-in-law hadn't fallen into the river, despite what the eyewitnesses described. Because whilst yes, the man had been inebriated, nobody saw, as he staggered along the riverside, a boot in the middle of his back which had helped him towards his murky, wet, final resting place. Portia had known then he was the right person to help her and now their partnership was a strong one, both of them intent on helping abused women to escape.

Over the time she'd known him they'd grown close and despite what he'd done to protect his sister, murdering another man, just thinking about him made her heart feel warm. She'd wondered on more than one occasion if her feelings were recip-rocated, but if they were he never spoke of it. Despite that, she'd noticed the way he seemed to deliberately brush his fingers against hers, that he had a special smile only she saw. He was quiet, stoic and she truly hoped that eventually he would find it in himself to ask her to walk out with him, because she would agree in a second.

Thankfully, as she approached, she spotted him just heading towards the river steps in his small boat, and she waited until he arrived and his passenger, a well-dressed goodwife who inclined her head to Portia in acknowledgement, had departed, before she went to where he was now tying the rope from his boat to a steel mooring post.

'Tis good to see you,' John greeted her, his wide smile lighting up his face. Portia couldn't help but grin in return, her heart giving a little skip as it did every time she saw him. He wasn't over tall, but his rowing had built up his upper body and arms so they were wide and muscular, and she always felt safe when she was with him.

'And you,' she replied, following him to a bench where they sat side by side.

'You have a job for me?' he asked. They never spoke of what they did out loud, nobody must ever know of what she arranged.

'I do.' She nodded. 'Her name is Mary, and she will be here on Thursday at the usual time. She has her card to give you so you know that it is she.'

'Excellent,' John said. 'I will go now to Teddington to arrange her onward progress. Do not fear, you know that everything will happen as it should, as it always does.'

'Thank you,' she replied, leaning against him just slightly, feeling the firmness of his upper body. 'Here.' She took a handful of coins from her pocket and handed them to him. 'She couldn't pay much, as often happens with these women, but this is your share. I could not do what I do without you.'

'You know why I help,' he reminded her. 'If I can assist in saving even one woman then it is worth it. I wish we had been able to do the same for my sister. There are too many men who use their fists without a thought and no woman should endure that.'

With a lengthy hug goodbye, which lingered just a little longer than appropriate between a man and a woman who were not related or in a relationship, Portia stepped away and walked swiftly home through the now lowering twilight. The golden setting sun filtered where it was able through the tall, compacted buildings. It was no longer warm but that didn't matter because Portia felt a heat inside, the way she always did after she'd seen John. There was a lightness, a little skip in her step.

4

2025

Belting out the words to 'The Best', her favourite Tina Turner track, Beatrice's singing was, she admitted to herself, fairly raucous as she joined in with the radio. Even to her own ears she was off-key, but she was in a positive mood and the song reflected her new burst of confidence. She could do this.

When she'd met with the letting agent just six weeks before, she'd only managed a quick viewing of the shop and flat. He'd looked bored as he explained to her that the establishment had been empty for several months, traders preferring shops on the main thoroughfare, not tucked away down a quiet mews. She didn't believe him though. Together with hers were five other small independent establishments including a wonderful bakery. Earlier that morning, the smell of fresh baking had drawn Beatrice in to buy a croissant, and the owner, having discovered that she was a new neighbour, introduced herself as Jo. The adjacent shops had attractive, well-designed displays in their windows, and already Beatrice had seen customers going back and forth, despite the letting agent's gloomy predictions.

Now, looking around properly, her shop was even more

wonderful than she remembered. She may even declare it perfect. It was small, there was no denying that, and despite the tall ceilings and a beautiful Georgian bay window with small rectangular pieces of thick, uneven glass, it was dark and exactly what she wanted. Once she'd dressed the space appropriately, the gloom would play to her advantage.

Behind the front half of the shop with its built-in shelving and old display cabinet topped with a dark wood counter, was a back room from which led the stairs to her flat. Beyond that sat a tiny kitchen. With barely any light penetrating from the shop and kitchen, this inner space was even gloomier, and it was just right for what she intended for it. A few lamps and maybe some candles, and this would be exactly the calm place she'd envisaged for her customers, and she was certain they would come.

She'd already spent the morning cleaning, and it was now almost lunchtime. Ignoring her growling stomach, she couldn't wait to bring her stock, which she'd been buying for months in preparation for this moment, downstairs and start putting it out on the shelves. To see everything as she'd imagined it so many times. Washing her hands, she ran upstairs and began to carry the boxes down, placing each of them reverently on the floor.

After she'd stacked up the packs of cards she'd ordered from an online wholesaler, she brought down the last four boxes. These were the special ones, the cardboard now faded and ingrained with dust after several decades in the attic at home. Within them were the cards her mother had collected over many years, imagining herself doing just what Beatrice was now undertaking in her memory, fulfilling her heritage and bringing her tarot readings to people who needed her.

The antique sets, the most precious ones, were placed carefully on velvet runners laid in the display cabinets. Not only were these valuable in monetary terms, more importantly they would become cherished by someone who felt an affinity with the cards, and only those who truly understood them would know that.

On the radio Tina Turner had been replaced with Robbie Williams, and Beatrice's voice became increasingly croaky as she continued to sing along. It was only as she paused to take a breath before launching into the refrain of 'Angels' that she realised someone was knocking on the shop door. Turning the music down, she let up the roller blind to find a man, she'd guess a few years younger than herself, grinning at her. He held his hand up in a greeting and mouthed, '*Hi*'.

Beatrice quickly opened the door. 'Sorry,' she apologised, 'I had the radio on.' The old-fashioned shop bell she'd noticed earlier remained silent, and she made a mental note to try and fix it later.

'I could definitely hear some, er, singing.' He smiled and she caught a glimpse of straight white teeth. 'I thought I'd come and say hello,' he continued. 'I'm Jack, your landlord.'

'Oh.' For a moment Beatrice was lost for words. In her mind her landlord was some sort of Dickensian old man with a hunched back, wearing a rumpled tail coat and slightly dented top hat. A Scrooge caricature to go with the dark, shadowy ambience of the shop, not a well-built young man with fairly wild-looking, shoulder-length, blond surfer-style hair and deep grey eyes. And his close-fitting white T-shirt, black jeans and canvas shoes weren't in keeping with the old-fashioned clothes she'd also mentally given him.

'Sorry, come in.' Remembering her manners, she stepped aside and held her arm out to welcome him in. 'You don't look how I imagined a London landlord to be,' she admitted. 'I was expecting some sort of wizened old bloke in an antiquated outfit.'

'Counting my ill-gotten gains like a Dickensian novel?' Jack asked, laughing. He didn't know how close to the truth he was. 'Most city landlords these days are big companies, I'm one of the few simple human ones, I'm sure. When my parents retired, I took over Hampstead Books on the corner of the main road. And also, the row of shops along this side of the mews. My grandfather bought them in the 1960s when they were dark and distinctly unfashionable, but they've turned out to be a good investment.'

'I'm very pleased to meet you,' she said. 'I'm Beatrice, although mostly people call me Bea. I've seen your bookshop, although only a quick peep through the window when I came to look at this place. It looks like you sell second-hand books?'

'Well spotted, although we do also stock new ones. We specialise in botany, plants, organic gardening, that sort of thing. My grandfather opened the shop, and then later Mum and Dad took over. I did a degree in art history and afterwards came home to help run the shop until I eventually became custodian when my folks retired. They now live in Cornwall in what used to be our holiday home, although they do sometimes miss the hustle and bustle of city life so come and stay and give me a bit of a break. The shop is my life now; I love it and I can't imagine doing anything else.'

'Well, as you have no doubt guessed, I sell tarot cards. And I'm going to give readings too, in the back room.' Beatrice waved her hand behind her. 'I need to dress it all first, some lamps, a table and chairs and a nice rug, that sort of thing. And, if I can ask whilst you're here, I'd like to put a sandwich board out at the end of the mews to attract passing customers, or nobody will know I'm here. Apart from my website which I'm still building, and my social media. Would that be okay? I'll make sure it's positioned so it doesn't trip anyone up.'

'Yes, of course,' Jack replied. 'Wow, tarot card readings. Can you see into the future?'

'No, although everyone asks that.' Beatrice laughed. 'My readings aren't like some sort of end of the pier show, or a tent in a fairground. I have a skill with the cards, but they can only help you to work out answers to questions, perhaps ones you haven't yet asked yourself. My mum was able to do it, and her mother, and all the women in the family going back generations. Who knows when it first started, which ancestor. Mum always wanted to do readings and have a shop, she collected packs of cards for years but unfortunately, she passed away before she was able to fulfil her ambition, so here I am doing it for her. She grew up in Hampstead and always spoke of how much she loved this area. I'm really excited to be here.'

'And are you local, a Londoner like me?'

'Nope, I lived with my parents in a village in Nottinghamshire all my life. I helped my dad look after Mum when she got sick, and I also worked in a shop selling crystals and holistic remedies,' she explained. 'And I gave tarot readings too.'

'I imagine this is very different then, compared to a rural village,' Jack said.

'It is,' Beatrice agreed, 'but it was time to make a move, and the right decision to make.' Except she knew she had no choice, she'd made her feelings clear and couldn't live with what was going to happen. She hadn't jumped, she was pushed.

5

1644

Sunday was the first of May, a day for celebrations. Portia, her close friend Elsebeth who was married to a well renowned draper, together with Vittoria and Maria, had spent the day at Cornhill, where a permanent maypole was erected. The larger houses owned by merchants and lawyers were decorated with boughs of greenery, as was the tall pole. They'd enjoying the Morris Men, puppet shows and the crowning of the May Queen, followed by several hours of revelling. People danced to the fiddles, tambour drum and recorders in the light from a large bonfire, which at one point looked as though it was going to topple over onto the bystanders.

Eventually Maria announced that she must go to buy a pie or there would be no supper, and Vittoria decided to accompany her to enjoy the last of the celebrations still going on in the city. Portia left them and returned home.

She had been back for less than an hour when she heard the sound of footfall outside and Vittoria's high, lilting, song-like voice. Bursting into the room, she instantly filled the room with her vitality and vibrance. In Portia's eyes she lit up a room like a blazing fire on a winter's night, a brightness which drew people to her, wanting to be encompassed in the circle of warmth she spread. She loved her so wholly, it was all consuming.

'Mama,' Vittoria exclaimed as she hurried to the table and dropped the bag of vegetables she was carrying onto it. 'The market place is in uproar. Another merchant's wife has been murdered!' Her eyes were big with the thrill and excitement of bringing such news home. As ever, Portia couldn't help but see what Vittoria had never done. The strange way the centre of her beautiful eyes – their unusual pale hazel shot through with vibrant gold jewels – leaked away to the edge like the keyhole on their door. The house didn't have a mirror and even if it did, it would be of little use. The affliction in Vittoria's eyes affected her sight and – although she could get about with care and with either Portia or Maria to accompany her – she could no longer see as well as others did, her eyesight increasingly failing as the years marched on. As Vittoria busied herself removing her shawl and taking their purchases to the kitchen in an alcove in the corner of the room, Portia turned to Maria and raised her eyebrows.

'Another murder?' she murmured. 'Is this true?'

'Indeed,' the other woman replied. Maria, older than Portia by twelve years, had lost all vestiges of youth. Her younger years had been hard, and it showed in the lines on her face. It was no wonder when Portia had engaged her as a wet nurse she had willingly agreed to make the journey to London and not stopped to ask questions. Now the two women were as close as sisters. And Portia needed a sister.

'The news sheet sellers are shouting from every corner. A rich spice merchant with a big warehouse close to Queenhithe Quay, his young wife murdered, or so they say. The second goodwife to disappear since Lady Day, that is why the city is up in arms.'

'How dreadful,' Portia said as she sat down on the chair she'd just vacated.

'Here.' Maria passed a crumpled piece of paper from her pocket, its surface covered in tiny type. 'I bought a penny pamphlet so you could read it aloud to us.'

Portia often thanked the Lord that as a young girl she'd been taught to read and write. Despite offering to teach Maria on numerous occasions, the other woman refused to learn. Vittoria had at one point been able to read some rudimentary words, but now, as her eyesight deteriorated further, she could only see if they were printed large enough. And these certainly were not.

'Mary Brown disappeared from her bed during the night of Thursday the twenty-eighth of April. Master Brown had been drinking at the Chequer Inn and when he returned home, their bed showed that someone had been sleeping in it, yet the house was empty. Her clothes and belongings were still in their usual places.' She looked up at Maria. 'It does not say she has been murdered though, there is no mention of a body being found.'

'That is only a matter of time. They live close to the river, everyone knows that if a body goes in there, it may never be found. Or perhaps it might wash up somewhere between the city and the sea. Master Brown obviously believes she has been taken and killed, why else would she be missing? And this is not the first woman to be taken from her bed. As I said earlier, I overheard someone saying that another goodwife in Saint Clements Lane also recently disappeared, murdered in the night. Now people are beginning to realise there have been others over the past few years – a pattern of women vanishing into the dark whilst their husbands are away from home or in the tavern. And they are becoming increasingly frequent. It sounds as though someone is watching the women until they are alone, a man out there who is killing women.'

'That is also mentioned here.' Portia waved the news pamphlet. 'But perhaps it is just a coincidence?'

'More than a coincidence I would say.' Maria had tied an apron around her waist and was cutting slices from the pie she'd just bought whilst beside her, Vittoria poured beakers of ale and placed them with bread and a dish of deep yellow butter on the table.

Portia carefully folded the news sheet and placed it in the cupboard beside her cards, stroking her fingertips across the smooth silk and feeling it catch on her rough skin. It was a long time since she'd worn such fabrics, back when her hands were soft and white. Joining the other two, she started to slice the bread. They were now chatting of other things, the murdered women forgotten, and Portia hoped it would stay that way. Although there was no blood on her hands.

6

2025

After Jack left, the shop felt smaller and darker. Beatrice was pleased to have met him and hoped that in time he might become a friend. Picking up the empty boxes, she began to flatten them. She'd already spotted a row of industrial bins at the end of the mews and suspected one of them would be for recycling. There was certainly nowhere to store them in the shop or flat.

As she picked up the final one, she felt a thud as something she'd missed slid down the box and landed in the bottom corner. Rummaging in with her other hand, her fingers closed on a small package in the bottom, and she pulled it out for a proper look, dropping the carton on the floor as she did so.

She was holding something wrapped in a piece of silk, so thin it was almost transparent, the threads stretched apart she could almost see through them to what they enclosed. The insipid gold of the fabric held little trace of the vibrancy it must have originally done. Balancing it on her palm, she slowly lifted the covering away to display its contents, drawing her breath in slowly as she took in what she was holding.

It was a pack of tarot cards – that was immediately evident – but they were unlike any she'd ever seen, not even the older, more valuable cards displayed so carefully in the shop. These were far more antiquated than any of those, and instantly, instinctively, she realised what they were. Carrying them through to the shop where she had a stool behind the tall counter, she perched on the edge of it and laid the cards down in front of her.

For as long as she could remember, her mother had talked about the cards. Tarot cards – reading them, consulting them – it had been as natural a part of her life as breathing. She used to tell Beatrice that she'd read them before she'd agreed to go on a date with her father, and again when he'd asked her to marry him. She'd learned how to use them from her own mother, Beatrice's *nonna*, and grandmother, the skill having been passed down from mother to daughter for as long as anyone knew. And when Beatrice was eighteen, she too was taught.

They'd visited a shop not unlike the one that she was now sitting in and examined many sets until one particular one revealed itself to her – the backs glorious with the deepest green and bronze constellations and the Major Arcana, the picture cards, a facsimile of old medieval designs. Nothing physical happened, and yet the moment her fingertips touched them she knew they were for her. Now those cards were sitting in her bedside table drawer and she read them to seek advice whenever she needed to. As she had done so before she'd escaped to London to open this shop and honour her mother's wishes.

But the cards in front of her now weren't her mother's, the ones she always used. These were far older, ancient even, the aura of another time enveloping them, and even without properly examining them Beatrice knew they were the ones which her mother had spoken of, a pack which had reputedly been in their family for generations, originally from Italy. Cards that could allegedly alter the path of someone's life. Beatrice had always just smirked inwardly when such things were said. Certainly, the cards could give advice, suggest options, but they couldn't change lives. She had never been shown them, even though she'd been told they were packed away in the loft.

Despite their obvious age – though she had no idea exactly how old they were – they'd remained in good condition. As she slowly started to shuffle through them looking at the hand-painted illustrations, she noticed that some of them had muddy scuff marks on them, and one of them, The Lovers, had a dark brown stain across the corner, which looked unpleasantly like blood.

On the whole, they were, however, glorious. The Empress in a vibrant red gown seated on a throne and surrounded by a golden hue which must have originally been radiant, and The Fool, the young man in his short tunic strolling along the road beneath the sun, full of optimism for a new adventure. How very appropriate, Beatrice thought. She could feel a warmth coming from the cards, the same sense of connection she had felt with her own pack the first time she'd been introduced to them. But there was something else, something uncomfortable, a sadness she didn't understand.

Going through them carefully, conscious of how old they must be, Beatrice laid the top three out on the counter and began to do a reading for herself. She'd only been in London for twenty-four hours. Had she made the right decision to run away? Really, she knew it was too early to know, but still she turned the first card over and looked at what was before her.

The Moon, depicting doubt, second questioning herself. Not a surprise, given how many times she'd wavered about whether she was making the right choice to move to Hampstead and open a shop. It was a huge undertaking, even with the money her father had given her when he'd sold the family home, but it was what her mother had always dreamed of and it felt the right thing to do. Silently she nodded to herself before turning the second card.

The Star, the beautiful glowing design despite its age making Beatrice smile. A sign of healing and renewal, shining its light towards a bright new future. She turned the final card and frowned, the Page of Cups, not what she expected to see. Usually, this card spoke of new relationships, although, she reminded herself, it could also mean new beginnings. That must be what it was telling her here. Flipping the pack over, she looked at the card on the bottom, the 'shadow card'. Most readers, herself included, rarely paid much heed to this card and she wasn't even sure why she'd looked, but sometimes it told of something hidden, perhaps an underlying energy within a reading. She was looking at The Fool, indicating the start of a journey, something which lay ahead. Uncertainty, new experiences she couldn't yet envisage but would encounter. She wasn't sure if that meant the shop, or her life here in London, but she knew it was telling her something she'd understand in time, and she would have to wait until the answer showed itself.

The pictures on the cards were so intricate and exquisite that Beatrice started to lay them all out face up across the counter top until the full seventy-eight were displayed. She marvelled at the brightness of the colours, how they'd barely faded over the years, wondering how long they'd been hidden away in various boxes over the years. Her mother hadn't ever taken them out to use them for a reading. When Beatrice had asked, the reply had been that they didn't speak to her mother as they needed to, she had no empathy with them. That was simply the way with cards. You bonded with a set, or you did not. But Beatrice had known the moment she held these in her hand that, unlike her mother, she was tied to them, they had been waiting for her.

As she finished laying out the cards she frowned and began to scan them all. Having laid them in rows, it was now obvious the pack wasn't complete, she didn't have seventy-eight, she only had seventy-seven. There was one card missing, and it only took a few seconds for her to realise that The Devil card was absent. Going to the packing box in which she'd found the cards, she looked inside, turned it upside down and shook it, then took it apart in case the card had slipped into the base of the box, but it was nowhere to be seen.

Carefully Beatrice picked them all up again, and with no other suitable container to put them in, she re-wrapped them in the piece of cloth in which they'd been stored in for goodness knew how many years. How could there be one missing? Yes, sometimes a clumsy customer, unaware of the cards' impor-tance, knocked one to the floor with an elbow or a scarf, but the reader would immediately notice. Nobody allowed their pack to be split, it rendered them useless. The reading she'd just done meant nothing, no wonder the shadow card, The Fool, had made little sense. And now she understood the emotion she could feel coming from the cards. They were missing a part of their being, their whole.

As she slowly moved around the shop, closing the blind and locking the door, she tried to recall every discussion she'd had with her mother about this special set, the 'family' cards. Snip-pets of conversations came back to her as she racked her brains.

Both her grandmother and mother had talked of an ancient Italian heritage and the roots of the cards, but Beatrice couldn't remember anything about the pack no longer being whole. Although now she thought about it, there had been some puzzling comments which meant nothing at the time but now seemed strange. That the cards were searching for something? Had she remembered that correctly? She shook her head as she tried to retrieve old memories, long since forgotten. A story about them helping women to escape. No, that couldn't be right. Escape from what? Something about those who were in danger could be present, then gone, as though slipping between two curtains and vanishing.

None of it made sense. She hadn't slept well the night before, the first night in a new bed and her head was fuzzy. As she'd told Jack earlier, cards could help people to come to a decision, but they didn't hold any powers. They certainly couldn't make people disappear, there was no magic involved in reading them. And whatever these rumours were, they had no doubt become distorted over the years, spoken from generation to generation and the truth lost in time. More so, they didn't explain why the pack was no longer complete.

7

1644

Sitting back, Portia viewed the intricate black hand-painted sword woven with elaborate flowers in gold, red and blue on the backs of the cards. The illustrations were on thick, heavy parchment, several sheets glued together to ensure they remained robust. They were already over one hundred years old, passed down from her Italian grandmother and doubtless her ancestors before her, but they still looked vibrant, as though the images they held might dance off the face.

Italy – with its heat and dust, its lyrical flowing language she still spoke to herself in her head – was a fading memory now. Shaking off the memories, she looked up at the eager young woman sitting opposite, her face alight with expectations. Portia knew instinctively this was just an ordinary reading.

'Are you ready?' Portia asked. She received a nod of confirmation, and Portia turned over the first card.

'The Hanged Man,' she announced. The image depicted a man bound in ropes hanging upside down. His breeches were a vibrant red and he was wearing a green jerkin. He was sometimes referred to as Judas, the traitor. Across the top of the card could be seen the wooden gibbet, wound with greenery from which he hanged by his feet. Her customer drew a breath in sharply, her fingers in front of her mouth.

'It is not as you think,' Portia reassured her, used to this response for what appeared a terrifying card to be presented with, an omen of bad fortune. 'He is suspended there, waiting. This suggests a period of quiet, and of reflection. It tells you that you may need to sacrifice something now, in order to wait for better fortunes later.'

Looking relieved, the woman placed her hands back in her lap and nodded slightly. What Portia was saying seemed to make sense. She turned the next card.

'The Hermit.' The old man on the card with his stick was all in grey, the hood of his heavy cloak pulled over his head. In his right hand he carried a glowing lamp. Around him the dark skies were illuminated with stars.

'This card denotes someone who may come into your life or perhaps is already here as a guide. To assist you in making a decision. He is quiet and thoughtful and considers his actions and advice before committing. It is not unusual to turn this card at the same time as The Hanged Man. The two men often appear together.'

Picking up the final card, she turned it over, and immediately her customer gave a wide smile. The figure on the card was wearing a magnificent red gown, placed on a throne which was surrounded by gold leaf, shining out as though the card were a candle to light the way.

'The Empress,' Portia said, smiling back. 'She brings abundance, to shower us with the world's riches. She symbolises maternal good fortune and fertility and is a good card to turn if there is a wish for a family.' Now the other woman was nodding rapidly. 'You must remember what all the cards tell you, that waiting, having patience, will in time result in riches.'

Now wreathed in smiles, her customer got to her feet and hugged Portia. 'Thank you,' she said. 'Now I understand what I must do, I must wait with fortitude then all that I wish for shall come to me, in time.'

* * *

Portia's pleasure at being able to give such a joyful reading was, however, short-lived. Two hours later she was sitting at the table painting another of her spare Devil cards when her careful intricate strokes were interrupted by a knock at the door.

She had been taking the opportunity of being on her own, Maria and Vittoria having gone to Smithfield Market; there was reportedly a travelling fair with a bear in a cage and she did not expect them to return for some time. It was imperative the other two never discovered what she did, it would place them by association in as much danger as she herself already entertained. Calling out, 'Wait one moment, please,' she quickly placed her paints and the still wet card in her cupboard, before opening the door to a young girl.

'I wish to see the woman who does tarot readings, and I was told at the market that you are she.'

'Then you have come to the right place for that is indeed me, and I am presently at home on my own so if you have time, I can do it now. Come in.' Portia ushered her visitor into the parlour.

Once she'd taken the girl's voluminous shawl, Portia took her payment, slipping it into her pocket, and indicated the three-legged stool on one side of the table. More to go into her coffer, where she endlessly saved what she could towards the future. When something might happen and their safe, steady life could be rocked like the waves which had rocked the boat bringing them to London all those years ago.

Her customer sat down, her voice coming out as a whisper as she introduced herself as Nell. Portia went to the narrow built-in cupboard beside the entrance door and removed the small package wrapped in gold silk, an offcut of a roll originally brought from the Far East, to be made into a gown for her mother, many years ago. A whole lifetime ago. Now faded in places and frayed around the edges, gossamer threads floated and paused momentarily in the air as though suspended there by an unseen hand. She moved to the table and sat down.

Unwrapping the package, she took the cards, their weight so familiar in her hand, and began to shuffle them. Once she was content, she lay them in the middle of the table. She heard a shuddering intake of breath and, looking up, she smiled, hoping to reassure.

'Your fate awaits you now.' Portia lowered her voice to create a relaxing but mystical aura. It was imperative the room remained calm, or the reading may not be true. Nell's hands were shaking as Portia shuffled the cards, and now she could see the woman was barely more than a child, and yet here she was, potentially about to ask for help. As word spread from mouth to mouth and knowledge of what Portia could do was now carrying across London, she was being visited more and more often. Previously, it had only been maybe three or four times a year. No wonder the streets were ringing with the rumours that a murderer was spiriting women away from their beds. And yet still, the men did not stay at home to protect their wives, they continued to frequent the inns every night.

'I do not actually require a reading from the cards.' The silence in the room, darkened with the heavy clouds outside and punctuated by crackles and popping from the fire where a fresh log had been placed minutes before, was broken as the young woman spoke, her words coming out in a rush. 'But please, I need you to help me.'

Silently Portia placed the cards face down between them.

'If you do not need to know what the cards can tell you, I do not understand why you are here. How do you think I can help you?' Portia looked into Nell's eyes which were red and swollen from crying. Rummaging in the pocket of her skirts, the girl found a rag and blew her nose into it. There were no visible bruises on her, but that meant nothing. Plenty of men were particular about where they inflicted injuries.

'I must escape, somewhere that I cannot be found,' came the reply as more tears hovered on her eyelashes. 'I am with child.'

'If you are not wed, then the father of the babe must be made to marry you, your own father will ensure this comes to pass. Unless the man is already wed to another? And if you are married to another, then I suggest you keep your lips tied and let your husband believe the new babe is his.'

'No, you do not understand.' The woman's hand shot out and stopped Portia shuffling the cards. It looked so small compared to her own and felt icy cold. 'I cannot ask my father to do this thing and save my virtue because he *is* the father of the babe in my belly.'

Portia let the air in her lungs out in a long hiss between her teeth. Nell was nothing but a child herself; this situation was appalling. 'Have you felt the baby quicken yet?' she asked.

The girl nodded. 'I tried to tell myself I was mistaken, that there was another reason for my tiredness and that my courses had stopped. They do not always come every month. But two days ago, I thought I felt something, just a flutter as though I hold a butterfly within me, and this morning it came again, but stronger. The push of a tiny foot, a tiny hand. You must remember those feelings, I have been told you have a daughter of your own. Before long, my belly will show, already it is beginning to swell. And as the weather becomes warmer, I will not be able to swathe myself in shawls every day as I do now. And I am too afraid to visit one of the women on Kyroun Lane who may rid me of it. So many women also die alongside the unborn child.'

Portia didn't comment, instead she picked up the cards and started to shuffle them again. It wasn't the usual way things were done, but Nell wouldn't know that, and it was necessary to slip the card which had so far remained inside her sleeve to find its way to the top of the pile. She dealt the necessary three cards and instructed the girl to turn the first one.

'The Ten of Swords,' Portia announced. 'This card represents the culmination of an immoral situation. The dark before the dawn. But it also depicts that now the worse has happened and your life shall become better. The sun will soon be reborn.' She hoped Nell was reassured that things were going to look brighter now, indicating it was time to turn the second card.

'The World. The culmination of this part of your life, and the beginning of a new, more harmonious one. You will become a new person as a fresh cycle commences.' Finally, she paused as the third card was turned, the one which she already knew to be there.

'The Devil,' she stated. 'What is real, what is an illusion.' She looked up and stared Nell in the eyes. 'We will create an illusion. That you are taken from your bed and disappear, murdered. But what will be the reality is that you will flee in the dead of the night when all is still and dark. Taken, yes, indeed, but by those who care to a place of safety where you can reinvent your life and start again. Do you have money to do this with? You will need to support yourself and this child.'

'I can do that. I am already very able at sewing and embroidery, many rich women bring me cloth to embroider.' She held her arm out, displaying a series of flowers creeping up her sleeve. It was indeed beautifully done. 'Although I am young, I shall say I am a young widow, my imagined husband could have been ten years my senior. It will explain my current state.'

'You must take a copy of this Devil card,' Portia pointed to the one that she had just turned, 'and return home. In two days' time, Sunday, you need to be at Venours Wharf when the clocks chime ten at night. When all is black and the streets are quiet. Will you be able to leave your home at that hour without being seen? At the river, a waiting boat shall take you away to where you and your baby can start a new life. There will be women there to help you, especially given your age and condition. To take you to safety.'

Nell nodded, and for the first time since she'd arrived, a tentative smile crept across her face. 'Somehow, whatever it takes, I will ensure I am there at the correct time. As soon as my father goes to the tavern as he does every night, I shall leave.'

'That is good. The boatman, John, will know to look out for you.' Portia went back to her cupboard and removed a copy of The Devil card. Even she admitted to herself that now after so much practice it wasn't as easy to tell the difference between the original and the copy. 'Take this now, give it to John when you get to the river. It is the sign so he knows you have been sent by me. I must ask for payment, whatever you can afford. This is dangerous work, and I have to pay John and the women who will help you with your onward journey.'

A small purse, heavy with coins, was passed over and as she stood up to leave, Nell threw her arms around Portia and hugged her tight. She could feel the girl's rounded belly pressed against her. There was indeed little time to waste here.

'Thank you, may you be blessed by the angels above,' she whispered, 'for you are truly an angel yourself.'

As the door closed behind her and Portia went to store the money, she couldn't help a small grimace at being called an angel. She certainly was not, for she had done something terrible in her life of which she could not speak, ever. A lie she was still living, which would tear her life apart were it ever revealed.

8

2025

The first week in the shop was quiet, but Beatrice was thankful for the time to arrange the back room as she wanted and set up the various utilities which needed organising. After her discovery of the old cards, she started making enquiries about separate insurance for them, wincing at the figures that she was being told. As soon as the broadband was installed, she got to work building a website. She had limited skills, but she'd done an online course and spent hours watching YouTube videos, so she was sure she could achieve something basic, but workable.

The rug, bookcase, table and some lamps that she'd ordered arrived, and she enjoyed arranging them in the back room. Now it looked just as she had imagined, welcoming, with an occasional antique – well, reproduction – piece to give a nod to the age of the building, and indeed the lineage of the tarot.

After entering all her stock on her website and making it live, she turned her attention to the sandwich board she'd asked Jack about. She hadn't seen him since his first visit even though she found herself looking towards his bookshop whenever she popped across to visit Jo and buy bread or a pastry, or when she'd ventured to the local corner supermarket.

With her tongue nipped between her front two teeth, she carefully decorated around the edge of the board as best she could, her GCSE art skills now a little rusty, and then wrote 'Tarot Cards and Readings. Life Choices Eased'. She wasn't sure about the last bit, but people always seemed to worry about decisions they either needed to make or had already made. If they thought the cards could help, then it may increase the footfall to the shop. She added the phone number and her social media details on the bottom. If people looked for her online they should hopefully find the link to her website, and she'd already set up a form on there for people to book a reading. Perhaps she should also do them online, she could do it via video call and then she wasn't reliant just on people in London.

'You've got this, Bea,' she said to herself. 'You're going to smash it.'

The sandwich board proved to be more successful than Beatrice had envisaged, and the following day the shop door opened, the bell – which Beatrice had managed to revive with some WD40 and a polish – jingling as a young woman stepped in. Her hair, a vibrant orange reflected onto her glowing face and her bright eyes.

'Hi.' Beatrice looked up from her laptop where she was researching the logistics of offering online readings. 'Can I help you, or do you just want to browse?'

'I saw on your board that you do tarot readings,' the woman replied. 'Do I need to book an appointment or are you able to do it now?'

'Now is fine,' Beatrice replied, smiling. She went to the door and slid the bolt, turning the sign to 'Closed'. 'I don't want us to be disturbed,' she explained. 'We can go into the back room here, where it's quiet.' She led the way, quickly switching on the lamps. It had a restful ambience now she'd furnished it, and she was happy it had the right atmosphere for card readings.

Once her customer was settled she took out her cards and shuffled them, their weight and size as familiar in her hands as though they were a part of her own body.

'Do you have a reason that you wish to consult the cards?' she asked. It didn't have any bearing on the outcome, but she liked to know why people visited her.

'I'm getting married in a fortnight,' the woman explained. 'I suppose I just want to know what the future might hold, if I'm going to be happy.'

'Let's see then, shall we?' Beatrice smiled as she placed the cards on the table between them and dealt three cards face down in front of the woman. 'Turn over the first card,' she requested.

The woman did as she was asked, revealing a card bearing the picture of a young man.

'The Fool,' Beatrice said, looking down at the familiar figure standing on the edge of a cliff with his belongings on the end of a stick resting on his shoulder. A small dog danced close by. The woman looked up, her eyes wide.

'Seriously?' she questioned. 'That doesn't bode well, if the cards think I'm a fool to be marrying my fiancé.'

'That's not what this card is telling us,' Beatrice reassured. 'The Fool is excitable, looking forward to the beginning of a journey, which is what your marriage is. Sometimes he tells us that an action may be uncertain, doing something on the spur of the moment. But that's not you if you're getting married, they take months if not years to organise.' For a moment, her mind strayed to her father before she shut it down to concentrate on what she was doing.

'Actually, that's not so far from the truth,' her customer admitted. 'I'm so excited to get married, but we haven't been together that long. We've planned our entire wedding in eight weeks. I don't believe I'm doing the wrong thing though. I've always been a spontaneous person, and I know without a doubt he's the person to spend the rest of my life with.'

Beatrice hoped the other cards would reflect this. Carrying on, she instructed the woman to turn the next card, displaying two people entwined, looking into each other's eyes.

'This one is easy to explain in your situation, The Lovers. It speaks of commitment and the union of two people, two energies, for eternity.' As she spoke, she could see the woman relax further, her shoulders which were up around her ears when she'd started the reading had now descended to where they'd normally be.

'And your final card,' Beatrice said as it was turned to display The Star. 'A beacon, the promise of forthcoming pleasure. Look to the future, your wishes and dreams can come true.' She smiled at the woman who was grinning, her palms pushed against her face.

'Thank you,' she said. 'Thank you so much. I know it's the right thing to do. I'm marrying the right man at the right time, and your cards have shown that our future together will be happy.'

Beatrice nodded. 'Nothing in life is certain, but this is a positive reading. I'm pleased they've put your mind at rest, and I hope you have a wonderful wedding.'

She led the woman to the shop counter to pay and also gave her a leaflet with her website and social media channels on it.

'If you can tell everyone about me and leave a review, perhaps follow me online, that would be great. I've only just opened here, so the more footfall the better.'

'What about these cards you've got for sale?' her customer asked, indicating the shelves around the shop. 'Do you give lessons in card reading? Can anyone do it?'

'I don't give lessons, no,' Beatrice apologised. For her, reading the cards was something in her blood, as though she'd always been able to do it. She couldn't teach that aspect to someone else, it was part of who she was, and that wouldn't happen with just anyone.

After her customer had left, still enthusing about her reading and chatting non-stop about her wedding, the shop felt strangely silent. Beatrice had become used to the quiet and it hadn't worried her, but now for the first time since she'd come to London there was a wisp of loneliness curling its way inside her and settling down as though it intended to stay. It was a strange feeling, and not one that she liked. She knew no one locally, she needed to get out and find some new friends. Everyone from home had promised to come and visit and they often sent messages online, but it wasn't the same as spending the evening out with them. And their photos on social media showed they were, of course, still doing that, but there was a Beatrice-shaped hole in them.

This was the first time she'd lived on her own, having returned home after finishing university. She hadn't had any proper long-term relationships, just boyfriends who'd lasted a few months before drifting away. Then after her mother fell ill all that went on hold, boyfriends were too much of a commitment. As soon as she got home from work she'd take over caring duties from her father so he could have a rest. They were a tag team, a partnership, and even after her mother passed away it was the two of them against the world and they'd dealt with their grief together. Until suddenly they weren't, and everything had changed.

Now, it was Dad and Kerry who were the team, and further-more he'd announced that they were to marry. It had been three years since her mum had died, and he told Beatrice that although he'd never stop loving her, now he'd fallen in love again and wanted to make Kerry his wife.

Beatrice just couldn't accept it. How could he? Nobody would ever, could ever, match her mother. Kerry was always perfectly pleasant, friendly even, but suddenly out of the blue, her dad had announced that he was selling their home and moving in with Kerry. Of course, he told her, she could go too but he was wrong – she just couldn't, it wouldn't feel right. And then, as if one bombshell wasn't enough, he informed her that they were going to be married, a Christmas Eve wedding.

However hard she tried, Beatrice couldn't accept the betrayal of her mother's memory and almost immediately she'd started planning her escape. With half the proceeds from the house sale which her father had given her, she was fulfilling her mother's ambition: opening a tarot card shop whilst also giving readings. She was keeping her mother's memories alive. And even though she was now in her late twenties, with a blank spreadsheet of former relationships, it was time to live not just her mother's dream, but her dream too.

9

1644

Portia waited for a message from John to let her know that Nell had disappeared successfully, moved from her dangerous existence to a place of safety. It was now Tuesday, two days since the girl should have made her escape, and Portia was feeling increasingly worried. Previously, he had always sent a message the day after he'd taken a woman to Teddington, but this time she'd heard nothing so she was relieved when finally, she heard a rap of knuckles at the door and opened it to find him on the doorstep. His usual cheerful countenance was missing though, instead his forehead was tracked with deep lines.

Behind her, Vittoria and Maria both paused what they were doing. Vittoria was always pleased for a reason to stop doing chores, and the arrival of a friend certainly constituted that.

'Will you come in?' Portia stepped to one side, holding her arm out to usher John into the room. Her heart was thumping painfully in her chest, her worries about Nell now significantly increased, and rising further.

'I cannot.' John's eyes flicked for a moment to the other two women. Now Portia was certain his visit was about the girl. Not once since she'd started helping women to escape their violent lives had she told the others what she was doing when she read for those who needed her help, and she wasn't about to discuss it in front of them now. The less people knew, the better. Her skin was prickling with the dread of impending bad news.

'I am just stepping outside for a moment,' she spoke quickly over her shoulder before joining him on the street, shutting the door with a decisive bang so Vittoria wouldn't take it upon herself to join them.

Once on the street she took his arm and walked quickly to the corner of Walbrooke Street, where it was empty of people and there was no danger of them being overheard.

'Tell me what happened,' she whispered. 'Did Nell not get away safely?'

'I do not know what went wrong, but she did not arrive at the river as you instructed. When you came to tell me to expect her, you said Sunday, did you not? I also waited yesterday evening, in case one of us had the day wrong, but she did not come and I have heard nothing. Do you know where she lives? Can you go and see her?'

'I never know where my customers live,' Portia reminded him. 'I must protect Vittoria from the danger of what I do, so the less I know about the women the better. We can do nothing now, except wait and see if she comes back to see me. I have a very bad feeling about this though.'

'As do I.' John nodded. 'I will pray there is a simple explanation, that she will still be able to escape her cruel father.' Portia always gave a brief explanation to John about the women he rowed upriver; he was helping them every bit as much as she was.

They said goodbye and Portia returned home, her heart heavy. She too was praying for Nell.

* * *

It was a further three days before Portia got some answers, and they were not what she was hoping for. She was standing at a market stall, one that was her preferred place to shop, the vegetables coming from a farm in Kent and fresher than those arriving from further afield. Behind her, two women, their woven baskets at their feet, were talking rapidly, their words falling over each other as they made no attempt to keep their voices low. Portia had already been party to the description of an ailment that sounded revolting and had required two visits to the apothecary.

'Found dead? Where? Poor mite, she was barely more than a child, really.' Portia's attention was alerted and she began to listen more intently, trying to discover what they were now talking about.

'Left in the house, their neighbour found her. She'd been strangled and her father was nowhere to be seen. She was with child, apparently, too. They caught up with him beyond the city walls on the Great North Road, he was riding as though the Devil himself was at his heels. According to what I heard, they'd only removed half of his fingernails when he confessed to killing her and also that the babe in her belly was his. He's already been strung up. But...' Here she paused for effect, and Portia was now swallowing hard to stop herself being sick because she was certain that she knew who they were discussing. '...when I speak of the Devil, it is the truth that he was involved, because a card depicting Satan was found in a sack filled with her belongings, as though she intended to run away. What do you make of that?'

Portia didn't wait to find out what the other woman made of it, instead, clutching her hemp sack of shopping against her, she stepped away before turning and hurrying towards the river as quickly as she could without drawing attention to herself. She knew there was little likelihood of finding John there; on such a fine day he might be anywhere on the water, but one of the other boatmen there would take a message asking him to call on her.

As she walked, breaking occasionally into a trot, her head was filled with the image of Nell, her pinched, sad little face, her stomach slightly extended with the baby put in there by her father. Abused and then murdered. Had he seen the card and beaten the truth out of her before he killed her? The idea that her assistance in helping Nell escape may have brought about her death was so appalling, so dreadful, that Portia tried to stop thinking about it, but the thoughts crept insidiously into her mind. At one point she had to stop, putting her hand on the church wall beside her as she darted across a graveyard to bend over and wait for a wave of nausea to pass.

When she arrived at the wharf, never had she been so relieved to see John's boat, its familiar, blue-painted oars laid inside. Of him though, there was no sign. She walked back and forth across the dock looking for someone to ask if they knew of his whereabouts when she heard a call and she spotted him walking down the lane, a pie in one hand and a leather flask of ale in the other. With her mind so taken up with what she'd just heard, the time had escaped her and she realised that it must be dinner time. Maria and Vittoria would be wondering where she was with the shopping so she couldn't stay long, much as she wanted to.

'Hello, my sweet,' John greeted her as he grew close, 'it is lovely to see you.' With one hand on her elbow, he steered her to a corner of the dock away from the warehouse where men were stacking bales of cloth and they sat on an old wooden bench, warped and bleached by the weather.

'John, I believe something terrible has happened to Nell.'

Before Portia could go any further, he held his hand up to stop her speaking.

'You need say no more,' he said. 'For I have just heard what you must have also. That her father discovered her plight and murdered her before she could escape.'

Portia felt her eyes fill with tears. It was the first time that she hadn't been able to fulfil her mission and for such a young girl, younger even than Vittoria, she was devastated.

'And apparently, the card I gave her was found in her baggage,' she said.

'Indeed, that is what is being spoken of in the taverns,' John replied. 'You must not worry though, there are others in the city who read the cards, nobody will point a finger at you. And certainly, nobody knows of what you do other than those who will always keep your secret. Women do not betray other women.'

'I hope not, or I will be there upon the gibbet too,' Portia said. 'I must go home now; I have been out too long. I am fearful to continue with what I have been doing, yet how can I not help those in dire need?'

Getting to her feet, she began to walk home, her whole body feeling weary. She'd failed Nell and she didn't know if she could carry on. Who else might she fail?

10

2025

'Hello.' Jack stuck his head around the open shop door, his hair falling across his eyes. 'Are you busy?'

Beatrice made a big pretence of looking around the obviously empty space before grinning and shaking her head. 'Nope, nothing that won't keep. What can I do for you?'

'Just being neighbourly.' He slipped in through the door and closed it behind him. 'You've been here for two weeks now, I thought I'd come and see how it's all going, if you've settled in okay. Do you have anything that needs doing down here or upstairs?'

'Everything's great, thank you.' Beatrice led him through into the back kitchen and switched the kettle on. She picked up a jar of instant coffee and raised her eyebrows and he nodded. 'I've really settled in; it feels like I've been here ages. Weirdly, I can understand why my mum loved it around here so much, it's getting under my skin too. I've had a few customers walk in off the street, and I did a reading for one woman who's about to get married. She then told all her bridesmaids, and they now also have readings booked. They're coming on Sunday in a group. I don't actually intend to open on Sundays or Mondays, seeing as it's just me, I need a break occasionally to keep on top of admin and have a bit of a rest, but it's too much money to turn down and they all sounded so excited when they rang. I'm actually looking forward to it. Apparently, they're treating it as a part of the hen party, so who knows what state they'll be in when they arrive!'

'That sounds fantastic,' Jack replied. 'I was going to ask you if you fancied going for a drink on Sunday afternoon, but it sounds like you'll be too busy.'

'I'll be done by lunchtime. They're all due to be here at ten o'clock so I should easily be finished between eleven o'clock and midday. I usually do a longer reading, but they said they intend heading to Westfield afterwards to do some last bits of shopping, so we agreed to keep each one to fifteen minutes. Like tarot speed dating.'

Jack laughed. 'You could market yourself like that. Do you do online readings too? If it works for dating, perhaps it might work for readings too.'

'I have thought about it, although I confess, I do like a proper, deeper connection with the people I'm reading for. Even when they say nothing, I can feel their anxieties, their concerns, see their emotions across their faces and I believe that influences the cards. Having said that though, online readings would definitely expand my clientele and earn some extra money.'

'So why do people come to see you? Is it when they're worried about something?'

'No, not always, but there's always a reason why they seek a reading. A question, a confusion, something they want the answer to or are wishing for. The cards can't give them a definitive solution, but they will offer knowledge which can help.'

'It must be nice to have a talent like that,' Jack said. 'I like being able to help customers choose books, but it's not a skill like you have. You could change people's lives.'

'I hope I do,' Beatrice admitted. 'That's why I do it. And my mother did before me; reading the cards so they help another person's life for the better is a wonderful legacy to have.'

'And those antique sets of cards in the display cabinet in the shop, are they really old or replicas? I never knew there were so many different designs of cards,' Jack said. 'They remind me of the beautiful old plates in some of the books I have in my shop, the elaborate illustrations of flowers.'

'Oh, there are so many, people have been reading tarot cards for hundreds of years. I have a set that has been passed down through the women in my family for centuries. At least I think so, they're Italian and they look really old. Unfortunately, when I went through them one of the cards is missing, which is a real shame because with the pack incomplete they can't be used.'

'Can you replace it with a card from another pack?'

'No, each pack is a family. It's as though a family member has gone missing; you wouldn't adopt someone else to replace them.'

'Could you try and find it? Perhaps it's still out there some-where,' Jack suggested. 'Then you'd be able to do a reading with the pack, is that right?'

'Well, yes, I suppose I would be able to if the cards were complete. Given how old the pack is, it's very unlikely I'll ever find the missing one, but if I do some research I might discover something to help me. And if I don't it'll be an enjoyable activity anyway.' For a moment she wondered if she had the skills to do such a thing; she had no idea where someone would start look-ing. But somehow, she knew if anyone was going to discover it, then it would be her.

'And talking of enjoyable activities, how about that drink on

Sunday? The weather forecast is good so we could go for a walk first?' Jack drained his cup and went into the kitchen where he washed it up.

'That sounds great, thank you, I'd love that.' Beatrice smiled as, just for a moment, a tremble of anticipation fluttered inside. A tiny crack in her wall of loneliness.

* * *

Sunday, as Jack had promised, arrived with vibrant cyan-blue skies criss-crossed with contrails as planes high above headed to far-flung countries. Beatrice wondered if they were carrying people who were also running away. No, she told herself sternly, she wasn't going to think of coming to Hampstead as running away, but instead moving onto her new life, her future.

The hen party arrived a few minutes early. Beatrice could hear their raised voices as they approached the shop, being led by the bride assuring them they were in the right place.

Welcoming them in, she offered tea and coffee whilst they waited as each person had their reading. She'd already warned them that she needed a quiet and relaxing atmosphere, but they waved some bottles of Prosecco and asked if she had some cups. She only had the mugs from the kitchen so she handed those over and left them in the shop as she got started.

All went as she expected until her last customer, slightly older than her friends, came through. She seemed nervous, her hands clasped in front of her and a frown on her face and she wasn't as exuberant as the others. Beatrice asked her if she was all right.

'Of course.' The woman, who introduced herself as Sandy, gave her a bright smile, but it didn't reach her eyes, which were dark and hooded as though she was hiding her true thoughts. 'Can I ask the cards a question? Do I have to say it out loud?'

'You can, but they won't give you a simple answer,' Beatrice said. 'They offer ideas for you to think about, and from that you can hopefully tease out the solution you need. And you don't have to tell me what it is, but if you do feel able, then I can better explain what the cards are suggesting. It is entirely confidential in here,' she added.

Sandy nodded. 'I'm not like those other girls...' She pointed over her shoulder at the shop behind her. 'They're all planning their own weddings, they're young and idealistic. Impulsive, like my sister – the bride today. Anyway, I'm already married.' She lifted her left hand and held it up, showing Beatrice the simple gold band on her third finger. 'Marriage is not how I imagined it would be though. I can't say anything when I'm with my family, not when all the talk is of the big day and how exciting it is, and we all live close to each other so I see them almost every day. My husband didn't want a big wedding, so we just went to the registry office with a few people. None of his family came, although they do live in the North West so quite a long way for them to travel.' Beatrice didn't say a word, she couldn't imagine anyone not travelling to their child's wedding.

'And now?' she asked.

'Now it's all different. He's not the same man I married but I'm too afraid to say I want a divorce, so I'm just suffering in silence. Everyone in my family loves him, they don't see the real person. How he behaves at home. Because he's like Jekyll and Hyde. And with the wedding coming up it's one big lovefest, and yet here I am, my life is a misery. To tell you the truth, I'm worried for my sister... Suppose her marriage ends up the same way?'

'This is 2025,' Beatrice said, 'you don't have to stay with him. Your family will want you to be happy.'

'Unbelievably, I suspect not as much as they want him to be a part of us all. They wouldn't believe me if I told them how horrible he is when we're at home.'

'So, what do you want the cards to tell you? Whether you should leave? It seems you've already made your mind up.'

'I don't know.' Sandy's voice wobbled slightly. 'I want them to tell me *how* I can leave, to help me. Can they do that?'

'Well, not the details. As I said, it's not like that. They might give you suggestions, options, but then you must work out the details yourself. Cards can't help someone escape.' As she spoke the words they seemed to hang momentarily in the room and Beatrice felt a prickle crawl down her spine. Swallowing hard, she quickly picked the pack up, then she shuffled them and laid three cards out before instructing the woman to turn the first one over.

'The Eight of Swords. This card denotes confinement, restriction,' she said. 'Sometimes in our life, even if not physically, we are stopped by others from being who we wish to be.' Sandy was staring at the card, and in the silence Beatrice asked her to turn the second one.

'Now we see The Magician. He is telling you that although you feel you are in a situation from which you cannot see a way to escape, if you believe in yourself, you will be able to instigate change. And finally,' she leant forwards and flipped the third card over, 'The Devil. He is telling us to look with open eyes and see what is true, and what is an illusion.' At the sight of Satan with his horns and fiery tale dancing with a wild, wicked grin on his face, her client grimaced.

'For you, this is the card that matters the most,' Beatrice reassured, tapping it with her finger. 'It tells of a different life. What is actually the truth, and that which is shown to others, the illusion. Remember that, and remember you are strong and you *can* leave. The Devil has told you so.'

'Thank you,' Sandy whispered as she gathered up her bag and jacket and went to join her sister and friends. 'You have told me what I needed to hear.'

'The cards have told you, not me,' Beatrice reminded her, placing her hand gently on the woman's arm as she guided her out.

* * *

The group finally left at twelve thirty and Beatrice gave a huge sigh of relief as she locked the door behind them. She didn't have long before the time she'd arranged to meet Jack in front of his shop. Running back up to her flat, she touched up her make-up and changed the loafers she wore in the shop for her trainers which would be more comfortable.

They walked to Parliament Hill and sat on the grass, which was looking tired in the late Indian summer sunshine, watching people enjoying their weekend. Couples walked hand in hand and Beatrice looked at them, remembering how she'd been feeling when Jack had invited her. It was as though the world was conspiring to show her what she'd missed out on all these years. She hoped it wasn't too late to find love now.

'So, tell me more about these ancient cards of yours, the pack with a card missing,' Jack said. 'Have you thought yet of any way to begin researching them?'

'Not really,' she replied. 'I've looked online and found some history about when tarot cards first came about, although I did know some of that from what my mum and *Nonna* had told me. It was in medieval times and looking at the pictures, I'm guessing the pack I have possibly dates from around the fifteenth or sixteenth century.'

'Wait, what? Your cards might be six hundred years old? Surely not. How come they were in a box in your loft and they're not in a museum? Do you think they might just be good copies?'

'I don't. I honestly think they may be the real deal, especially with the family tales I know of. I really hope they are. The parchment is thick and feels rough and old, and the paint looks like the ones I've seen online. They haven't faded as much though, probably because they aren't being displayed and they've been kept somewhere dark, although there are a couple of small patches where the paint has flaked off. A few of them are a bit grubby and one of them has a horrible stain which looks like blood, although I'm hoping I'm mistaken about that. I don't know, I'll have to do some more investigations. The thing is, now there's nobody left to ask in my mother's family why one of the cards is lost.' For a moment her voice broke and she took a deep, shaky breath and stopped talking.

'Sorry, I don't know why I'm getting all emotional.' She gave a little laugh and smiled at him. The last thing she wanted to do on this sunny Sunday afternoon out with a gorgeous man was bring the mood down.

'Don't be daft, there's no rules on how to feel,' he told her.

'It's just that I helped my dad look after my mum for a few years when she was ill. When she died it meant there was no one in her family left, just me. Now he's met someone else and they're getting married, so I feel rather alone.' She stopped talking abruptly, not wanting to explain how distraught she was that he'd found someone else and forgotten her mother. Despite all his excuses and long-winded explanations, he had moved on as though she, like her tarot cards, was ancient history.

'Right,' Jack smacked his hands down on his knees, 'let's find a pub and have something to eat and drink and you can make a plan to discover the story about your cards.' He changed the subject as though guessing, correctly, that she'd said all she wanted to on the subject. 'Who knows what secrets they may be hiding?'

Beatrice nodded. She had the feeling that Jack was right. She was certain they held a secret, but would it then explain why one of the cards was missing?

11

1644

Portia felt empty and exhausted, her dismay over what had happened to Nell haunting her every waking moment.

It brought back the terror of her own flight, the constant checking over her shoulder gripped with a fear that Lorenzo had somehow received word that his baby had in fact survived. She could almost feel the hot breath of his hounds which would have surely hunted her down if he had known the truth. And now she had a deep empathy with the women who, as she'd once done, were running towards, and not away from, dark shadows in a tunnel in which they couldn't see the end. Always praying that all would turn out well, and devastated this time that it had not.

She would always thank God that Vittoria, Maria and she had survived their flight across Europe, docking in Portsmouth after the long and arduous journey on a Venetian cog ship. At times she'd thought they'd all perish, especially when the waves towered above the deck and she and Maria huddled in their tiny cabin praying for deliverance as the roaring sea threatened to swallow them down to its depths. It was three gaunt, sickly and half-dead people who had disembarked onto the quay with their few sacks of belongings.

During the better days of the voyage, when the sun shone and the wind dropped away, meaning the ship barely moved in the still waters, she and Maria had sat on deck altering and re-sewing the tiny shifts to ensure they would fit Vittoria for as long as possible. Tiny, hand-stitched pinch-pleats which could be let out. Her clouts which needed to be washed frequently could only be cleaned in seawater, the salt making them stiff and harsh against the baby's soft skin, but there was no alternative.

After the hours sitting on the ship's deck, by the time they reached London three weeks later, their Italian skin, already darker than the pale English sailors amongst the crew they trav-elled with, was a deep brown from the sun. Even Vittoria was a warm golden colour, making the anomaly in her eyes even more prominent. Portia soon became used to comments about the strange irregularity. She, however, barely noticed it. The same abnormality had affected her sister Agnese.

As though by thinking about the young girl had made her appear, she heard high-pitched chatter on the stairs and the door to their home opened to admit Maria, laden down with bags of food, Vittoria, and behind her another young girl who looked a similar age. Seeing the girl's dark eyes and brown skin, which matched her own, Portia wasn't surprised when Vittoria introduced her as Caterina.

As the girl said 'Hello', there was the cadence of a familiar Italian accent, just as she and Maria had, although theirs had diminished over the years. Having been raised in London, Vittoria had less of an accent, although with Italian typically being spoken at home, she could understand and speak her native language fluently.

'*Buongiorno,*' Portia exclaimed in delight. 'We meet very few Italians in London, have you been here long?'

'No, we arrived this past month,' Caterina explained. 'I have come with my father – he is a merchant dealing in spices from the Far East. We accompanied a large cargo coming from Venice, and he intends to remain here for maybe one or two years. I met Vittoria and Maria at the glove-makers and instantly I recognised Maria's accent. I could not help introducing myself, I have met no others from our country since we arrived.'

'And do you hail from Venice?' Portia asked. She could see the delight on Vittoria's face at finding a new friend, but there was always the unspoken danger still lurking across the seas and she had to be on her guard at all times.

'No, Mistress. Although we sailed from Venice, we live in Bologna. And here it is so cold, I am used to a fierce sun by this time of year.' The girl pulled the sides of her mouth down and Portia laughed. She remembered how for her first few years in London, even at midsummer, the English sun didn't feel as hot as it did in Italy.

'This is pleasant weather,' Vittoria chided. 'You should be thankful you were not here at Lady Day when we had many weeks of heavy snow and it lay thick on the streets. It became so icy underfoot that Maria fell over and had a bad pain in her back for several days. It looked beautiful at first, sparkling and white on the ground, but within a day it became brown with the droppings from the animals and the contents of the buckets as they were collected by the night soil man. After that I was not so enamoured of it,' she confessed. 'And the Lord save me, it was so bitterly cold, my lips split and my cheeks stung despite wearing a scarf across my face when I went out. You should give thanks that you come here in spring.'

Caterina laughed. 'In that case I promise to never complain

about how cold I feel again.' Going to sit in front of the fire, the two girls huddled together, talking quietly, their heads together as they laughed, and it did Portia good to hear another Italian accent. She hoped it may encourage Vittoria to speak her native language more often, despite it being something she was reluctant to do. She'd shown little interest in the country from where she originated.

After an hour of the two girls talking together, Vittoria cleared her throat and asked, 'Mama, would you do a tarot reading for Caterina, please? I have told her about your skill and she has seen them being performed at home in Italy.' Portia couldn't deny the eager faces which were turned to her both smiling in anticipation and getting up, she collected her cards and placed them in the middle of the table, giving instructions to the girl now sitting before her. Vittoria sat to one side so she could see everything revealed.

'The Emperor,' Portia said as the first card was turned. 'He is a father figure, someone who guides you. Authoritative and expects to secure whatever he desires.' Caterina looked thoughtful as she nodded.

'My Papa,' she agreed.

'And your next card.' Portia paused as it was turned it over, surprised to see what was before her. 'The Moon.' It was telling Portia that she couldn't be certain of the facts of Caterina's situation, that mists can blur the truth. She did not voice this out loud, however, instead choosing her words carefully. 'Moonlight shines down and illuminates all so it can be seen clearly, but equally, through the clouds which the moon attracts, things may become distorted and not as we believe they are. Sometimes truths are obscured.' Without waiting for Caterina to question her, Portia leant forward and turned the final card, inwardly breathing a sigh of relief.

'The Three of Cups. Celebration and joy, this card often appears when there is a marriage to be made. It can also represent a special friendship; it tells you are compassionate and kind.' Now Caterina and Vittoria were both smiling widely and holding hands; it seemed the mention of marriage was the right one. And why wouldn't it? All young girls dreamed of a handsome and rich man to marry.

Once the girls were occupied eating some of the delicately flavoured almond and clove cakes Maria had cooked earlier, Portia sat with the cards on her lap, idly turning them over one at a time. The Emperor, The Moon, the Three of Cups, they were as recognisable to her as though an extension of her own body; she was bonded to these cards. As a child she'd watched her grandmother giving readings and learned to do the same. Now, she too, could see everything that was both spoken and unspoken as she looked at the faces on the cards. They had survived being brought to London and previous to that, a house fire in Milan when her mother had snatched them up as she ran, carrying Portia and her sister Agnese in her arms.

As precious as life itself to the women of the family, the pack drew them together, forever held them as one. And one day they would do the same for Vittoria, although as her eyesight worsened, Portia worried she wouldn't be able to use them. She'd had many lessons over the years, and she could already read them almost as proficiently as Portia did, but she needed to remember the meaning of each card instantly. Portia wondered if she could find a way to raise the outline of each design so if it were ever needed Vittoria could read each card with her fingertips.

A half of an hour later, Caterina left. With a father as rich as hers, she had a guard who'd followed her to the house and waited patiently outside. It would have been more than his life was worth to leave her there to walk home alone. Portia did wonder if Caterina had been truthful to her father about where she was visiting; given the difference in their status, with their home unlike the opulence in which without doubt the girl lived.

After she'd gone, Vittoria came to sit beneath the window with Portia. They were both sewing, although Vittoria was bent closer to her work and Portia felt her heart break that the young girl was now having more difficulty seeing things. Her eyesight had definitely declined at a faster rate in the past year and a half. But determined, she continued with everything she'd done before, only accepting help when she really needed it.

'Mama, tell me about Italy,' she said. 'You rarely, if ever, speak of it. Yet you looked delighted when you discovered where Caterina hails from, and now, I think I would like to know more about my heritage. You have never explained to me why we live here in London, always with an excuse that I am too young to understand, but I believe I am now old enough to be told.'

Portia laid her work in her lap. She was repairing a shift that had been torn. Although she had money to replace it, with some small stitches it would be serviceable for a while yet. Finally, it was time to at least tell Vittoria a little of why they now resided in London even though she could never tell her the whole truth. Her life was woven with so many lies, and she needed to be careful of every word.

'When we came to England, it was because we had to flee, we left Italy in a hurry. Your father was a violent man with a vicious temper and I was fearful for your safety. Especially as you are a girl and he was certain you would be born a boy, so you would have not been particularly welcomed. I made the decision within minutes of your birth that, to save you, we needed to leave immediately. Milan was teeming with the plague, and your father had already left for his villa in the hills. I was fortunate to find Maria to be your nurse, her husband and her own baby had succumbed to the plague a month earlier. The disease chose who to afflict; I myself was lucky to only have it lightly and then I grew well again. Thankfully, Maria agreed to come with us; she no longer had any reason to stay in Italy and it was better to escape the pestilence.'

'So you just ran?' Vittoria asked. 'And my father, or at least his servants, did not give chase? Even though I am a girl, surely he would not let you escape so easily if he was as domineering as you say he was. That he just let his wife and child go, it does not sound right.'

Portia swallowed hard. She hadn't expected Vittoria to question her story, having kept it deliberately simple. 'I believe that he too became ill and died as so many others did. It explains why he did not follow us, and as you know, we were not apprehended and were able to purchase a passage on the *Sea Bird* as soon as we reached Venice. Fortune smiled upon us, allowing us to set sail within a day; otherwise, a longer stay at an inn may have led to our discovery, if indeed we had been pursued. And I will always be thankful that we came safely to England, because we have been able to live a life here and I have not been looking over my shoulder fearful to see a familiar face. Although it's doubtful that anyone would recognise me now.' She laughed as she said it and gestured to her face which no longer held the baked golden brown of a life spent beneath the Italian sun but was almost as pale as her fellow Londoners. It was also tracked by numerous fine lines which had developed over the years. Even her hair showed threads of grey weaving through it. 'And nobody would recognise you either, given that you were a tiny, swaddled babe, barely seen, when we left.'

Vittoria nodded slowly. It appeared her desire for answers was assuaged, at least temporarily.

'I am very pleased that you were able to save me and bring

me here to safety,' she said, 'for I have everything in life that I need so long as I am with you.'

Giving Portia a hug, she moved away to help Maria prepare the vegetables for their dinner, and Portia looked out onto the street. She knew that – with her distinctive colouring and eyes – there was a way that, even now, Vittoria could be recognised by anyone who knew her father. And if that happened, her life, all their lives, were in danger. Everything would be shattered, all she Portia had built, reduced to dust. Her heart beat hard in her chest and, gathering the edge of her apron, she dabbed at her brow, which was now speckled with beads of sweat.

12

2025

Beatrice looked at the list of potential websites to investigate that she'd hastily typed on her phone three days earlier whilst she and Jack sat in the pub. She'd enjoyed spending time with him, he was funny and had a carefree attitude that she herself had been missing for a long while. Deep down she knew it was time to change.

'Right, Bea, get on with it,' she said out loud. Her laptop was open, and she started clicking on links, disappearing down research rabbit holes as she read the history of how tarot cards had been used centuries before. Looking at other sets which had survived, mostly in museums or private collections, they appeared to be similar in many ways to her own pack. Although the design on the reverse of her cards was more beautiful, more intricate. She was more certain than ever that what she had was very old and valuable.

There were also some articles about cards sold via auction houses, and an academic paper by an American professor, Henry Stanton, at Yale University. She made a note of his name, and then, with some further delving on a networking site, found an email address for him. Perhaps if she took some photos of her pack of cards she could send them and hope she wasn't instantly dismissed as some sort of eccentric. She still had no idea of how to begin tracing the missing card and, she admitted to herself, there was almost no chance of discovering what had happened to it. Nor when exactly it had been separated from its compatriots. With no other leads she opened a new email, addressed it to Professor Stanton and began to type.

* * *

The shop was becoming steadily busier and Beatrice was delighted that between word of mouth and her sandwich board, she'd begun to draw in more and more customers. Her website was also doing a steady trade.

After several requests she finally decided to try video readings, even though she knew she wouldn't be able to get a proper connection with those she was reading the cards for. Nevertheless, everyone seemed happy with what she told them, and Beatrice was pleased that even after a few short weeks her business was slowly, but increasingly, building.

One Thursday evening after she'd unpacked some replacement stock and stacked it on the shelves, she took her own set of cards into the back room and began to lay them out to do a reading for herself. It was a week since she'd emailed the professor and she hadn't had a reply and she was starting to wonder if she was doing the right thing, searching for the missing card. That it wasn't something which should be left in the past, sleeping as it must have been for many years. Centuries, even.

She turned over The High Priestess, followed by the Six of

Cups and finally The Tower. Seeing this last card, she frowned, it was not one that she would have hoped for. The Priestess was telling her to trust her instincts, and she knew she was doing just that, searching for the missing card. The Six of Cups spoke of the past flowing into the present as indeed it would if she could fulfil her quest. She didn't know who, if anyone, may have previously gone looking for that last card, but what she knew for certain was that she must undertake the journey. The time was right, almost as if the pack had been waiting for her to reunite them.

But the third card, The Tower, indicated disruption and confusion, possibly a rocky foundation. That was a message she didn't want to see. She couldn't deny that, despite now settling into her new home, she still felt unsteady, as though she were a ship on a churning sea. Previously her rock, her father, had always been there to support her but now he'd gone. Or rather, she'd gone.

Going upstairs to her flat, she took the remains of her previous night's dinner out of the fridge. She was so used to making enough food for two, herself and her father, that she frequently ended up with too much, eating leftovers for several days. She put it in the oven whilst she hopped in the shower.

Thirty minutes later, sitting at the table with her phone propped up against the salt and pepper, she began to eat whilst checking her website and emails at the same time. At home, phones at the table had been banned, but there was nobody now to remind her of the rules. She still felt a little guilty but carried on regardless.

There was another enquiry about an online reading and she quickly replied to that, before turning to her personal emails. Her face lit up as she spotted a reply from Henry Stanton, having all but given up on hearing from him. Opening the email, she slowly laid down her cutlery as she read it and then read it again.

It confirmed that, as her research had suggested, he was a world authority on tarot cards and their history. And having seen the photos she'd taken of her cards, he was very interested. In fact, reading between the lines, she suspected he was extremely excited, in particular about the fact that it was missing The Devil card.

There have been rumours for many years within the tarot collectors' community of an ancient pack used as part of a collusion to murder women. I know that seems bizarre in this day and age, but centuries ago it was believed tarot cards had magical powers and could influence or control people's actions. Over the years, various sightings of a single Devil card have been recorded, in fact someone else messaged me a year ago saying they were searching for information about this very card. I've double-checked but unfortunately, I don't have the email with their contact details any more. Certainly, nobody I know has ever seen it, so the stories have been nothing but an anecdote. Perhaps they aren't though. You seemingly have a pack missing the card which was reputed to have the power to make people disappear. What is true, what is an illusion? Perhaps – with your help – we can finally find out and solve the mystery.

Beatrice laid her phone on the table and pushed her plate away. She thought about what her mother had told her about the cards, how they could change people's lives, set them free. But now here was someone else saying that they caused women to be murdered. Surely that wasn't what her mother meant?

There was a mystery, a tale here waiting to be told, and it was one that she was somehow connected to.

There was a mysterious male voice waiting to be sold... but it was one that he was expecting to hear on this day...

13

1644

The sun was setting behind Tallow Chandlers' Hall as Portia returned from having spent several hours with Elsebeth who had given birth to a dear son, Peter, two days previously. They'd spent most of the visit cooing at him in his crib whilst also gossiping about acquaintances and those who lived in the streets surrounding their homes.

She'd met Elsebeth when she'd come for a tarot reading and the other woman had been so fascinated in the cards and their potential powers, that she'd stayed for a further two hours asking questions. Portia now valued their close friendship. Because she could never be open and truthful with anyone about her flight from Venice, she hadn't made many acquaintances in all the years of living in London, even though she was on speaking terms with their neighbours. Elsebeth was special though, and Portia smiled as she remembered the laughter they'd shared earlier that afternoon.

Ahead of her, loud shouts caught her attention and she hurried forward to see what was causing the commotion. It sounded as though it was coming from close to home. With the way the buildings were jettied overhead it was difficult to see what was happening, but whatever it was, it appeared to be near to the doorway to the cobbler's shop next door to her own home.

The owner of the shop, Robert Shoemaker, was a widower without any children and he lived in two rooms above the shop, renting out the attached cottage next door to Portia. Despite it being small, it was comfortable and she liked where it was, unobtrusive and barely noticeable, just a small wooden door and a single window onto the street. She also liked that Robert, despite being past his prime, had muscular arms and was within shouting distance if needs be. Although it wasn't currently his voice she could hear raised, but several other men. As she drew closer, she saw a circle of people gathered just yards from Robert's door.

'Probably someone who has fallen out of the tavern after his dinner and is now inebriated,' a woman next to Portia remarked. 'I would lay money on his wife being one of those crowded around him, called to take him home.'

Portia was on the point of agreeing when there was a collective gasp from those watching, and several women screamed. Everyone began to back away, and into her view came a young man staggering about and appearing, as predicted, to be drunk. Except it then became obvious that his inability to walk was caused by a knife buried up to its hilt in his side. Within a moment he fell to the ground face down and lay there, not moving.

'An argument in the tavern then,' the woman said as she turned to carry on her way. Although shocked, Portia nodded. Fights that ended up with someone being injured or killed were not uncommon, although she hadn't seen violence on St Pancras Lane and so close to home before. She gave a shudder. They were living somewhere that she'd previously considered safe, and this had deeply unsettled her.

Within minutes the body was removed from the street, and Portia hurried up to her home where she found Maria watching everything, leaning out of the window. Robert came out to throw a bucket of water over the blood and wash it away. Portia questioned him about the ruckus, but he told her he knew nothing.

'A group of men chased him here, they were shouting about the women who have been disappearing, murdered. Then when they caught up with him, despite him proclaiming his innocence they killed him. Thankfully, the city marshal and constables were swift to remove the body.'

Portia felt a trickle of foreboding inch its way down her spine. Surely the mission which she undertook, but kept so secret, could not have found its way to her door? It must have been a killing of a different woman; there were plenty who plied their wares on the streets and met an untimely end.

Her worries intensified when the following morning, Maria, having returned from collecting water at the Poultry conduit, passed her a freshly printed pamphlet.

'All the women are talking about it,' she said as she stood waiting for Portia to read it out. The lurid title told them everything they needed to know.

'"Murderer of Women Taken from Their Beds Now Found".' She read on as the other two listened intently. It was difficult to read it out, her voice wobbling occasionally.

'"James Chernock had been seen in the vicinity of The Crown on several occasions after dark and twice stopped by the night watchmen, who recognised him".' She paused. It seemed poor James had simply been in the wrong place at the wrong time. '"When questioned by a group of men including Master Brown whose own wife was murdered, her body, like the others, cast into the river and from there out to sea, Chernock denied it. But as a sure demonstration of his guilt, he immediately turned tail and ran. He was, however, apprehended and during a scuffle, knifed. The constables have been unable to ascertain whose blade was used, but they are not looking any further for a perpetrator. The city's men can sleep well knowing that their wives and daughters are now safe".'

Portia snorted. 'Naturally, there is no concern that perhaps the women of this city have not been able to sleep in fear of their lives. So long as the men are not worrying about their wives, all is well.' She screwed up the news sheet and threw it onto the fire where it flamed momentarily, before disintegrating into wisps of blackened ash. If only it was as easy to dismiss it all thus. She knew the women hadn't been murdered, and unfortunately now an innocent man had been. And everyone else would know the truth when she was asked to help another of her sisters to escape, because then a husband would be shouting once more from the rooftops.

14

2025

Since reading the email from Henry Stanton, Beatrice's mind kept deliberating over the same questions and not finding any answers. Instead, she felt an unease which was steadily growing, keeping her awake long into the night.

She couldn't decide what had disturbed her the most, the mention of the card being associated with the murder of women, or the fact that, apparently, someone else out there was also on the trail for it. Now there was a sense of urgency, her previous mindset that it was little more than an adventure suddenly felt more like a race. For what reason could someone else want it, given that she herself had the rest of the pack? And it seemed that potentially this other person was more than one step ahead of her. Was she chasing a lost cause?

Her initial thought had been to reply to Henry and ask him not to let this other party know that she had the rest of the cards, but he'd said he no longer had the email enquiring about it, so she'd have to hope that the knowledge would remain a secret. But if there was one thing she had now learned, there was something special about the missing Devil card.

It was now Monday afternoon and she and Jack were going to the British Museum on the off chance that there was anything to do with tarot cards on display there. It was a long shot but so had been her email to Professor Stanton and that had yielded results, even though they weren't what she'd been expecting.

He was already waiting on the corner, his long legs encased in pale denim which looked soft and well-worn, together with a faded navy-blue shirt. A tattoo was just visible at the edge of where his sleeves were rolled up. As she approached, he was looking at his phone so she could view him without him being aware of her. And she liked what she saw.

'Hello,' she greeted him and gave him a quick hug, revelling in the few seconds of how it felt with her arms wrapped around his warm solid back as she breathed in his woody, musky after-shave. 'Are you ready to go?'

'I am.' Jack smiled down at her and she felt a curl of desire twist in her stomach, creeping upwards to make her face flush. 'I was thinking that once we've finished our investigations at the museum, we could grab an early dinner if you like?'

'Sounds great.' Beatrice tried to stop her face from showing just how much she liked him. She was sure he only thought of her as a friend but there was no denying the way her heart was beating faster than normal, and she knew it was being with him that was doing it. And dinner later would be the perfect way to end an afternoon together.

* * *

At first, Beatrice thought there was little to help their search as they wandered around the museum. They frequently found themselves in the middle of exhibition rooms and galleries which had fascinating artefacts but weren't remotely to do with medieval or Renaissance Italy, which was all Beatrice could think of as a starting point.

She was about to call it a day when she noticed a display cabinet with an ancient board which looked a little like a backgammon set and beside it, a pair of ancient cards from an old Italian card game, Tarocchini. The sign with the description explained they had been donated by a private collector called Margot Williams. Beatrice knew from her previous research that Tarocchini had been the precursor to the tarot deck. It was a long shot, but she wondered if there was a way to find this Margot.

After leaving the museum they walked to Covent Garden and found a pub where they could order food. Whilst Jack was at the bar ordering their dinner, Beatrice started searching on her phone for any leads or signs of Margot. The details beside the cards said that they had been donated in the 1990s, and depending on how old Margot had been then, perhaps it was too late to be looking for her.

'I haven't found anything obvious yet,' she explained when Jack joined her. 'I've googled her name but the few people who come up are nothing to do with antiquities or tarot cards.' She pulled the corners of her mouth down. 'I was getting excited when I saw an actual name, but she isn't easy to find.'

'The trouble is, we get so used to being able to find people on social media that we're immediately stumped when someone isn't there. We need to be cleverer than that,' he said. 'Try and think of people that this Margot might be linked with, or places. If I wanted to find a certain book or dealer, that's how I'd approach it.'

'Hmm, I'm guessing she'd potentially have connections with antique dealers, assuming she originally bought the cards and didn't inherit them. It might be easier to search out dealers, they *need* to be visible to attract customers.' She rubbed her hands together with pleasure that they'd thought of another thread to investigate. Before she could get her phone out again, their food arrived and she pressed pause in her head so she could enjoy having dinner with Jack. Every hour that they spent together, she couldn't deny to herself how much she was increasingly enjoying his company.

The evening sped past as they followed dinner with several beers and chatted on and on until Beatrice's throat began to feel husky. Jack had entertained her with tales from his university days and holidays he'd taken surfing in Cornwall. She'd guessed correctly from his hairstyle that first morning he'd turned up on her doorstep that he loved nothing more than riding the waves. Although the shop meant he couldn't take extended time off, he managed the occasional few days when his parents ran the shop and in turn he stayed at their place, near Newquay.

After walking to the underground station, they hopped on the Tube home. Jack had his arm around her waist as he steered her on and off trains and as she stood in front of him on the escalators, he placed both his hands on her waist. They felt warm and she ignored any doubts she had about anything happening with her only friend in London and just enjoyed his close proximity.

It was ten o'clock and already dark as they arrived home. The leaves on the sycamore trees around the edges of the small private gardens they walked past were now turning yellow. Having clung on to their resplendent green for as long as possible they were now a vibrant chartreuse, as though daubed with a paintbrush. Summer was all but over, the last few days clinging to their vestiges of warmth, reluctant to allow autumn in its profuse, exotic finery to sweep in.

Their steps slowed as they headed towards Beatrice's shop

and flat. She was wondering whether to invite Jack in for a coffee when he yawned and announced, 'It's been a long day, I'm worn out. And I've got to be up early tomorrow, I'm expecting a delivery. Thanks for today, I've had a really good time. Let me know if you track down Margot or discover anyone else who can help you.' He wrapped his arms tightly around her and she held her breath, wondering if he was going to kiss her, but to her disappointment he just bent down and gave her a peck on the cheek.

'Goodnight then,' she tried to keep her voice light, 'and thanks for coming along and helping me today. I'll definitely let you know if I get any further in my research.' He waited whilst she unlocked the shop door, locking it behind her again. A perfect gentleman, but not one that had any romantic designs on her, that was now obvious. His arm around her earlier had seemingly just been courtesy, as they'd got bumped by other travellers. It was probably just as well, she told herself, she had a lot going on in her head and a relationship wasn't a good idea. Despite that though, she slowly climbed the stairs to her flat, her heart heavy with disappointment.

15

1644

Both Maria and Vittoria were sleeping, their regular breathing a soft background to the sound of Portia's quill scratching across the surface of the blank card she'd made as, once again, she replicated The Devil card in readiness for when the next woman in need of her help arrived at her door. She never knew what happened to these cards, whether those she helped took them as a memento of a woman who had aided them in their hour of need, or if they were cast to the wind as John in his boat took them upriver to a new life, one that was safe from the dangers which threatened them in London. She sometimes worried that what she did may be etched in her face for others to read, giving away her secrets. And she had so many.

Now so familiar to her she didn't need to look at the original to replicate it, the lines and colours imprinted in her head and flowing in the paint onto the card. Whilst the pack were like family to her, their recognisable faces, this one was special, a favourite child. Once it was complete, she placed it in the cupboard to dry before climbing the stairs to lay down on her bed pallet and pull the blankets across herself. Beside her

Vittoria mumbled in her sleep and, with a smile, Portia moved quietly across the space to tuck the blankets around the girl.

The following afternoon, once the three of them had cleaned the house and Maria had been out to buy bread, together with a game pie, for dinner, Portia took the sack of hops and started to brew some ale. It was a fine line between making sure they had enough to drink and not making too much, so it started to turn rancid, a waste of precious ingredients. She'd asked Vittoria to help, but when she started adding the hops to the water bubbling over the fire, she told the girl to step away. If there was anything spilled, she might not be able to see in time to move out of its way.

'I shall play patience,' Vittoria said. As well as the tarot cards, Portia had brought from Italy a beautiful set of playing cards. Although not as exquisite as the tarot, they were beautiful in their own right. Unlike her own pack, there was no bond with these; she didn't need to understand what they told her, and she'd previously outlined the details in gum Arabic. Where Vittoria didn't recognise the pictures she could feel the raised bumps and understand which it was.

Just as Portia poured the boiling water over the hops, two things happened. The first was that she remembered she'd left the newly painted Devil card to dry in the cupboard the previous night and it was still there, and the second was that, at the same moment, Vittoria exclaimed she'd found it and held it up.

The shock caused Portia to pour some of the water over the floor and also her foot. Shouting, she shook the water away as she placed the pot down and hopped to a stool to sit down and pull off her boot and hose. The other two rushed to see and, despite the pain, Portia couldn't help noticing Vittoria still held the card, even though her attention was now firmly on the injury. For a moment, she put the card down on the table beside the pot and, fearful of the wet ruining the design, Portia snatched it up and slipped it into her pocket. Aside from the pain she was in, she heaved a sigh of relief, hoping she'd avoided a difficult conversation regarding the appearance of a replica card.

Within minutes, Maria was busily applying a salve of honey and oil to the skin; despite the protection of Portia's heavy leather footwear, the water had managed to seep in through the gaps between the laces and the tongue to scald her foot. It was a deep pink and already three small blisters had formed.

'You have been lucky,' Maria said. 'I think it won't scar, but it is going to be sore for several days. How did you manage to spill the water? You pour from that pot almost every day and have never done so before.'

'I know,' Portia said. 'I felt a little faint and my attention wavered for a moment.' She knew that wasn't what had distracted her, but it was a simple lie which would suffice. And, she considered, the pain in her foot was the price she'd had to pay in order to retrieve the card and keep it safe. She was surprised that Vittoria recognised it, but then again, she'd seen Portia's cards so frequently and the image on the front was seemingly distinctive enough, even for someone with limited eyesight.

'Then let me finish making the ale and you put your foot up to rest it,' Maria said.

'Nonsense.' Portia laughed. 'Bind my foot with some of those strips you tore from my old shift, the one that was beyond repair. They're so thin and the linen now very soft they will not hurt me any further, and I can then put my hose and boot back on once they've dried in front of the fire.' She pointed to where Vittoria had already placed the items, the stocking hung over the settle in front of the flames, which, after the addition of a big piece of applewood, were now licking up the chimney and throwing out a fierce heat.

Once her foot was bound, she walked gingerly to the cupboard and took out a bottle of spiced wine. They'd all had a shock, and this was an occasion in which they needed it for medicinal reasons, where something stronger than the small beer they drank day to day was required. It also gave her the opportunity to hide the card still in her pocket, and now with the tiny mark of Vittoria's fingerprint on one corner, beneath the pack. And only a moment too soon.

'Where did that card go that I found?' Vittoria asked. Her eyes were scanning the floor, her head bent close so she could see it properly. 'I am sure I found The Devil card beside the set of tarot. But it wasn't the actual one, the colours were not as vibrant, it was more like a copy on what felt like inferior card.' Portia's forehead quirked slightly into a frown.

'You are mistaken, my dear,' she replied. 'It *was* the actual Devil card. I found it on the floor after my most recent reading, it must have slipped out when I packed the others away. I just placed it there intending to wrap it with the rest but then forgot. Over the years all the cards have started to fade.'

She placed a small cup of wine in front of each of them and thankfully the card was soon forgotten as they sipped the drink and murmured their appreciation of something so delicious. Her racing heart slowly returned to normal, but she knew just how close she'd come to her secret being revealed.

* * *

The following day, one of Elsebeth's servants arrived at the door, his face pink and sweating from where he'd been running. He held onto the door jamb and bent over, trying to catch his breath whilst also attempting to deliver his message.

It took several minutes of Portia asking him to repeat certain parts before she gleaned what he was saying. That Peter was dangerously ill and Elsebeth was asking for her dear friend to be at the baby's bedside.

'Tell her I will be with her directly,' Portia commanded, and the man immediately turned to run home.

'You cannot be going out with your foot as bad as it is,' Maria exclaimed as Portia picked up her boot and carefully eased it over the bindings, making it a tight fit.

'After Vittoria and yourself, Elsebeth is the most precious person in the world to me,' Portia said. 'I cannot refuse her request; I must go to her and see if there is any way I can assist. Although an apothecary I am not, I will take some of the medications you have made and stored in case of illness in our house. Hopefully, they can help. Honestly,' she reassured, 'my foot does not pain me at all, the liniments you used have greatly assisted in my recuperation.' Leaving her shawl still hanging on the nail on the back of the door, confident it would remain warm enough outside for another couple of hours, she left.

Once outside her house she called a quick 'good day' to Robert who was stitching the upper part of a much-worn child's boot to the sole. Its owner perched on a stool waiting for it to be returned, the other foot, clad in its twin, swinging back and forth whilst his mother watched on.

It was only a brisk fifteen-minute walk to Elsebeth's home on Aldgate, but with her foot protesting with every step, it was closer to thirty minutes by the time Portia arrived. The servant who'd called on her earlier must have been keeping an eye out because he opened the door before she'd even knocked,

pointing behind him to the stairs. Portia nodded and hurried up
to the nursery as fast as her now burning foot would allow.

The room in which Elsebeth sat beside the heavy, carved oak
cradle was dark and hot, a fire burning brightly in the grate. The
flames leapt up the chimney as they threw out a heat which,
with the breathlessness from trying to hurry, made Portia feel
weak for a moment. She pulled up a chair beside Elsebeth and
flopped down into it, pulling her cap from her head.

'Tell me what ails him,' she asked. In the crib, the baby was
swaddled in a blanket, his damp, dark hair stuck to his face
which had a dark hue. Beneath the blankets, Portia could see his
chest rising and falling far too rapidly than would be normal.

'I do not know.' Elsebeth's voice trembled as she spoke. 'He
did not want to feed yesterday, and nor did he waken in the
night. Now he seems to have become worse, and although I can
wake him, he falls back to sleep almost immediately.'

'Does he have any rash?' Portia asked. She didn't have a lot of
experience of ill children, perhaps she should have brought her
neighbour with her, who knew what to look for. Babies fell sick
and died within days, sometimes hours, they were so fragile, and
Peter did look seriously ill. Being in the hot room with its background smell of disease turned her stomach as it brought back
memories of those last few hours in Italy fifteen years ago. She
swallowed hard and tried to drag her mind back to the present.

'Not that I have seen.' Elsebeth unwrapped the bindings
around him and lifted his shift. Portia ran her fingers down his
torso, the skin tacky with perspiration and breathed a small sigh
of relief that it was smooth. None of the scratchy feeling of
measles, at any rate. And she couldn't see any other skin discol-
oration either.

'Leave him unbound,' she said as Elsebeth went to wrap him
up again. 'It will be easier to see if a rash develops, and see how

he breathes easier now?' Although Peter's chest was still rising and falling rapidly, it had indeed lessened slightly now he was cooler. 'Let the fire burn down too,' she suggested.

'Do you know what the matter is with him?' Elsebeth asked. 'He is so precious, I cannot lose him.'

'I do not,' Portia admitted. 'But I have brought a tincture of endive and marigold to help break the fever. You will have to spoon it between his lips when you are able to wake him. Do it often, as many times as you are able. Is your husband at home? He should be here at his son's side at this dangerous time.'

As she said the word son, she was certain she saw Elsebeth blanch a little, but in the gloominess of the room it was difficult to see.

'He is not,' Elsebeth explained. 'He has gone to King's Lynn to oversee a shipment arriving from Antwerp. But it is safer he is away from home. For reasons I cannot speak of, we all fare better with him gone from the house.'

Portia wasn't sure she agreed, given that Peter was hovering close to death, but she didn't make a comment. By now, her foot was in agony and after handing over the medication she said her goodbyes, promising to return the following day.

Her journey back was even slower than the one to Aldgate and hobbling down Walbrooke Street, Portia could only think of sitting down and taking the weight off her foot. The streets were now fairly empty as people began to head home for the night, but as she turned to cross St Stephen's churchyard, she caught sight of a man up ahead talking with someone, his face turned to his companion, in profile. For a moment it looked so familiar with its hooked nose and long chin that she stopped still on the path and the person behind walked into the back of her.

'Sorry.' Flustered, she stepped to one side and looked again, but the man had gone. Surely it couldn't be who she'd first thought, she hadn't seen him in fifteen years. And there was no reason why he'd be here in London; it was simply her mind playing tricks. If he knew she was here, and the precious cargo she'd brought, then her world would come crashing down and her life would be in danger. She would protect all that she had with everything she'd got.

Starting to feel hot, her forehead prickling as beads of sweat formed across it, she wondered if she too was coming down with a fever. Maria had been right, going out on her injured foot had been a mistake and she limped towards home, promising herself that as soon as Peter was on the mend she'd rest it properly. But right now, her mind was racing after what she just thought she'd seen.

16

1644

Within two days of burning her foot, Portia came down with a fever and she lay on her bed for almost a week feeling spent, alternately burning hot and then icy cold. Maria insisted that she procure a tincture of poppy seeds from the apothecary, and she continued to use honey on the wound. At some point, although Portia had no idea when, word had come from Elsebeth that Peter had turned a corner and his fever had left him.

As she lay on her bed pallet drifting in and out of consciousness, Portia's mind tumbled with hallucinations and nightmares as it churned over the man she thought she'd seen on her way home from visiting Elsebeth. He appeared to her, his face large and looming as he shouted that he would take her for his wife, that he would steal Vittoria away from her. She belonged to the Tabanellis, she was their possession and they never let that which they owned slip through their hands. Be it dead, or alive. Several times she roused from her deep slumber shouting and flailing her arms against him, even though she was the only person in the bed. It was as though she could feel his hands creeping upon her.

Thankfully, by the seventh day Portia finally felt sufficiently well enough to sit beside the window and look out at the small areas of the street which were visible to her. Now, the hallucinations of her fever had receded, and yet she could not properly shake them off. She found herself watching everyone walking past, terrified that she hadn't been mistaken and her greatest fear would be realised.

They needed to hide, to move to another house away from the area in which they currently lived. If the women who visited for card readings couldn't find her, at least for a while, then things would calm down. Goodwives talked and she'd be found again in due course, but lying low, like a fox in the grass, was necessary for a while. First, she would have to explain to the other two, to persuade them it was a good idea, without divulging her reasons.

Later that evening after supper she broached the subject. They'd eaten some cheese followed by stewed apple and blackberries and were feeling replete. There would never be a better time, Portia decided.

'I have decided that I wish to move to another lodging,' she announced. 'Since I burned my foot, this place holds bad memories for me. And we have enough gold saved to afford something a little larger. Now I am feeling well again it is my intention to go out tomorrow and ask around. Someone will know of something suitable.'

'Oh, but not far, surely?' Vittoria's mouth was turned down at the corners. 'You know my eyesight is no longer as proficient as it once was. I can find my way around the streets in our local area because they are familiar to me.' Portia felt a stab of guilt, before reminding herself that, ultimately, the dangerous work she did was for Vittoria. She hadn't chosen to move house on a whim, whatever she'd just told the other two.

'I promise it will not be far. And if you would like me to, I will draw a map of the new locale with a raised surface, as I have on the playing cards, and you can follow it with your fingertips,' she said.

'Thank you.' Vittoria nodded her acquiescence. 'Perhaps you could do that with other things when my eyes get worse. You keep saying that in years to come I might not be able to read the tarot cards, but doing as you have suggested would solve the problem, would it not?'

'I cannot deface my own pack,' Portia said. 'Not the ones which have belonged to our family for so many years. But perhaps I could create you a set of your own to use?' she suggested, and Vittoria smiled and nodded, her eyes lighting up with pleasure. Portia would do anything to carry on seeing her beautiful face, do whatever she had to, to keep the girl – and all their lives – from being harmed.

* * *

Having now made her mind up to move house, Portia went out the following morning in search of somewhere new. Beneath her velvet jacket, which she'd originally brought from Italy and was now faded, shining where the thick, soft pile had rubbed away, she carried a pouch tied around her waist, heavy with gold coins to pay the necessary first quarter's rent.

Still wishing to be reasonably close to St Pancras Lane as she'd promised Vittoria, but far enough away to avoid any suspicion which may come knocking at their door, she stepped out towards the river. She had decided that she'd like to be closer to John. If she ever needed brute strength, then having him close at hand would be sensible. And, she admitted to herself, perhaps she could visit him at the river more often. As she walked her eyes darted from side to side, and she was feeling sick as she kept remembering the man she thought she'd seen before. She had to be mistaken.

After asking around she was directed to a house on Philpot Lane which was empty and available to rent. In truth, she would have rather moved to Southwark, south of the river, but she knew that Vittoria and Maria would never concede to be so far from their friends and the shops they preferred. And it was the wrong side of the river to John.

Inside the building it smelled musty with the sharp odour of rats' urine. That was to be expected though; when a property lay empty it was only a matter of days before the vermin would move in. But a fire in the hearth and the noise of people would soon get rid of all but the most bold and brave. And those would be despatched with the upside of her shovel and thrown on the fire.

Despite the smell, it was perfect for them. Stairs to an upper level with two separate rooms, one of which was large enough to put up a hanging and divide into two, so that finally all three of them could have a sleeping space of their own. It often crossed her mind that by doing what she had done fleeing Milan, she'd denied Vittoria a life so much more luxurious than the one she now lived. But at what price? Here they may be poor, but they were safe. At least they would be, she was certain, after they moved to this new abode.

'I'll take it,' she said to the landlord who was waiting at the door. He'd explained that he owned the row of terraced houses of which this was the middle one, his father having built them.

Turning her back to him so he couldn't see from where she was retrieving her money, she counted twelve gold sovereigns out and handed them over. 'We will move tomorrow,' she confirmed.

'I'll send my lad down to light a fire in the morning.' He indicated the large stone fireplace set into the opposite wall to the door. The chimney would carry heat up too and they would be warm at night, Portia thought. 'That way any "visitors" currently here will be long gone before you arrive.' She thanked him for his thoughtfulness and taking the key from him she set off home, pausing for a moment to purchase some marchpane. It was a rare treat in the household but she was feeling in a celebratory mood.

The move, with John's assistance, went smoothly. The following morning Portia hired a cart to carry their belongings to the new house and John lifted their few pieces of furniture onto it.

As promised, when they arrived, there was a fire blazing in the hearth with a further supply of wood already stacked up. She'd agreed to pay an extra penny a week for the fuel, it was easier to not have to worry about where to procure it or to carry it to the house. Despite her initial reluctance to move, Vittoria now had a wide smile on her face as she explored their new, bigger, abode. Together with John, the carter carried in their possessions and placed them on the floor, lifting the beds upstairs.

It didn't take long to arrange their items in the larger space, and it highlighted how little they actually owned. Portia realised she'd have to buy some sort of cupboard now they no longer had one built in. Her precious cards were in her pocket, hard against her leg as she moved about, but she was too fearful to put them down for a moment in case they got mislaid. Despite the amount of gold she'd paid out to enable them to move, there was no denying more would have to change hands to purchase extra furniture, and she set off to the Shambles where she could employ a joiner to make something rudimentary for her at a decent price.

Within days the new furniture was delivered. She had also purchased some wool to re-stuff their thin, worn mattresses, and the house was filled with the soft scent of summer. It made her yearn for the countryside of her childhood where months of hot weather made everything around them smell fragrant; flowers and crops and sun-baked earth. Not the scent of wet cobbles and the Fleet ditch, or animal excrement left on the streets.

Now, a small oak cupboard stood proudly in their new parlour. Although roughly hewn, made at speed and with the occasional gouge in the timber where a tool had slipped, there was a sturdy lock and with relief, Portia placed her coffer of money, the remains of the Italian jewels stolen when she'd made her escape from Milan and her cards inside, along with their spare clothes, their medicine phials and bottles. Portia said a silent prayer of thanks. She knew those who needed her would find her again and she trusted the cards to invoke that, but she hoped she was concealed, at least for a while, from he who would kill her if he knew what she'd done.

17

2025

Beatrice checked she had everything she needed in her handbag. After Jack's suggestion, she'd emailed every auction house in the country asking if they had any records of sales of tarot cards. She also explained that she was looking for a Margot Williams, but as she'd suspected, nobody was going to discuss the other woman, if they even knew of her. Unfortunately, Margot seemed to be a dead end, as far as her researching went.

However, to her delight, she received a reply from a small auction house near Ipswich where the owner, Ian Barwell, informed her that ten years previously he'd been involved in the sale of an estate for a collector of historical divination and astrological items. Including, he recalled, several packs of tarot cards.

He'd suggested she visited him, so today she was heading to Suffolk on the train. Jack had offered to come with her, and she had readily agreed, excited at the thought of a day out together. Every time her stomach felt jittery, she reminded herself that they were just friends, but that did nothing to quash the anticipation and buzzing inside.

They'd agreed to meet at the end of the mews at nine thirty.

Jack needed to wait until his assistant, Alex, was in the shop and everything was satisfactory before he could leave. At least, Beatrice thought, she could lock hers up and just leave it. She was pleased she had chosen to take Mondays as her day off, it was an easier day to be out and about investigating.

She only waited a couple of minutes before Jack appeared, his wide, generous, ever-present smile lighting up his face.

'All okay?' she asked.

'Yes, Alex is fine and I'm just at the end of my phone if he needs me, although in all honesty, he rarely has to defer to me these days. I'm almost superfluous to requirements.'

They jumped on the Tube to Liverpool Street and were soon sitting on the train with a cup of coffee watching the countryside rushing past the window. Jack had sat down opposite her and was now asking her what she knew about the person they were going to meet.

'He sold some cards at an auction about a decade ago, including one which sounds similar to the one I'm searching for,' Beatrice explained. 'Apparently it was very unusual, that's why he remembers it. He suggested if he could see the rest of the cards,' she patted her handbag where they were safely stowed, 'he may be able to tell if they're part of the same set.'

'And does he have the details of who bought it?' Jack asked.

'He said he has; it was a dealer – so someone he has done business with from time to time. But he won't tell me, data protection and all that. But if he thinks it's the right one, he'll pass my details on. I can't believe that after so many years, centuries, I might be the one to reunite the pack. I wish my mum knew, she'd be so pleased.'

'Fingers crossed this chap has some answers,' Jack said.

They chatted for the rest of the journey, slipping easily from one subject to the next, just as they did every time they were together, and before she knew it, Beatrice realised they were pulling into their station. Grabbing her bag, she and Jack hurried to the train door.

It was a short taxi ride from the station to the auction house. They were both immediately captivated by the Aladdin's cave of items big and small in the large showroom where they'd been asked to wait whilst the receptionist went to find Ian Barwell. The rows of chairs lined up across the middle indicated it was also where the sales took place and, Beatrice considered, how could you not find yourself putting your arm up to bid when you were surrounded by hundreds of years of people's lives for sale? Their belongings once so precious, yet now relegated to sit on furniture also bearing labels denoting their sale number. A Georgian chest of drawers in oak so dark it was almost black and covered in scratches and nicks from use over the centuries was covered in random objects; a brass sextant, a carriage clock, a filigree egg on a gold stand that looked like, but almost certainly wasn't, Fabergé.

Jack was rummaging in a box of books he'd found, taking each one out and looking inside the front cover. Beatrice guessed he was hoping to discover a first edition of something rare. He was so busy that when a voice called out, 'Those books are a job lot, they'll probably go for a tenner a box. You can log on and bid online,' they both jumped.

Beatrice quickly put down the china teapot she was holding and turned to see the owner of the voice. He was tall, well over six foot and slightly stooped as if he'd spent his life physically apologising for his height, and he looked as though he should have retired years ago. His glasses were hanging on a chain around his neck.

'Ian? Ian Barwell?' Beatrice asked, walking over and holding out her hand to shake his. Jack quickly replaced the books he'd been piling on the floor as he reached into the darkest recesses of the box for any more treasures, and followed her.

'I am,' Ian confirmed. Just like the rest of him, his hands were enormous. 'You must be Beatrice?'

'Yes. And this is my friend Jack, he's come along too. I hope that's okay?'

'The more the merrier,' Ian said, smiling. 'Shall we go into my office and have a cup of tea, and you can tell me about these tarot cards you have.'

A few minutes later they were ensconced in what was, Beatrice considered, possibly the smallest office in the world, especially for such a physically big man. If he moved some of the furniture and *objets d'art*, there might be more room for some chairs, she thought as she and Jack perched on a pair of mismatched wheelback dining chairs.

Bringing in some cups of tea, Ian handed them over before sitting down behind the heavy mahogany desk. There were yet more random items balanced around the edges, as though he'd put them down and forgotten why they were there. Thankfully, the centre was clear; Beatrice didn't want to display her cards anywhere which she wasn't certain was clean.

'So, you are on the search for a particular tarot card, one that is missing from a pack in your possession,' he said. 'Did you bring them with you as we discussed?'

'Yes, of course.' Beatrice took them reverently from her bag and placed them on his desk. She took the first couple of cards from the top of the pack, The Empress and the Ace of Pentacles, which both still looked almost as bright as they must have the day they were painted.

Ian put a loupe into his eye socket and, switching an angle poise lamp to better illuminate the cards, he picked one up carefully and held it close to his face as he scrutinised it. After five minutes, during which the only sound in the room was their breathing and the rattle of china as she and Jack drank their tea – given the faded rose patterns and patchy gilt edges on the cups and saucers, Beatrice wondered if they were also auction lots – Ian moved on from the two overturned cards to then carefully examine the back of one.

'You are correct in your assumption, these cards are probably late fifteenth or early sixteenth century – the inscriptions are in Latin. I'm pretty certain they are Italian in origin. May I ask how you came by them? If these were to have come up in auction, it would have caused a big stir in the industry, and I'd have known about it.'

'I inherited them,' Beatrice explained. 'My mother's ancestors were Italian and they've been passed down through the generations. But there's a card missing from the pack, that's why I'm here. I'm trying to track it down, to make the set whole again. The trouble is, I have no idea even where to start looking. Hence why I sent you, and pretty much all the other auction houses in the country, an email. I haven't heard back from anyone else though.'

'Indeed,' Ian said as he nodded slowly. 'Bear with me, let me look something up, I need to double-check. If these are what I think they are, you may have an important element in a fascinating mystery.' He went to a bookcase beside Jack and after a couple of minutes found what he was looking for. Sitting back down, he began to riffle furiously through the pages, muttering to himself.

'Yes, yes, I thought so. Here we go.' He passed the book over, open at a page with a small photo of the back of a card which looked identical to Beatrice's pack.

'That's it,' she exclaimed, grinning at Jack and then Ian. 'That must be my missing card. I'm certain there won't be another pack like this, because it's hand-painted and who would have a random Devil card on its own unless it was missing from a set? Is there a photo of the front of the card?' She flipped the pages back and forth.

'Sadly, it appears not,' Ian said. 'This is all I have; it's the auction catalogue. As I said in my email, the card was sold to a dealer in London; he used to take quite a few pieces from us back then. The business is still there though, I sometimes hear about them on the grapevine. Let me give him a quick call and make sure he doesn't mind me passing his details on. One minute.' Picking his phone up off the desk, Ian hurried out, leaving Jack and Beatrice looking at each other in astonishment.

'I can't believe I've managed to track it down so quickly,' Beatrice said. 'I honestly thought it would be a lost cause.'

'Don't get too excited yet,' Jack warned. She knew he was right, the voice of reason, but she couldn't stop her hand from shaking a little as she squeezed his.

'There we go, all sorted.' Within minutes Ian marched back in and threw himself back in his chair, making it roll back a little, hitting the cabinet behind him. 'Let me write this address down.' He looked over the detritus on the desk until he found a biro and an old envelope. 'Tristan Pritchard, he's expecting a call from you. He's the son of the dealer who bought it, but he's running the company now. Poor old Jacob is no more, I must have missed the notice that he'd passed away. It's a sad state of life when all one's friends start popping off.' His momentary morose expression was replaced almost immediately with a smile as he handed Beatrice the envelope on which he'd written Tristan's address and the name of the company. She put it in her bag and carefully packaged up the cards again.

'He remembered the card I was speaking of it because it caused quite a stir when it surfaced. And he reminded me there was someone else after it too. A few weeks after the sale I was approached by a woman, I can't remember her name, she'd heard I was in possession of the card and she wanted to buy it. Quite insistent in fact. I sent her to Tristan so he might have her details. He's very excited that you may have the rest of the pack. Don't let him start badgering you to sell them to him.' He laughed to himself. 'Dealers always consider everything can be purchased for the right price.'

'I definitely won't,' Beatrice assured him. 'These cards are precious to me. They're part of my family, my heritage.'

'Do let me know what you discover,' Ian said. 'I love a quest for a specialist object.'

'Of course I will,' Beatrice promised as they left the office and said their goodbyes. 'You've been so helpful, thank you. I truly appreciate it.'

She and Jack decided to walk back to the train station. He offered her his arm and she tucked hers through his. Their breath was visible in tiny clouds in front of them; the sky was a vibrant cerulean blue, but the temperature had dropped significantly in the past couple of days and the weather was now noticeably cooler as autumn began to properly tighten its grip. Beatrice scuffed her feet in the crisp, dry leaves which were piled up in little drifts on the pavement.

'Well, that went even better than I'd hoped for,' she said. 'I didn't even consider that he'd have a photograph of my card and a possible trail to it. It seems all too good to be true.'

'I hope it's all as straightforward as it's been today. Did he give you the email address for this Tristan chap?'

'No, just his name and business details, but once we're settled on the train, I can start looking online to see what I can discover.'

The phone signal on their journey back to London was

frequently, and frustratingly, non-existent and she hadn't managed to find any further information by the time she got home. Once she was upstairs in her flat with a sandwich and a cup of coffee, Jack having gone straight back to his shop, Beatrice was desperate to start searching properly.

Despite what Ian had said, she couldn't find anything online to indicate that Tristan was still running his father's business, and Beatrice felt her previous excitement begin to dissipate. Even searching for his name brought up few clues until, after ninety minutes of unsuccessfully following threads which eventually led nowhere, she found someone who may possibly be him, on LinkedIn. It was the right name and he looked in his fifties, which seemed about the right age to have lost a parent and inherited a business. A business which subsequently seemed to have disappeared. He described himself as a purveyor of *objets d'art*, this had to be him.

She quickly sent him an email mentioning Ian Barwell and what she was searching for, then messaged Jack to give him an update. Was this finally a step towards reuniting the pack? Of doing what her mother would have done if she were still alive? This, she realised, wasn't just a search, a journey for a card, but also for herself. And it was the memory of her mother that was pushing her on. Her mind drifted back as it so often did to when she'd first been shown how to do a tarot reading and how her mother had hugged her so tight as she'd instinctively understood the connection between a reader and her cards. Would there ever be a time when her memories didn't hurt as much as they still did?

18

1644

Three days after they'd moved house and with their lives now settled back into a normal routine, Portia was interrupted in her making of some more honey and oil salve. Maria had used their entire supply of it on her foot, and now it needed to be replenished. The scald was thankfully much improved, the blisters gone, although there were still two patches which were pink, the skin wrinkled as though it had been stretched and pulled in different directions. Despite her hopes for the contrary, she knew it would scar and remain like that.

The door burst open to admit Vittoria, together with Caterina. Behind them came Maria, as usual left to carry all the shopping, a hessian bag bulging with vegetables and a rabbit hanging from a piece of string, blood congealed around its neck. The fur would be cleaned and cured and later utilised for winter collars and muffs. It was more expensive to buy than if the rabbit was unskinned, but the snow at the start of the year remained at the back of Portia's mind and she wanted to make sure they were well prepared if similarly harsh weather occurred again in six months' time.

Given that it was only days since they'd moved home, she was surprised to see Caterina. Although the two girls' paths would have likely crossed again at some point, given they were continuing to use the same merchants and traders as before, she hadn't expected to see her quite so soon.

'Hello.' She smiled at them both as they continued talking and laughing together, just as they had been as they arrived. 'I am surprised to see you have found us already, Caterina, but it is lovely to see you.' Vittoria was already pouring them both small beakers of beer sitting in a jug on the cold shelf, a slab of stone which would help keep things cooler when the sun outside was at its hottest. Already midsummer's day was less than a week away and then the city would erupt in celebrations, music, dancing and a lot of wine. Sore heads would abound for days afterwards, and there would be a sharp increase in babies born the following spring.

After the revelries, the heat of the sun usually blazed down until the autumn solstice and as time went on the pall of stench from the Fleet ditch would creep out until it hung like a canopy across the city. There was no escaping it. Having experienced nothing similar in Milan, despite living in London for fifteen years, Portia still couldn't get used to it.

'I told her where to find us,' Vittoria explained. 'The day before we left St Pancras Lane, I went to find Caterina to tell her we were moving. I know where she lives with her father, and with everything to organise, I do not believe you even realised I was gone.' She was right, Portia mused, at no point had she noticed the girl wasn't there. It was dangerous for Vittoria with her limited eyesight to be out on her own; thank goodness she'd navigated her way there and back successfully. Portia made a note to make sure in future that she knew where the girl was at all times. At least Caterina was no danger to her. 'And wait till she tells you what has happened!' It was at that point when she realised that the two girls' eyes were bright with excitement.

'Tell me then,' she said, putting her pestle and mortar down and placing her hands on her hips, smiling as she looked between their bright faces expectantly.

'You said that there was marriage in the air and ten days ago my father brought home a young man, Filippo, who has just arrived from Rome. He is wonderful. Handsome and kind, I believe he is sweet on me and I do not think my father will object if he were to ask for my hand. We have spent many hours together in the parlour talking of all kinds of things. Of home, Italy, London. Of his work for my father – he is very good with mathematics and works on the ledgers. I believe I am falling in love.' She gave a big sigh, a smile on her face. Portia could see that Vittoria was entranced with it all.

'And after you are wed,' she said, 'then it will be my turn. I must have my cards read, Mama, I need The Empress to show her face and a husband to walk into my life too.'

Portia felt the smile slide off her face. She had never considered that Vittoria would want to leave their home, to fall in love and have a family of her own. In her head the girl was exactly that, a child to be protected, not a young lady of marriageable age. There had been so much danger involved in getting them to London, she hadn't ever thought ahead to that point in their future, only ever imagining them with Maria, living together forever. She'd been putting aside money for Vittoria after she was no longer there, and yet the girl might be expecting it to be used as her dowry. How could she have been so naïve? Naturally, Vittoria would want what all young women dreamed of. Especially when her friend spoke of it too.

'It is not always easy to find a husband,' Portia warned. 'And not all men are kind; once you are wearing a wedding band upon your finger, he may do whatever he wishes.' She hadn't told Vittoria in explicit detail how her father had been, wishing to spare the girl, but now she wondered if that had been the wrong decision. Portia was thankful though that – in spite of Vittoria's beauty – it was very unlikely that a man would take a wife who may in the future lose the rest of her sight. In time, she might not be able to cook or sew at all. Her heart felt heavy with sadness. It was the natural course of things, the way of the world, and she didn't want to speak the truth out loud and upset the girl.

'Certainly not easy when your eyes are as yours are.' Maria's sharp voice carried from the scullery. Whilst Portia avoided subjects she'd rather not talk about, Maria said what was on her mind, even if it was not what anyone wanted to hear.

'No, that is not true,' replied Vittoria, hands on her hips and lips pouting. 'I have pretty looks, you have always told me that, and a husband will be found for me. And of course he will not harm me, or be unkind for I shall choose wisely, find a man who falls in love with me. Come Caterina, we will not stay here. Let us walk to your house, perhaps your papa will have another guest who is looking for a wife.' She flounced out with Caterina in tow, the girl looking apologetically at Portia as she ran after her friend. Just as Portia had feared, Vittoria lived in a world in her head where all was touched with gold and good fortune. They had shielded her from the harsh realities of life.

'I will make sure she gets back safely,' Caterina reassured as she closed the door behind her, calling to Vittoria to slow down before she tripped on something.

'Why did you say that?' Portia turned on Maria who continued folding the clean washing which had been spread on bushes in the small piece of garden behind their home. 'Now she is upset.'

'Because it is the truth.' Maria shrugged. 'Her eyesight has deteriorated over the past two years, we both know that. Even this week she was having to bend close to the hair slides on the haberdashery stall to see them properly. No man, however pretty she is, will be burdened with a wife who cannot keep house for him, or look after the babes.'

Portia knew the other woman had only said what she was thinking, and she told her so. 'But you should not have said it aloud. She will soon notice when there are no offers of marriage and it would have been better if she had realised it herself. Now she is upset and it will be worse when Caterina marries and is then with child; showing Vittoria all that she may well never come to have.'

'It is sad, yes, but it is the way things are in life. And at least she has you and me to take care of her...' She stopped talking at that point and continued with her folding. Portia knew the words she had not spoken, that at some point they would not be there and, even if she was provided for financially, Vittoria would need someone to help her in the house. The need to save enough felt more of a burden than ever.

* * *

As Portia suspected, it didn't take long for her customers to find her once more, and a week after Caterina's visit, there was a knock at the door and it opened to reveal an elderly woman. Her clothes were old-fashioned, a stiff stomacher holding her upright and her skirts wider than was more common now.

Vittoria had been quiet since the discussion about marriage and, realising the visitor was a customer wanting a reading, she pulled on her boots with a deep sigh and stomped out of the door behind Maria. As it closed, Portia heard Maria suggest they went to find someone selling cinnamon cakes and there was a grunt of agreement. Hopefully, the heavy mood in the house would soon start to lift.

Once they were on their own, Portia invited the woman to be seated and collected her cards from the cupboard. It was the first reading she'd done in their new house, and it felt good to get them out again.

'What do you wish the cards to tell you?' she asked. Sometimes, women who came to her because they needed to disappear didn't offer this information immediately and she needed to ensure The Devil card was removed from the pack before she started, if she was going to replace it at the right time.

'I have a dilemma; I need some pointers of which way I must go. A fork in the road, a decision with far-reaching consequences. I need some guidance of which I must choose. You seem like a woman who will have the answers, who knows how I feel.'

Portia felt a tickle of unease make the hairs on her neck stand on edge. The woman was absolutely right, she had made some tough decisions in her journey through life, although if necessary, she would do the same again. It was as though her customer had sight into her heart. Placing three cards out in front of the woman, she instructed her to turn the first card over. She heard a sigh of relief as the card depicted a man and a woman entwined with each other.

'The Lovers. It speaks to us of someone you knew in the past who brings with them a choice you must now make about your life. A decision about love, your heart, a joining of two people.' The other woman didn't take her eyes off the card as though she was expecting it to tell her something more. Portia knew it wouldn't. The only person the cards truly spoke to was herself because that was the way they behaved, just as they had with her mother, with her grandmother. They had an affinity with the woman who owned them, not with the person for whom they gave forth their knowledge. Who would read them when she had gone? Because Vittoria could not. She turned the next card and laid it down. The woman's eyes widened in fright.

'The Hanged Man,' Portia explained. 'This card can mean one of many things. Today it is telling you that you need to consider carefully which road to travel. To pause and not to rush into a decision you may later regret.'

Turning over the third card, she felt a jolt in her chest and her heart began to beat faster. The Hierophant. The Pope in red sacred vestments seated on a throne. But instead of facing the woman, it was facing herself and that potentially gave a different meaning to it.

'The Hierophant, inverted,' she said. 'He is a teacher to lead us spiritually and tells us that the unlocking of truths will bring us freedom. In this world, or the next.' The more she spoke, the more the woman smiled and nodded.

'I knew I was right to seek you out,' she told Portia. 'Others had told me that you hold life's decisions and future in your cards, and they are correct. Thank you, I know now what I must do.' She didn't divulge what her dilemma was but left the house with a spring in her step, one which hadn't been there when she'd arrived.

Returning to the table, Portia picked up the final card, The Hierophant, again. She knew what it truly meant, and she couldn't help wondering if it was bringing a message for her. Because upside down, the card told that what she believed was somehow distorted and that information was being kept from her, purposefully or not. Something was stirring beneath her feet, and the strong walls she'd built around herself and Vittoria were starting to tremble. She couldn't allow them to fall. There was danger lurking. She'd suspected it for a while, except she didn't know what it was and how could she fight something she had no knowledge of? An unknown adversary. Despite living peaceably and without fear in London for so many years now, something was waiting, a sharp scent of threat. She was frightened, and yet she did not know what of. Perhaps she would do a card reading for herself and see what they told her, they were never wrong.

Portia picked up the cards and then paused. To be forewarned had to be an advantage, but she was scared to see what may be waiting for her. From the way she could sense something in the air, whatever was awakening wouldn't be for the better.

Sitting back down, she shuffled the cards and lay them down. Closing her eyes, she placed the three cards before her and turned the first one.

19

2025

Five days after their trip to Suffolk, Beatrice received a lengthy reply from Tristan. She was desperate to show Jack, but she had a reading booked at the shop and couldn't close until five o'clock. The rest of the day threatened to crawl past extremely slowly. Especially after she'd messaged Jack and he'd suggested they go out for dinner later so she could tell him everything.

Her customer arrived on time for her three o'clock appointment. She wasn't what Beatrice had been expecting; Heather Wright was middle-aged and she was wearing jeans and a hoodie. Her voice over the phone when she'd booked had been polite but brusque, and she'd sounded like a city solicitor or investment banker. Beatrice had expected her to be suited and booted.

As she showed Heather through to the back room, she noticed the woman was repeatedly wiping her hands against her jumper as though they were sweating.

'Have you ever had a reading before?' Beatrice asked, keen to put her customer at ease. She wanted a visit to her shop to be an experience so people left an excellent review and hopefully suggested to friends that they too visit.

'No, never.' Heather shook her head. 'I don't even know why I'm here really, but I have something going round and round my head and I can't decide what to do. I'm hoping the cards can shed some light.'

'They cannot give you direct answers,' Beatrice warned as she started to shuffle the pack. She loved the way they instantly felt warm in her hands, as though glowing with pleasure at her touch. 'However, they can show you different ways of thinking, other roads you may not have travelled and perhaps give you a new direction to explore your questions a different way.' Laying the cards on the table, she drew a deep breath as she looked at the first card turned. It wasn't a good place to start.

'The Three of Swords. This signifies grief, sorrow, a separation perhaps. Some sort of emotional turmoil.' She paused for a moment, but Heather said nothing, so not wanting to dwell on it further, she turned the second card.

'The Hermit.' The card showed an old man dressed in rags, as though a homeless person. He was depicted in monotone and wasn't as attractive as her other cards. 'A card which tells of introspection, mulling things over. Taking time away from the rest of a busy life to reflect on important matters.' Still Heather didn't say a word, just cleared her throat and appeared to be awaiting the final card. Beatrice turned it over.

She stared at the card. It was upside down, facing her instead of Heather. Was this also a message for her? The Devil card, what was true and what was an illusion. She wasn't expecting it and nor did she understand it, although that was the thing with the cards, as she'd just explained, they didn't automatically give an answer. It was up to the person to understand them. Clearing her throat, she explained what it meant.

'And finally, The Devil card. It is telling you to distinguish between what is real and what is a lie. An illusion.'

Opposite her, Heather drew her breath in sharply. 'It's all a lie,' she whispered. 'I've created an illusion and I don't think I can keep it going any longer. The card is right, now the truth is going to come pouring out and I cannot stop it.'

Beatrice waited to see if any further information was forthcoming. She'd long since learned that people had to assimilate things in their heads before they could explain them out loud.

Heather kept her head down, looking at her hands twisting and turning in her lap.

'I had a baby. A long time ago, I was fourteen.' Her voice was low, and Beatrice had to lean forward to hear her. 'I didn't even tell anyone I was pregnant, I knew my dad would blow his stack. So, I hid the pregnancy and had the baby in my bedroom. Luckily, the rest of my family were out, no one heard all the noise. It was a little boy, he was gorgeous. He had a thatch of dark hair and huge, deep blue eyes. I couldn't keep him though. I was so scared. I wrapped him in one of my jumpers and left him in the stairwell of a block of flats nearby. It was a busy place, I knew he'd start crying and be found quickly. Which he was, there were lots of reports in the papers and on the telly. All that *we need the mother to come forward, she might require medical treatment* stuff. As if a mother who has concealed a pregnancy and birth is then going to out themselves. Of course, I said nothing. He was taken to St Thomas's Hospital, and the nurses named him Thomas. I go past it almost every day on the bus and I think about him.'

Beatrice was still silent but this time from surprise; she hadn't been expecting a tale such as this.

'My entire life since then has been a lie. As you say, an illusion. Because I've never told anyone, in fact this is the first time I've spoken of him out loud. I've been married for thirty years,

I've got two daughters and a grandson. But then four weeks ago out of the blue I received an email; Thomas has tracked me down. Can you believe it? One of my girls got me a DNA kit for Christmas last year, it tells you where your ancestors originated from, in my case Hackney with a smidge of Sweden. I didn't realise when I did it that it also shows any other people to whom you are related. Although at the time it only showed my cousin Chris. But then Thomas must have done one too, because it showed that he was a close match to me. Close as in, I must be a parent.'

Finally, Heather looked up, her eyes full of tears. 'I have no idea what to do. I so desperately want to meet him, to say sorry for what I did. He deserves that, even if he gives me a mouthful of abuse. And I wouldn't blame him. But if I do, I'm going to have to tell my family. My dad is no longer with us, but my mum is. She's very old, the shock would probably kill her. I hoped that coming here might give me some answers of what to do.'

'I did warn you it isn't as straightforward as that,' Beatrice reminded her, softly. 'But look again at what the cards have told you. The Hermit, taking time out to consider things. Nobody is telling you to make your mind up immediately. Does that make it any easier to see a way forward?'

As Beatrice went through the cards again, she suspected Heather had barely listened the first time, her head so full of the reason why she was visiting.

'I understand it better now you've explained a second time, thank you,' she said. 'And the Devil is right, my life is an illusion at the moment and I need to confess to what I did, whatever everyone thinks of me. And then I can meet Thomas. Finally, my life will have come full circle.' She got to her feet. Beatrice thought she looked a hundred times stronger than when she'd arrived, and she hoped there would be a happy ending to her tale.

After saying goodbye to Heather, Beatrice went back to her reading room to tidy the cards away. Why had The Devil card been inverted? She could think of no way that her own life was an illusion, there were no skeletons in her closet. Was it someone else's secrets she was destined to discover?

* * *

Beatrice was still thinking about Heather that evening when she arrived at the restaurant Jack had suggested. It was about a mile from where they lived, but he had a meeting in the afternoon, so it was easier to meet up somewhere on his journey home, especially as the venue had been highly rated in the local press and he was keen to try it out. He had arrived before her, and she was surprised to see him in a suit and shirt, though he lacked a tie.

'I feel a bit scruffy now.' She laughed as she indicated the black jeans and soft cashmere jumper she was wearing. 'I wasn't expecting you to be in a suit.' She didn't add that he looked even more attractive than he did in his usual shop uniform of jeans and a T-shirt. However lovely he was, and every time she saw him he looked a little bit cuter, she needed to remind herself they were just friends. He had given no indication that he thought of her as any more than that, and she needed to remember it.

They ordered dinner, Beatrice choosing what appeared to be posh macaroni cheese with a long Italian explanation and Jack selecting the biggest ravioli she'd ever seen, stuffed with porcini mushrooms and ricotta cheese.

'Tell me everything,' he said as soon as their order was taken. 'You've heard from Tristan?'

'I have.' She grinned at him as she opened her email and read out what he'd sent. '"Thank you for your message. It's been a while since anyone has spoken of the family business, I closed the shop when Covid hit and then decided to deal exclusively online. My customers usually come to me because they are looking for a particular piece and if I can, I source it for them. It's a lot more lucrative than selling people's unloved items, often the weird and wonderful which have been inherited. Now, my job entails going on a treasure hunt with someone else's budget which is much more fun. However, luckily for you, I kept all of my father's ledgers. The shop was opened by my great-grandfather and all of the paperwork has been kept. It seemed daft to throw it out, so much family history there. It is going to take a long while to find the card you are searching for though, if we are even able to. I do remember it though, because back in those days my father used to get me to research certain items if we didn't have any specialist expertise, and any provenance I could find would help push the price up. Whilst I was investigating this card, I discovered some interesting rumours that it was part of a pack connected with the murders of women in seventeenth-century London. So I am as fascinated as you are, if you truly have the rest of the pack."'

At this point Beatrice paused, her eyes meeting Jack's. She was waiting for what she'd just said to sink in, just as it had taken her a few moments when she'd read it earlier.

'Wait, what?' He almost spat out the mouthful of wine he'd just taken.

'I know! Another mention of the cards being associated with murders. I wasn't expecting that, it is more than a bit creepy. I've already replied asking if I can go next Monday. If I can, I'll let you know what we turn up. I *really* hope he can find some information to help direct me to whoever now has my card. It means everything to me, it's one final thing I can do for my mum, it belongs with us and nobody else. I feel as though I'm the only person who still remembers her, who still relives the memories.'

It was painfully obvious that her father had stopped. Now it was all, 'Kerry this, Kerry that' and 'Let's go to Spain for Christmas'. After all, why would Beatrice want to visit her dad for the festive season? Well, they were right there, she didn't want to. Nor to see how her mother had been eradicated from his life, as though she hadn't ever been the biggest part of it. In truth, Beatrice knew she was behaving badly, but she still had a huge hole in her chest which her mother dying had left, and now it felt as though her dad was gone too.

Her reflections were interrupted by their dessert arriving and, thankful for the distraction, Beatrice dug her spoon into the creamy zabaglione and listened to Jack talk about his meeting that afternoon with a book dealer.

* * *

She didn't have to wait long for a reply from Tristan, confirming that the following Monday was fine for him, suggesting she arrived at eleven o'clock. *'In time for coffee and cake,'* he'd added. Beatrice thought she was going to like Tristan. Unfortunately, this time, Jack was unable to take the time off work to accompany her.

'I'm sorry,' he said when she called him with the update. 'We have a big delivery on Monday morning, and I can't expect Alex to be hefting all the boxes about, books are very heavy. I wish I was able to come, I had such a great time on our Suffolk excursion. Make sure you remember everything, write it down if necessary. Then perhaps we can go out for a drink on Monday night and you can tell me what happened?'

Beatrice was disappointed he couldn't join her, even though she'd suspected as much. He couldn't devote the time that she could to find the card and really, why would he? After all, this was her search, not his, and she needed to remind herself of that. It did occur to her that perhaps he was making an excuse, but if that were the case he wouldn't have suggested meeting up later.

She noted down Tristan's directions of how to find his house. He lived in Marylebone, and she looked up the address online, zooming in on Google Earth to take a closer look. Somehow, she wasn't surprised to see his home situated in a square of tall, white Georgian town houses set around a private garden enclosed by railings. There was no flat number, but she couldn't imagine he lived in one entire house unless he had a huge family. Perhaps she'd arrive to find a nanny chasing hordes of young children around the place.

Beatrice was certain he was too old for that, although how old was too old? Even though she was now in her early thirties, she hadn't yet given up on finding someone to marry and have a family with, but she was aware her biological clock would soon begin to slow down. She couldn't just let the years roll past indefinitely. Perhaps she should be actively seeking out a potential long-term boyfriend, except now wasn't the right time. Her mind strayed to Jack and how he made her feel, before reminding herself that they were just good friends. Just because he created a buzzing, restless feeling of delight in her every time she saw him, he hadn't given her any indication he felt the same way. She needed to stop thinking of him like that.

Almost before she turned the final card, Portia knew which it would be. Doing a reading for herself gave her an insight into what she'd turn even before she did so. Sure enough, staring up at her, *laughing* at her, was the leering grin of The Devil card. A constant reminder of what was real, and what was an illusion.

At that moment she understood instinctively that her previous conviction that their lives in London were safe was an illusion. Nothing previously had happened to give her this feeling, and yet since that fleeting glimpse of a man who bore an uncanny resemblance to someone she'd known a long time ago, the foundation she'd built their lives on felt precarious. As though the illusions she'd so skilfully crafted and adhered to were about to crumble. Should she too, like the women she helped, now be disappearing under the shadow of night, taking Vittoria and Maria and running? Every part of her said yes, even though she didn't understand why. But the cards were telling her, and she knew not to ignore them.

It wouldn't be so easy this time though. Vittoria was no longer a tiny child without a voice of her own, both she and

Maria were now settled here in the city. And, more importantly, here in London Vittoria was known by most of their neighbours and friends. If for some reason she was out on her own and found herself in a street she didn't recognise, unable to navigate easily with her failing sight, there was always a market trader or a goodwife who could guide her home. And she now had her new friend; if they moved away she wouldn't have someone of her own age to chat and laugh with. Even moving a few streets away had already provoked a scene.

For them to run, as the women she'd helped escape had done, it would require her to tell the other two about being in grave danger, otherwise they would never agree. And it would mean leaving Elsebeth, her dearest friend, and John who, even after their years of friendship, still didn't know what her most inner thoughts of him were. Only if she was discovered here would she uproot their lives and tell Vittoria everything. From outside the door, she heard the sound of a news sheet man calling out to those who wanted to know what was happening in their fine city, and Portia shuddered.

* * *

The day after she'd read her own cards, Portia needed to visit St Pancras Lane again and ask Robert if he could provide her with some replacement leather cords for her boots. She had pulled and tied one cord too many times, finally stretching it until it broke in two.

Maria was making ale, Portia having been banned from doing it again, so she left them both – Vittoria sitting beside the window and making use of scant light as she bent low over her sewing, barely able to make out the stiches these days without being very close, but determined to continue doing it – and

headed back to their previous accommodation. Unusually for
the time of year the weather had taken a turn for the worse and
Portia pulled her shawl over her coif to stop it becoming wet
from the rain which had been falling steadily all morning. She
and Maria took great pride in their starched headwear, which
was always laundered just as it had been in Italy, but water
would instantly reduce it to a rag upon her head. She hurried
along, trying not to slide on the wet cobbles, her now lace-less
boot slipping up and down on her foot and making her ankle
burn as it rubbed.

As she walked along Walbrooke Street, her head down,
watching where she trod, the sound of a shout ahead made her
look up. A horse had bolted and people were leaping out of the
way as it careered along the street, chased by its rider, the cause
of all the shouting.

It wasn't the horse that caught Portia's attention though. It
was the man standing at the end of a passageway, who, like
everyone else, had turned towards the ruckus. Gasping, she
dived into the nearest doorway to avoid being seen. Thankfully,
as everyone around her were also jumping out of the path of the
advancing horse, her sudden movement didn't attract his attention and he turned away, pulling his cap down against the
weather. It didn't matter though, she'd seen him, and now she
knew her worries about the glimpse of a man she'd once known
had been correct. The inverted Hierophant card had told her
what she had known all along, that her belief they were safe in
London was distorted and essential information was being kept
from her, purposefully or not. Niccolo Tabanelli, the brother of
Lorenzo Tabanelli, was here in London. Long ago she had run,
escaped, but she hadn't hidden as well as she'd believed she had,
and now her deceptions were going to find her out. This is what
her cards had been telling her.

Staggering into Robert's shop, she perched on the stool provided and showed him her boot so he could find a suitable leather thong. She was grateful to sit down, her legs shaking so violently she doubted she could stand on them much longer. Thank goodness they'd moved when they had, because it appeared possible Niccolo was staying somewhere in the vicinity. Perhaps she should have gone south of the river after all. If she could find out how long he was staying in London, she'd know if they should flee to Winchester. Except attempting to seek out that information was to risk alerting him to her presence.

As she'd feared, it was now even more likely that she'd have to ask John to help her flee, just as she'd asked him to do for so many women before. But to do so she'd have to tell him her truth. The secret she'd hidden for so many years. As soon as she had finished at Robert's, she'd go to the river and see if she could find him.

* * *

With her boot now securely fitted to her foot and no longer slipping with every step, she made her way to Queenhithe. The rain had eased off a little, just a fine mist still hanging in the air, but she kept her face covered. Constantly her eyes darted from left to right to check if Niccolo was in sight, every part of her body rigid with fear. He was nowhere to be seen, but this time she knew without a doubt that it'd been him she'd thought she'd spotted before. Then, she'd persuaded herself she was mistaken, but not this time. Under her breath she quietly prayed that he hadn't seen her. If he had, then she'd need more than Maria's rosary beads and prayers to save her.

She was relieved to find John sitting on an old, upturned

barrel on the edge of the wharf. Three other men were loading goods onto barrows from one of the warehouses behind them and were good-naturedly shouting at him because he would not give them a hand.

'I must preserve my strength for rowing,' he told them as Portia approached. He gave her a wide grin and immediately added, 'and see here, a passenger, so I must bid good day to you all.'

'I must speak with you urgently,' Portia whispered.

'Come in the boat with me then, on the river we can speak freely without eyes or ears following us,' he said, nodding his head slightly towards the other men.

Portia nodded and let him hand her down into the wherry, which dipped to one side beneath her weight, and she hastily sat down on the wooden plank across the aft.

Once they pulled out into the river he continued rowing slowly. 'So what, pray, do I owe the pleasure of this visit? If indeed it is for pleasure? You do not usually ask that we speak in private. Our usual dealings can be discussed in public given that you simply refer to "goods which need transportation".'

'It is not for pleasure,' Portia admitted. She only wished it were. 'This is nothing to do with our usual arrangements, it is for a different reason that I seek you out today.' She paused, holding onto the sides of the boat as the backwash from a large barge heading down river threatened to tip them out, although John didn't seem worried and just continued with his steady rhythm pulling the oars.

'I have seen someone, a man from my past who would wish me dead if he knew of my whereabouts. I do not know why he is here in London, but he must not discover I am also here, or I too will be forced to flee. And Vittoria – she will also have to escape. I hope Maria would come too.'

John nodded slowly. 'So, you knew him in Italy?'

For a moment Portia was surprised he had worked it out so quickly, but she reminded herself whenever they'd talked previously, she'd realised how quick-witted he was.

'Indeed, his name is Niccolo Tabanelli, he is a member of my family, although not an immediate one. However, he is close enough to recognise me instantly if he saw me, and I must avoid that at all costs. I am in grave danger if he discovers we are in London. Even being associated with the Tabanellis makes me one of their possessions and they do not like to lose what they believe to be theirs.'

'And Vittoria too?' John asked. 'She too belongs to them, or they consider that she does? What do you require of me, whatever you need it shall be arranged. Do you wish for him to disappear?'

Portia let her breath out slowly. She had hardly dare breathe since she'd seen Niccolo but here, now, John was going to make everything well again, just as at the back of her mind, she knew he would. If Niccolo were to go in the river, as John had arranged for his brother-in-law before, she would feel no sorrow. London without Niccolo in it would be a far safer place.

'Quite possibly,' she acknowledged. 'But not yet. First of all, I need to discover why he is here and how long he intends staying. If his visit is only transient, then I will keep myself hidden until he has left, but if he intends remaining here for a while, then my life will be in terrible danger. If you are able to search him out and help me, then I can watch him from a distance to understand why he is here. After that I will start making plans. I am sorry to ask this of you, you help me so much in other ways. I find myself depending on you more with each passing day.'

'I am pleased to do so,' John replied. 'You must know by now how much I admire you, I will do anything you ask of me. Our relationship may have started as a business arrangement, but now I have feelings in my heart. I should have spoken before; I realise that now my life here in London shall not be complete if you are to leave.'

Portia felt her face warm with a glow of happiness which she was certain John could see. She wished she could take hold of his hands but they were both gripping the oars as he continued the rhythmic pull through the water. 'I feel the same about you,' she admitted. 'I did not want to open my heart as I feared you did not share my thoughts. Despite my current worries, what you have just told me has made my heart brighten.'

By this point they were opposite the Ebbgate steps, and he turned the boat towards the quay, rowing more easily now they were out of the main thoroughfare of the river. 'You have told me his name,' he said, changing the subject as though they hadn't just confessed how they felt about each other. 'For now, I need nothing more from you. I will let you know when I have news.' Resting the oars on his knees, he reached across the boat and took her hands in his and squeezed them gently. 'Fear not, my sweet,' he said. Leaning forward, he pressed a brief gentle kiss to her lips and she couldn't help a small sigh of pleasure. His place in her life had taken on a new meaning.

Saying a reluctant farewell, she stepped out of the boat and climbed the steps. Now she must wait for whatever John could discover. She felt guilty that even now she hadn't told him the whole truth. Not even half of it. And now that he had professed an affection that she reciprocated there was even more reason why she shouldn't be keeping her secrets from him.

With Tristan's detailed directions, Beatrice left the Tube station and walked to his house, its number on a subtle narrow piece of slate. At the top of a flight of wide, shallow steps flanked with tall columns holding up a portico, was a large glossy black door with a brass knob placed in the middle. Just as she'd guessed, looking either side of the door, there was no sign of a row of intercom buzzers to indicate the building had been divided into apartments, so she pressed the only bell she could see before taking a step back and keeping her fingers crossed someone inside would hear it.

Her worries were unfounded as seconds later, the door opened. The man in front of her looked to be in his mid-sixties, wearing a checked shirt and dark corduroy trousers, and for a moment Beatrice had to swallow hard. It was just the sort of outfit her father often wore, and she felt a sudden stab of pain, a sharp unexpected pierce of loss, of missing him.

'Beatrice?' he said.

'Yes, hello, you must be Tristan, pleased to meet you.' She stepped forward and offered her hand.

'Please, just Tris is fine,' he said as he shook it.

'Likewise, Bea is good for me,' she replied. He stood to one side and ushered her in.

The hall she now found herself in was magnificent, reflecting the grand exterior of the house and she gazed around in admiration. If she had a home like this, she'd probably never go out. The floor, covered in elegant black and white tiles in a neo-classical design stretched away down a long corridor towards the back of the house. The walls were painted dark green and broken up with a barely visible dado rail in the same colour. Above her head hung a crystal chandelier. She guessed it no longer sparkled as it once had, cobwebs clinging to the droplets, but it gave an insight into the glamour the house must have once had in a glittering, bygone age. Several doors led from the hall and to one side a wide staircase, with a central carpet held in place with shining rods, swept upwards.

'What a beautiful house,' Beatrice exclaimed. 'It's straight out of an episode of *Bridgerton*!'

'Oh dear,' Tristan replied. 'I think you'll be disappointed when you see I live in twenty-first-century bachelor comfort, despite all the original features. See here.' He led her through the first door, almost as wide as it was tall, and panelled. 'This is my living room. It would have been the drawing room at one point and as you can see, it doesn't now look as though it's straight out of a costume drama.'

Turning around on the spot, Beatrice had to agree with him. The walls were a deep putty colour, but the furnishings weren't remotely of the Georgian era, the room dominated by two huge, turquoise, velvet sofas covered in yellow cushions. They looked comfortable and well used, the cushions indented by many years of people sitting in them. She wondered how anyone managed to stand up once they were buried deep within the seat, and she hoped she wasn't about to find out. On a modern glass stand in the corner sat an enormous widescreen television and the substantial pale marble mantelpiece was covered in letters, photographs in tarnished silver frames and a dented brass lantern. It surrounded an empty fireplace which still held the vestige of a fire – ash spilled out across the hearth and onto a threadbare but once-expensive-looking Persian rug.

'It's a beautiful room though,' she said. 'And everyone has a telly these days,' she added.

'Let's sit in the kitchen,' he said, ushering her out. 'I've found a load of paperwork, so we can have a coffee and see what we can discover.'

Beatrice followed him down the hall to the rear of the building and into the kitchen. Given the size of the rest of the house, it wasn't as big as she'd expected. The pale-cream-painted cabinets reached up towards the high ceiling and she wondered how anyone was able to reach them unless they had a step stool. A long, scrubbed pine table sat in the middle of the space and an Aga at one end in a chimney breast was belching out heat.

'The kitchen hardly seems in proportion, does it?' Tristan said, as if reading her mind. He waved her towards the table and she sat down, watching him as he poured boiling water into an already prepared cafetière. 'There are lots of little pantries and offices out the back here, I suppose any renovator would have them all knocked through, but this is quite big enough for me.'

He joined her at the table with the coffee and a plate, on which stood a lemon drizzle cake.

'Not for me, thank you,' Beatrice said as he offered her a slice. 'Perhaps once we've finished?'

'Good idea, we don't want sticky fingers.' Tristan pushed it to one side. 'Let's get started then.' He dragged the first of several stacks of ledgers towards him. A cloud of dust rose up making

Beatrice sneeze. 'Sorry, housework isn't really my thing,' he said. 'I have a lovely cleaning company who come in twice a week, but they only do the rooms I use, not the numerous ones filled with the detritus of my life, and those of my ancestors. My father was all too fond of buying sundry items which came through the auction house. This was our family home, so the rooms upstairs are full of furniture, artefacts and books. Useful though in our case, or I wouldn't still have all the paperwork associated with the business.' Beatrice thought about the chandelier in the hall but said nothing. He was probably so used to the cobwebs, he didn't notice them.

'So, these are all the most recent ones, for when we think the card was sold?' she asked, her head sideways as she read the dates along the spines.

'Indeed, one for each year. Now, I have everything on a computer system of course, but my father was very old-school, he said that we deal with antiquities and it was only right that we recorded them as our ancestors did. One of the many things he and I disagreed about, I must admit. Anyway, I've only brought down those which cover when my father was still working because it was he who sold it on. I can remember him talking of how he'd had several enquiries about this particular card, that there were people who seemed desperate to have it. Indeed, you're not the only person to have made enquiries about it since, the most recent was about a year ago. However, you are the only person with the rest of the pack, that's why I agreed to see you. Whoever we did sell it to, hopefully the answer will be here somewhere. Let's start with the ledger from the date of the catalogue Ian showed you.' He sorted through the books until he found what they hoped was the correct one and, turning to the page which included the date in the catalogue, slowly they started to read through the handwritten entries.

Twenty minutes later Beatrice said, her voice rising as she started to feel excited, 'Hold on, what's this?' as she pointed to an entry. 'Might this be it? It isn't easy to read.'

'All the men in my family have atrocious handwriting,' Tristan admitted as he turned the ledger towards him and grabbed the notebook and pen he'd left on the table, passing them to Beatrice. She'd already got her phone out and taken a photo of the page.

'I'll dictate, you write,' Tristan instructed. 'Right, the description says, "Fifteenth-century tarot card. Italian. It depicts the Devil, with horns, seated on a wooden throne. The back of the card is decorated with a black sword, and gold, red and blue flowers. Sold for five thousand pounds." Wow, that is a lot more than I would have expected, but if there was more than one person chasing it, I suspect he was made an offer he couldn't refuse. Otherwise, he would have taken it to auction. Someone must have really wanted it. And the buyer was a Margot Williams, a collector who was living in Brighton at the time. No idea if she's still there, of course.'

Margot Williams, where had she heard that name before? Beatrice thought for a moment before remembering that she was the person who'd loaned some artefacts to the British Museum. It felt as though everything was starting to come together.

'Fantastic,' she said, before explaining where she'd heard of Margot before. 'Now if I can find her, and fingers crossed she's still got the card, perhaps she'll sell it to me. And hopefully not for an extortionate amount.' She thought of how it appeared Margot had been as desperate as she was to own it, and didn't feel very hopeful at all. Perhaps the fact that she had the rest of the pack may persuade her.

'Worry about that if you're able to track it down,' Tristan said.

'And we haven't yet discussed the murders it was supposedly party to.'

'I was also told this by a Professor Stanton; he's an expert at Yale University. And now you've mentioned it too. I don't understand though,' she admitted. 'Why would my cards have anything to do with women being murdered?'

'I honestly have no idea. But you can see why there might have been a lot of interest in this particular card if it is believed to be the one at the centre of the grisly rumours. You could try going to the British Library and ask to see the London pamphlets from 1600 onwards.'

Beatrice felt her insides churn with excitement – and fear. She was a step, albeit a small one, further on towards finding the last card, and reuniting the pack. But did she want to find it, if it was the cause of a number of women's murders? She remembered the stain which looked like blood on one of the cards and felt sick. Tarot cards didn't have any sort of supernatural powers, although she knew some people did subscribe to the idea, yet how could one card, the one she didn't have, have been the centre of murder accusations? She was becoming increasingly confused, and her search was taking an increasingly unpleasant turn.

22

1644

Portia was too frightened to go out for fear of seeing Niccolo again but was rapidly running out of excuses each time it was suggested she visited the market with Vittoria and Maria. Her reasons were beginning to wear thin, even to her own ears. The days wore on and Vittoria became more and more confused as Portia became more of a recluse. If only she could explain that, once more, she was doing what she needed to, if it was indeed needed, to save the girl.

One day, three weeks after Portia had spoken with John, Vittoria sat down beside her on the step at the door leading to a small yard behind the house. With this albeit-tiny piece of land, they now had the opportunity to raise some chickens, and Portia was throwing scraps of food and corn out to them.

'Mama,' Vittoria said as she took hold of one of Portia's hands in her own and held it, 'please tell me more about my father. You talk of the bad things, of his violence which caused us to journey to England and escape him, but surely you have some happy memories? And what did he look like? Tall, short, thin, fat? Did he also have the same affliction in his eyes? Is that why I am so?'

'No,' Portia replied, 'your eyes are not like his.' She felt her own well up and she remembered life in Milan, the happier days before everything had turned so drastically bad. Their childhood, hers and Agnese's, a carefree time with their parents.

Lorenzo had changed from the charming and generous man professing love. The ink was barely dry on the marriage contract when almost overnight he became dismissive and cold. His coffers full of gold from the dowry, and shortly afterwards a babe on its way, his visits to his mistress in Verona began to last for longer and longer until he was barely at home. He wasn't averse to using violence either, if he thought his wife and servants were not being respectful enough.

'As you know, when you were born, the plague was blazing its way through the city. Quite literally – as houses which were full of the dead were burned to the ground, nobody would enter them to retrieve the diseased bodies.' She didn't mention that everyone knew that sometimes the afflicted within had not yet passed but were burned along with the bodies of their family anyway.

'So why were you still there?' Vittoria asked. 'Surely a wealthy family as you have told me you were would have had another home to flee to?' She was too astute, Portia thought, remembering the villa high in the hills above the city, which they travelled to each summer. Where the air was clear and the food fresh.

'We were due to leave,' she explained, 'but then we realised you were going to make an appearance earlier than expected, so we had to stay in Milan until you were born.' She was telling the girl more than she had before, but perhaps now she was ready to hear it. Or at least the parts Portia wished to speak of. Some of her tale would forever remain a secret.

'But after I was born, why did we not then go to the hills?'

'Because by then it was not safe. The pestilence was rife, the plague doctors with their hideous hooked masks walking the streets, and the servants had all fled or died. I had to run with you to escape the disease and the only cart I could find was going to Venice. When we arrived, with the plague still hot on our heels, I did what I believed to be right and found us a passage on a boat about to leave.'

'And I am glad that you did,' Vittoria said. 'I am truly thankful that you are my mama, I could not wish for anyone better. I am sure nobody else would have undertaken such dangers to save me and I love you so much for that.' She wrapped her arms around Portia and held her tight. It warmed Portia's heart to hear Vittoria express her love but would she feel the same if she knew the full story?

* * *

The day after her questions about her father, Vittoria arrived with Caterina, who came in the early evening to ask Portia if she might have another card reading. With her nuptials now approaching fast, she wanted to know what the future held for her as a married woman. Portia was happy to agree to her request, telling Caterina to put away her purse as she offered the sixpence that Vittoria had told her was the cost.

Laying out the three cards, Portia began, smiling as she turned over the Ten of Pentacles. 'This is a good card,' she told her. 'It is telling you of stability in your forthcoming marriage, of comfort and wealth. A life without worry.' Caterina's eyes lit up and Vittoria, who was seated next to her, gave her arm a little squeeze. It was a card that any young girl on the cusp of marriage would wish for.

The next one, the Page of Cups, was every bit as beneficial. 'This young man,' Portia indicated the youth on the card between them, 'he represents your beloved. He has an open heart, full of love which he will share with you.'

The third card though, The Wheel of Fortune, caused Portia to become silent for a moment. Once again she was seeing something in the reading that she wasn't sure she understood correctly. The Wheel of Fortune, but yet again a card inverted. She paused for a moment.

'The Wheel of Fortune,' she began. 'She is telling us that someone new is coming into your life. That does not mean someone you do not know, in this case it likely means your new husband and your imminent wedding when you and he will be tied forever.' But it wasn't the stranger in the girl's life that she was worried about, it was the one the card indicated would be arriving in her own. The wheel of fortune was spinning, and she was petrified of what it would throw out.

Caterina had only been gone a short while and the church bells of nearby St Gabriel Fenchurch chimed four after midday when there was a banging at the door. Opening it, Portia was pleased to find John waiting on the step.

'One moment.' She held her hand up and closed the door again whilst she picked up a partlet. Usually she arranged the small swathe of fabric across her chest as an act of modesty if her dress was a lower cut one, but today she needed to tie it around her head and keep her face hidden when she was away from the house. She didn't want the other two to see her deliberately obscuring herself or they may ask questions, especially as she'd been reluctant to leave the house in the past few days. As it was, Maria asked who was at the door.

'It's John,' Portia said.

'And is he not coming in to visit?' Maria asked, the surprise in her voice evident. Although he didn't often come to the house, when he did, John always came in to take a cup of ale with them all and pass the time of day. Portia knew Maria had a soft spot for him.

She had to think on her feet, and quickly. 'He said he wishes to speak to me privately, I will just step outside for a moment.' Not waiting for any more questions – she saw now Vittoria was also interested and was opening her mouth to speak – Portia slipped out of the door and hurried to the corner of the street, covering her head and face as she went.

'You know where he is?' she asked. She couldn't think of any other reason why John would come to her house so soon after she'd seen him. Her heart was racing, her breath coming in short, jagged bursts.

He nodded. 'I do. Come and sit with me here where it is quiet and we can talk freely,' he said. Portia followed him to a rough bench beneath an old yew tree in the corner of the churchyard beside them, where they were shaded by the branches and spiky foliage. 'I am certain I have the right man; I have followed him for a few days and he is currently with a merchant in the Royal Exchange. His usual pattern of behaviour has shown that normally he will stay two hours or thereabouts whilst he makes his business calls. If we leave now, we should be in a position to see him when he re-emerges.'

'Then come, we must leave right away so I might view him myself. Only then can I be sure.' She placed her hand on John's arm. 'Thank you,' she added, 'you are a true friend and more to me. So much more than I can ever speak of. And not just to me but also the many women you have helped over the years. And they seem to multiply with each new moon. When we first started there were just a couple each year and yet now see how word has spread.'

'And it is a good thing,' he replied gruffly. 'How many lives you have protected. It is amusing that the city is in uproar believing these women have been killed, when in truth you have saved them from exactly that.' Getting to his feet, he held his hand out and she took it. Hers was so small compared to his big rowing hands with calloused palms from the oars, but it felt perfect as his fingers closed around hers. He tucked her arm through his and patted it as though making sure it wouldn't move.

They hurried along Cornhill to the Royal Exchange. It was the first time Portia had been inside and despite the urgency of her visit, she couldn't help being enthralled as she found herself in an enormous courtyard. Surrounded by a cloister, she saw behind the stone arches were numerous small shops. Looking up, she saw another gallery together with more shops on the second floor above them. It was magnificent and she wanted to stand and take it all in but instead, mindful of why she was there, she hurried to keep in step with John as he walked briskly towards the gloom of the walkway. He ducked into the entrance to a spice merchant and she joined him. Her nose tingled as it was assailed by the myriad of smells that hit her: the warmth of cinnamon and ginger, the sweetness of vanilla and the unforgettable unique scent of liquorice.

'See that shop there with the glass bottles in the window?' John whispered in her ear, his hot breath tickling her. 'It is a supplier of fine wines. I have asked questions and apparently, he visits often, sometimes as frequently as twice per week.' Portia could hardly miss it, the sunlight from the open atrium above making the coloured glass glow as though they had candles within to light them.

'Is he there now?' she asked.

'I cannot be certain, but that is the shop he disappeared into when I tailed him earlier. I do not know if he remains there, we can only wait and watch.'

Waiting and watching was what they proceeded to do. Portia's feet began to hurt from standing still for so long, but she couldn't give up, just in case. From time to time, she stamped up and down to relieve the aching.

Their patience was rewarded more than two hours later when the shopkeeper appeared, followed by someone else. Portia drew her breath in sharply, emitting a small gasp of horror. She could see his face clearly now, and all her suspicions were founded. It was indeed as she feared, Niccolo Tabanelli, Lorenzo's brother. If she was seen, or worse, if Vittoria was, then all her lies, the house of cards she had built and lived within, would be gone. She needed to make some decisions, and quickly.

The morning of Caterina's wedding dawned brightly. There had been showers of rain earlier in the week but today it was once again clear beneath blue skies, the cobbled streets dry. Portia and Vittoria walked to St Mary le Bow where the marriage ceremony would take place, joining other merrymakers outside the church door to await the bridal party. The betrothed, Filippo, was already there with his family and the pastor, and in the usual way the service would take place outside the door before they all entered the church for prayers, and communion.

Portia saw two young girls walking towards them dressed in pale yellow gowns and carrying aloft a bower of rowan tree decorated with swathes of pink and white flowers, together with sprigs of rosemary. She described it all to Vittoria and then also what her friend was wearing as she approached too. Portia could tell Caterina's gown was new, a rich taffeta in a copper gold split open at the waist to display a deep burgundy skirt. Upon her hair was a matching headpiece. As she spoke of this too, her voice tailed off until she stood in silence, too appalled to utter another word. For behind Caterina came her parents, her mother also resplendent in stiff, shining dark green taffeta, the colour of ancient yew. Walking beside her, her husband and Caterina's father. Niccolo Tabanelli.

How could this be so? That of all the Italians in the whole of London, Vittoria's best friend was the daughter of the one man she was desperate to avoid. And now her friendship had inadvertently led them both to him.

There was no way they could leave the wedding; Vittoria had been looking forward to it since the betrothal had been announced. Portia could only hope that if they were last to enter the church they could stay in the shadows at the back and then depart without being seen. They hadn't been invited to the celebrations after the wedding, despite the friendship. This arrangement was for Niccolo, all about making business connections, expanding his web of friends and associates. Not about his daughter's marriage or it being her wedding day.

She waited silently as the vows were spoken, and after the congregation entered the church, she steered Vittoria inside and to a dark corner at the far end of the back pew. Although the rest of the nave was bright with sunlight pouring in through the windows, none of it reached where they were sitting and there were no candles lit here where it was dusty and unloved. Portia desperately hoped their presence in these gloomy shadows would remain unnoticed.

Once the ceremony was over – neither of them partaking of the communion, given Portia couldn't risk them being seen – she whispered that they would wait for the main party to leave so the crowd didn't jostle against them. Vittoria nodded, and it was several minutes before they inched along the pew and stepped out once again into the sunshine.

To Portia's dismay the other celebrants had not yet reached

the street as well-wishers and members of the congregation stopped them to offer congratulations. Before she could stop her, Vittoria had called out to the group to wish Caterina and Filippo good health. The bride stepped away from the others to embrace her friend and, as one, everyone seemed to turn and look. Portia felt her blood run cold and she quickly stepped backwards into the shade of the church walls, but she wasn't quick enough. Niccolo had glanced over at his daughter with her friend and then lifting his gaze, he looked straight into Portia's eyes.

It was everything she'd been trying to avoid, his stare locked on hers, as though she were a rabbit caught in a trap, at the mercy of a poacher who would think nothing of flicking his wrist and breaking her neck. Rooted to the spot and unable to move, she watched him saunter over. Beside her, Vittoria, still chatting with Caterina, didn't observe what was happening, somehow hadn't noticed the way the air had stilled. Right now, all Portia wanted was for the girl to wander away, so that Niccolo didn't properly look at her. If he saw, then all Portia's secrets would come pouring out like pus from a putrid, infected wound.

'Well, this is a surprise,' Niccolo drawled as he looked down at her. His English, despite its strong Italian inflection, was flawless. She'd somehow forgotten how big the Tabanelli men were physically, akin to menacing bears playing with people's lives. 'I believed you had died, along with everyone else. Lorenzo was dead within a day of arriving in the mountains but somehow, I evaded the sickness, as it seems you did too. When I returned from the villa the house was empty, all signs of the plague eradicated, many precious jewels and possessions taken. Whatever bodies had been there were gone. Yet here you are living in London, so the question I am wondering is, how and why are you here?'

'None of that need concern you.' Portia pulled her shoulders back as she spoke, as though by doing so she would somehow gain some inches in height and not feel as vulnerable as she currently did. 'As you have said, I did not succumb to the disease and I chose to make a new life here for myself.'

Out of the corner of her eye she saw the movement of Caterina returning to her other guests and moments later she heard Vittoria say, 'Mama?' as she stepped across the churchyard to stand beside Portia.

'We are leaving,' Portia said as she put her arm around Vittoria's back and turned her around, but it was too late. She heard a hiss of surprise and Niccolo's big hand, covered in thick dark hairs, just like the animal she had compared him to, landed on the girl's shoulder as he pulled Vittoria to face him, and Portia's grip around her waist tightened.

'Wait a minute now.' Niccolo's voice was lower. From the street someone called his name, but he just waved his hand in acknowledgement and ignored them. 'You did not come to this country alone, did you? I can see that you stole something before you left, something very precious belonging to my brother, to all the Tabanellis. Now I know exactly what you did.'

'No, you are wrong. I did not bring anything which was not rightfully mine. That was best placed in my care,' Portia replied, her voice almost inaudible. Again, a voice called him.

'I must go.' Niccolo clicked his tongue behind his front teeth as his attention was taken. 'It is my daughter's wedding day, but rest assured, I will come and visit you very soon, I am sure Caterina can tell me where you live. She often talks of her Italian friend, Vittoria. Do not think to run either. For wherever you go, now I know you are alive, I shall hunt you down.'

Abruptly he let go of Vittoria's shoulder, causing the girl to stagger slightly as Portia began to walk, and then trot, away, her arm looped through Vittoria's, trying to put as much distance as she could between them.

She knew Vittoria would soon start asking questions and as she hurried along she muttered, 'Ask me nothing, I will explain who that man is when we are at home.' Her mind was racing, hoping that by the time they had completed their journey, she'd have thought of a reason how she knew him, because she couldn't tell Vittoria the truth and risk her rejecting Portia, for that would without doubt happen if her lies were exposed. Fifteen years she'd kept the secret, and even upon her deathbed it would not be freed. Which might be sooner than she'd hoped if she didn't do something, and soon.

Once inside their house, Portia battened the door with the long wooden shaft which fitted into iron hooks on the frame to prevent it being opened. Vittoria was watching her, and it appeared she was still waiting for an explanation. Sitting down on the settle, Portia patted the seat beside her and the girl sat down.

'Do you remember me telling you how your father was not a kind man? That he hurt people – even those he professed to love? The fact was, he considered people – especially the women in his life – to be his belongings, his chattels to do with as he wished. Which is why I realised I must take you away as soon as you were born. Lorenzo was not there when that happened because he, together with his brother Niccolo, had already run from the plague, up to his villa in the hills. I knew it would be assumed we had died, and indeed it seems that was the case. Niccolo, Caterina's father, is the brother of your father and now he knows we are here.'

'So Caterina is my cousin?' Vittoria homed in on the one piece of information Portia hadn't even considered, and the one that the girl was most delighted with. 'You speak as though this is a bad thing, but it fills me with so much joy. She is more than just a friend to me now; she is family. I cannot wait to tell her, if her father, my uncle, has not yet done so.'

'Yes, she is. But now we cannot stay in London. We are in great danger. Niccolo will insist on taking you back to Italy and he may hurt you, and will certainly kill me,' Portia said.

'Why would he harm either of us? He is kind and loving to Caterina. He is not like my father, I am sure.' A stubborn pout appeared on Vittoria's face as she crossed her arms. 'If I were married, and lots of girls are at my age, then I would be able to make decisions about my life, so I believe I am of an age to choose for myself. I wish to stay with my cousin and whilst Caterina is here, then I too shall remain. And however angry my uncle might be, of course he will not kill you, you are my mama.' She rose from the bench and went to speak with Maria who, with a rare burst of intuition, was keeping out of the way, making butter in the scullery.

Portia leant back and looked into the fire, the embers just glowing. Although they kept it lit every day for cooking, it was far too hot to have the flames burning high. Thankfully, she'd managed to keep the biggest secret from Vittoria yet again. The more time passed, the years went by, it became harder to tell her the truth. But Niccolo had realised immediately, as she'd known he would. What his next move would be, how much longer she had before her actions fifteen years ago were laid bare and she lost everything she held dear, she didn't know.

Maria pulled Portia to one side to ask her what had happened at the wedding given they had arrived home earlier than she'd expected and then quite obviously had a disagreement, the effects of which were still continuing. She gave the other woman a brief recount of what she'd told Vittoria. Although Maria knew she'd escaped a violent household, she had omitted to tell her everything and even now with her world about to crumble around her, still she kept the most vital piece of information to herself.

24

2025

'So, I'm off to the British Library,' Beatrice explained. She was in a local bar with Jack, relaying what had happened on her visit to Tristan. 'And I've been trying to locate this Margot Williams, but I still haven't found her yet. I really hope I can somehow track her down and that she still has the card, or I may be on a wild goose chase for the rest of my life. The story about it being connected to a spate of London murders is bizarre, I don't believe it for a moment. I've always felt that these cards were special to the women in our family, how they've been handed down from mother to daughter, or niece if needs be. They were used to help women, that's their purpose, so why would they have been alleged to have been involved in women being murdered? There is more to it, I'm certain, and whilst I'm searching for the card I'm also going to try and seek out the real story behind the women's deaths.'

'It's certainly keeping you busy,' Jack said. 'I feel exhausted just thinking about it. Is there any way I can help you, when I'm not in the shop? Otherwise, I'll barely see you.' He pulled down the corners of his mouth in a mock sad face, although his eyes were creased, giving away his laughter.

Beatrice's heart gave a thump of pleasure. Was he saying that he wanted to spend more time with her? Even though every part of her rational self told her that a relationship, should one develop, wasn't a good idea and would doubtless end in heart-break for her, she couldn't deny her attraction to him was grow-ing. She'd had enough sadness over the past few years and yet here she was considering, if anything happened between them and it all went wrong, of potentially laying herself open to more. And, she reminded herself as she watched Jack go to the bar to buy more drinks, his long legs in their dark jeans with a plaid shirt accentuating his wide shoulders and muscular arms, he hadn't actually made any romantic gestures towards her. So far, this was all in her head and she'd do well to remember that.

He returned and put two glasses of wine on the table.

'When are you going to look at these pamphlets?' he asked. 'Would you mind if I came too?'

'Of course, I'd love you to come with me,' Beatrice said, smiling at him. 'It will have to be a Monday though, given that I don't yet have anyone to watch the shop for me. Business has really started to pick up now, I could probably do with an assistant. I'm almost fully booked with readings for this month, plus I have some arranged into next month too. And I also have those I do online in the evenings. It would be useful to have a second pair of hands when I'm busy, but I need someone prop-erly interested in the cards.'

'So why don't you advertise for someone?'

'It's not that easy. Nobody can do the readings; that needs to be me. And, as I said, even someone working in the shop would hopefully have at least some knowledge about the tarot, as people who come in ask questions about the different packs, their origins. Often, they've done lots of research before they go shopping. It's a considered purchase, it's important a reader bonds with the right pack, so it's not the same as just taking something off the shelf and ringing it up on the till. So, in answer to your question, I am considering it, but it has to be the right person, someone who either has some prior understanding or that I can train quickly. Also, I need to consider that although the shop is doing well, it would be an additional call on my finances to pay someone else. At the moment, I can afford the rent,' she dipped her head towards him, her landlord, and gave him a grin, 'and I'm slowly replenishing the savings I raided to set the shop up. But it *is* very quiet always being in there on my own, I must admit, it would be nice to have someone to talk to occasionally too. Anyway, I think I'll go to the library next week. Will that be too soon for you? Only I really want to go and investigate.'

'It'll be fine, I'm sure. I'll just send Alex a quick message now to check. Otherwise, you go and you can just fill me in when you get back. I don't want to hold you up.' Getting out his phone, Jack quickly typed out a message and within a minute he had a reply, confirming his assistant was fine with the arrangement. Beatrice felt a smile spread across her face.

* * *

Monday morning was wet and cold, a sharp wind blowing the leaves from the trees where they collected in corners and alleyways as they danced and whirled. Beatrice sheltered in the entrance to Jack's shop waiting for him. She was bundled in her winter coat, the first time she'd had to wear it since arriving in London, and she was grateful she'd decided at the last minute to throw it in the car.

'Sorry,' Jack hurried towards her, shrugging on a puffer jacket as he walked, 'a slight disaster with the till not working, but all sorted now. Let's go before anything else goes wrong. In all honesty, if I'm not here, Alex will sort things out, he's perfectly capable.'

They made their way towards the Tube station, Jack taking her hand and tucking it through his arm. Despite all her denials, her internal monologue telling her that nothing would happen, Beatrice couldn't help a frisson of excitement vibrating in her veins. Whatever happened she'd let it, she decided. Perhaps she should stop worrying about everything and try to live her life. It was a scary thought.

Once they were at the library, Beatrice signed herself in, pleased that Jack already had membership from when he'd previously needed to research some second-hand books. Having requested the pamphlets she guessed would have the most likelihood of finding an account about the killing of innocent women, they made their way to a desk to wait for them to arrive. All around them it was quiet, other than an occasional tap of fingers on a keyboard or the scratch of a pen. Beatrice could feel her heart beat faster as she sat and waited. Whilst she was desperately hoping to find a connection to her cards, she didn't want there to be any link with the rumours of women being murdered.

When the papers arrived, they divided them up and started reading. The tiny words, together with the unfamiliar spellings, made them difficult to understand and slowed down their efforts. Eventually though, Beatrice gave Jack a nudge with her elbow.

'I've found something,' she said. 'At least I think I have.' She pointed to the pamphlet in front of her.

The headline in capitals across the top spoke of a woman

murdered, and her body thrown into the river. They both bent closer to read it.

Beatrice felt her heart plummet as the story unfolded to explain that a woman had been dragged from her bed in the middle of the night, where later a Devil card had been discovered on the floor. It then referenced other occasions when something similar had happened, many women were going missing in exactly the same sort of circumstances even though no card was found. It seemed the tale which had followed the missing card down the centuries had some semblance of truth, although it still made no sense. Tarot cards were used as an aid for people, there was no way they'd be used to bring about the death of someone. More than one person, according to the news sheet.

'And look at what I was just reading, another story about The Devil card and a woman murdered.' Jack passed her a leaflet. 'This talks about a man who came home from the tavern to find his young wife missing and that he saw two men in the distance dragging her towards the river. It seems he also found a tarot card with The Devil on it seemingly dropped on the street.'

'It just doesn't make sense,' Beatrice said. 'Also, is it really possible it was The Devil card from *my* pack involved?' She picked up the next piece of paper and started reading. 'This one says that a young man called James Chernock was accused of the murders and during a struggle when he attempted to escape, he was stabbed. Did he have the cards back then? He shouldn't have done, they must only be kept by the women of my family. Whatever it is about these cards, they feel attached to me, as though they are trying to tell me their story. I am convinced that the heart of the tale isn't the murders, somehow there is something honourable and good connected to them. That's what I can sense when I hold the pack, their honesty and integrity.'

'What about if we try and get these leaflets into date order?' Jack suggested. 'See if that helps at all.'

Beatrice agreed, and they spent the next hour reading everything they'd been given whilst she made a note of the date for each pamphlet which reported that a woman had been murdered. There were eight in total.

'Eight.' Beatrice leant back in her chair and looked at what they'd laid out in front of them. 'And they are just from these leaflets, there may well be more if we widened our search dates. Or those which just weren't reported.'

'I don't think they got the right person for the murders,' Jack said. 'Poor James. Because look, this is dated June 1644, but there are a few more murders after that date. I wonder if anyone felt remorse that they'd stabbed the wrong person.'

'So, let's get this straight. These women, and it was only women, supposedly had The Devil card from a tarot pack – possibly my tarot pack – and were then taken from their beds in the middle of the night and murdered. No wonder the city was in an uproar. But why on earth would my ancestor be murdering women? That's the bit I don't believe. I don't like to think I'm descended from a killer, even if it was nearly four hundred years ago.'

'Is it to do with what the card means?' Jack asked. 'The Devil doesn't sound like a very cheery card to turn, and not the sort of thing you'd be pleased to see.'

'It's actually not a bad card to have,' Beatrice explained, 'that's a common misconception. Its meaning when I'm reading the cards is to challenge what is genuine or what people want us to believe. *"What is real and what is an illusion."* It makes people question things. Just like I'm questioning now what seems to have been real, that women were taken from their beds and killed, and what might have been really happening. Whether it was all an illusion. Although currently I have no answers to that.'

'Well, you are a tiny bit further forward in your quest as you do now have confirmation the murders did definitely happen,' Jack said as he followed Beatrice back out of the library. They started to walk towards Euston tube station. 'But more importantly now, it's one o'clock and I need some lunch, so shall we find somewhere to grab a sandwich and discuss your next steps?'

Beatrice agreed. She didn't want their day out to end, so extending their time together suited her perfectly.

They found an old Victorian pub on the corner of Chalton Street and were soon both tucking into mushroom burgers and fries, washed down with beer.

Halfway through the meal Jack had to take a call and, mouthing an apology, he slipped outside to talk. Beatrice carried on eating, scrolling through her phone as she did so, eventually checking her email and almost choking on her mouthful as she saw an email from Margot Williams. She opened it up and started reading.

Miraculously, it seemed she was indeed the buyer of the card Beatrice was searching for. She'd received a letter from Tristan, and thankfully she was still living at the same address. He had included Beatrice's email details and, she explained, here she was now making contact. Beatrice could hardly believe her luck as she read on.

Margot confirmed that not only had she bought The Devil tarot card from Tristan's father, she loved it so much she'd had it framed and more importantly, still owned it.

Jack returned from outside, and before he was back in his seat Beatrice started to relay the contents of the email, waving her phone about as she spoke as though to emphasise the importance of what she was saying.

'That's brilliant,' he replied. 'Totally brilliant. You'll soon have the pack reunited again. Great detective work! Where does Margot live?'

Beatrice looked at her phone, quickly scanning the rest of the email. 'She's in Brighton, so not too far on the train. I'm going to reply as soon as I get home and ask if I can go and see it. And if it is what I hope it is, try and persuade her to sell it to me. You're welcome to join me, work permitting.'

Jack started eating again, but Beatrice was too excited, laying down her knife and fork. Her research about the murders had been fruitful, and now she had a lead on the very card which had supposedly been instrumental in them. She couldn't wait to see it and hopefully return it to her pack. But nagging at the back of her brain was the fact that she was apparently not the only person who wanted it. And if she had been able to track Margot down, would somebody else do the same and get there before she did?

25

1644

For the first time in her life, Portia had no answers. Her inner voice, on which she depended to tell her what to do, was now frighteningly silent. Whilst her immediate instinct was to ignore Vittoria's wish to remain in London and prepare to flee immediately, she didn't want to cause a rift that might push the girl straight into Niccolo's hands.

The day after the wedding, the moment the church bells at St Benet Gracechurch tolled nine o'clock, she pulled her cap on and announced she was going out.

'May I come, please?' Vittoria, who was helping Maria with the washing and looking for any excuse to stop doing what was one of the least agreeable household chores, was already drying her hands on her apron. Portia had spent over an hour helping with the heaviest parts of the task, so she felt no guilt leaving the other two to finish the job.

'Not today, my dearest,' Portia replied. 'I must visit Elsebeth. I have not seen her since Peter was so ill and I am looking forward to seeing how he has grown. And to an enjoyable gossip with my closest friend.' *And to ask her advice urgently*, she thought, although she kept counsel and didn't say the words out loud. Suddenly, the nightmares she'd had when she was ill had now materialised and they were no longer in her head, she was living them.

Today the short walk to Elsebeth's house wasn't the pleasant stroll Portia had enjoyed on previous occasions. Instead, she was scanning the street ahead and every building as she walked, constantly expecting to see Niccolo's menacing silhouette. Nowhere felt safe now, not even her own home, and she was relieved when she reached her destination.

She was shown into the parlour where her friend threw her arms around Portia and hugged her tightly.

'I have been waiting for you to come again and see Peter now he is well. I cannot thank you enough for what you did that day. He is in the nursery, let us visit him and then afterwards we shall take a cup of wine together.'

Portia followed her to the nursery. As a wealthy merchant, Elsebeth's husband earned enough to provide them with a reasonably sized home, and she had several servants to help with the housework. A maid, who bobbed a curtsey as they entered, was busy folding laundry and putting it into a drawer.

'Here he is.' Elsebeth crept into the small room and over to the cradle. Inside, laid on a wool-filled mattress and covered by several knitted blankets, was the sleeping baby. Whorls of dark hair had escaped the cotton cap he was wearing, curled around the edge of his face against his plump flushed cheeks.

'He looks so much better than when I last saw him,' Portia whispered, running the back of her finger down his soft face. For a moment it made her heart hurt, thinking of the babies she wouldn't have, now that she was too old for childbirth. From where she was bent over the crib, she could smell the warm sweet milky scent of innocence. She'd missed that with Vittoria, as the newborn days were spent on board the ship and the only smell was that of fish and briny seawater.

Together the two women tiptoed out of the room and then returned to the parlour, arm in arm. Elsebeth poured them each a cup of wine and they settled down for a long-missed heart-to-heart.

'My friend, I have a terrible dilemma,' Portia blurted out before either of them had even managed to take a sip of their drink. 'I need advice, but I do not know who to ask. I cannot speak of this with Maria, for reasons that will become obvious when I explain, and you are my very good friend, the only person I can talk to. If I speak about this with John, he will try and dissuade me from what I believe I must do.'

'My dear, tell me what has happened.' Elsebeth, her brows pushed together, put her cup on the small table beside her and knelt down in front of Portia, taking her hands in her own. 'Nothing can be as dire as you think it to be.'

'It is,' Portia replied, her eyes filling with tears. She'd kept them inside knowing that if she let them out, they'd never stop. Rubbing the back of her hands across her face, she took a deep breath.

She went on to explain who had appeared and the place he held in her family's history. 'You know why I had to escape the violence in Milan,' she concluded, 'yet it seems now that Milan has followed me here. I believe we must leave London, although I know Vittoria will never willingly agree to go. But if she does not, she will be taken by Niccolo back to Italy. I cannot bear that thought, that everything I did will have been in vain.'

'I would be heartbroken if you were not here,' Elsebeth admitted. 'You are my closest friend. I tell you everything.' Portia noticed that she'd paused for just the merest moment before she said *everything*, but who was she to question it, when despite their close friendship she was still keeping her darkest secret.

'I have not yet absolutely made my mind up,' Portia admitted. 'I do not yet know for certain what Niccolo wants from me, but if it is Vittoria, as I suspect, we shall not stay. If I do decide it is the right thing to do, I promise you and John will be the first to know.' Getting to her feet, she said goodbye, promising to visit again soon.

Later, arriving home, she placed her basket containing bread she'd just bought on the table.

'Goodness but it is hot outside,' she exclaimed, flapping her hands in front of her face, trying to move the still, sultry air. 'But it was very pleasant to see Elsebeth, and Peter is much better and growing up so quickly.'

'And what did you talk about? Did you confide in her, tell her you are thinking of leaving London?' Maria asked. Portia cursed herself. She should have realised that Vittoria would have gone crying to Maria, there were no secrets between the two of them. The other woman was like a second mother to the girl. And like a sister to herself; she shouldn't have kept it a secret.

'Elsebeth has knowledge of a woman who helps those who wish to leave the city and start a new life in Winchester, and on my way home, I went to visit her.' She winced inwardly as she stretched the truth. There was only one woman in London offering this service and she was standing in the room. 'I hanker for the fresh air of the countryside, just as we had in Italy in the villa, and she can arrange it. I think Winchester would suit us well. Better than London, in fact.'

'No. I have told you, I will not go.' Vittoria, who was sitting at the window, threw down the cards she was playing with so they scattered over the floor. Wordlessly Portia began to pick them up again. 'What about my friends in London?' she continued. 'Not just Caterina, but also she has introduced me to her neighbour, whom I like very much. And I can walk to their house on my own, because I know the way. If we move away, I will have to start again, even as my eyesight fails further. Already you have made us uproot ourselves from St Pancras Lane. I shall remain here. If you wish to go then go, but as I told you before, I will stay with Caterina. Just because my father was not a good man, Niccolo, my uncle, is always very kind to me. I am sure he would welcome me into his family. I *am* his family.'

'I too will not uproot myself again,' Maria announced. Portia's heart fell. She had been depending on the other woman to help her persuade Vittoria, and now she too was refusing. How could she make them agree without explaining the danger she was in? Maria was not vulnerable, as she and Vittoria were. If she wished to stay, although Portia would dearly miss her, Maria could live peaceably in the city without fear. No longer could Portia say the same for herself.

'Good. Then that is agreed,' Vittoria announced as she began to shuffle the now reassembled cards, 'you may go to Winchester if you wish, Mama, and we shall remain here. Then, when you realise how much you miss us, you can return and all will be as it ever was.' The girl's hands were shaking slightly and Portia knew that despite her brave words, she was distraught at the thought of them being separated. It was stubbornness that was speaking through her, a trait she recognised. They could both command it when the circumstances called for it, and she would now have to do so.

If only she could explain that if Niccolo had his way, they'd be separated forever. She suspected that already he was preparing plans to have her murdered. There had been several instances in Milan when business associates who had crossed either him or Lorenzo had conveniently disappeared. Everyone knew not to question them or they too would follow. And if that happened, Vittoria would soon be heading back to the city of her birth. If she was appalled at the thought of Winchester, then she would be horrified with Milan. A city where not only would she not know her way around, but her command of the language was weak in comparison to the people who'd lived there their whole lives.

None of that could be spoken aloud though, and without another word Portia climbed the steps to her bed above and lay down. The air up there was stifling, and she undid the ties of her shift at the neck to allow her sticky, sweaty skin to dry off. She'd reached a crossroads in her life once again. In Milan, she'd had but minutes to think, and that decision had followed her here, putting her life forever in danger. But despite everything beginning to unfold in front of her, she would make the same choices again. It had been the correct thing to do then, and now she must choose the correct course of action again.

26

2025

Just days after she'd received Margot's email, Beatrice was sitting on a train heading to Brighton, watching the countryside flash past. Jack couldn't accompany her on this trip, and although she missed his cheerful presence, she couldn't delay the visit a moment longer. She was desperate to see if what the other woman possessed was indeed the card she was searching for. Her heart was beating fast with both apprehension and excitement. When they'd chatted on the phone, she realised they were both as fascinated as each other about the broken pack and why it had been split. She had a feeling that Margot was a kindred spirit.

Once she left Brighton station, Beatrice followed the map on her phone and headed towards the street where Margot lived. It was only a few hundred yards from the beach, and she could understand why the other woman had chosen to retire next to the sea. Brighton was full of lovely little shops and Beatrice promised herself she'd have a wander round before she got on the train home.

Stopping off at a florist, she bought a bunch of roses. There was already a box of expensive macarons in her bag; unsure how much pleading she may need to do to buy the tarot card, she hoped arriving with gifts would be a good way to start. She was also praying she had enough money left in her savings to pay whatever price was asked, because it would be steep, given that Tristan had told her how much Margot had paid for it. And everything appreciated in value, especially as Margot already knew she was desperate to reunite the cards. Nestled in her handbag alongside the macarons and carefully wrapped up, was the rest of the pack.

The flat was on the ground floor of a Victorian terraced town house. The rooms were tall and airy, elegantly decorated in pale yellows and greys which bounced the light flooding in from the large sash windows around the walls. She proudly gave Beatrice a tour, until they ended up back in the living room with its big bay window looking out over the street.

'My mother would be horrified if she were still alive to see I don't have any net curtains,' she chuckled. 'The whole world can look into my living room as they walk past, and I don't care. I like to be able to see what's going on out there, as my neighbours come and go. And,' she gave a bark of laughter, 'who they're with. I'm probably the nosiest person in Brighton.'

They were sitting at a low walnut coffee table inlaid around the edges with a pale geometric design. It was French polished and glossy and similar to all the other furniture Beatrice had seen on her tour of the apartment. She suspected it had come from the auctions she now knew Margot had frequented when she was younger.

In their email exchange Margot had explained that she and her late husband had not been blessed with children. Instead, she'd sat at home as the years turned to decades, with no babies arriving, and she'd turned her nurturing instincts towards their house and began haunting furniture shops and auctions, searching for beautiful pieces to fill it with. *'If I couldn't fill it with a family, then I may as well fill it with items which we couldn't have had with small children,'* she had written. Despite her joking, Beatrice could read between the lines at the sadness there, and it had made her wonder about her own childless state.

'So, here is what you've come to see,' Margot lifted a small frame, one of an eclectic arrangement of artwork, from the wall and brought it over, laying it carefully on the coffee table.

Beatrice hadn't realised she was holding her breath until she heard it leave her chest in a slow stream. She could see immediately that what she was looking at was indeed what she'd been searching for. Getting the rest of the pack out, she lay them next to it, spreading some of them out.

'It looks just like mine,' she said. 'Although,' she paused and leant closer to scrutinise the card further, 'it is perhaps missing some of the finer details, I think.'

'You're right,' Margot agreed as she also bent nearer to compare the cards. 'If you saw it on its own as I have all these years you wouldn't know, but each of yours are like a work of art, a tiny, beautiful masterpiece. They look as though Michelangelo has painted them. But this one, not so much. Let me remove it from the frame and we can look at the reverse. I can remember it's gold with red and blue flowers and a black sword as yours are.' Getting to her feet, she took the card and frame out of the room, returning ten minutes later carrying a tray lined with velvet with the card laid on it.

'Back in the day, as well as buying beautiful furniture I used to do some gemstone dealing,' she explained. 'All above board, I hasten to add! That's why I have this tray, but it's perfect to put the card on and make sure it doesn't touch any grease or dust.' She laid it on the table and, holding her breath, Beatrice ran her eyes over every detail of the card. Now, without the frame around it, she was even more suspicious that there was something awry with it.

'There's definitely something not quite right,' she said. 'Would you mind if I turn it over to see the reverse?' Margot gave her permission and, holding it at the edges gently, Beatrice turned it over. She didn't even need to examine the back, because she could immediately tell that, despite all her hopes, this was not the card she was looking for. It may look similar, but it wasn't the one missing from her pack.

'This card is much thinner than mine,' she said. 'Here, hold one of mine...' She passed Margot the closest one, The Empress. '...and now pick up your card.'

She did as Beatrice suggested and nodded slowly, placing them both back on the table, reversed so they could see the backs.

'It's not the same quality of card, is it?' Margot said. 'It feels more like a few pieces of vellum bonded together, compared to yours which seems to be one piece of very thick parchment. The set of cards you have are a much nicer quality. And the design on the back, the painting is cruder on mine.'

'Appropriate for a card which asks what is the truth and what is an illusion, isn't it? Because this card is an illusion,' Beatrice said. She managed to force out a laugh, even though inside she wanted to burst into tears. All her hopes had been raised for nothing. Had the other person searching for the card already found it before her? Turning the card back, she looked once again at the front of Margot's card. 'Look at this.' She breathed out slowly. 'There's a tiny smudge in the design at the bottom here by the Devil's foot, can you see it? Like a fingerprint.' She sat back to allow Margot to pick up the tray and hold it close to her face, tilting it slightly towards the window, taking advantage of the sun streaming in.

'You're right,' she said. 'I've never even noticed that, although given that they're hand-painted, there must be the occasional error.'

'Not on any of the others though, I've examined them over many hours.' Beatrice laid the cards gently on the table and they each looked at several until Margot sat up, her hand pressed into the small of her back.

'I think my back won't thank me bending forward like that,' she admitted.

Beatrice tidied her cards and wrapped them up, feeling a lot more despondent than she had a few hours previously, sitting on the train down, her heart racing with excitement. Now she knew she hadn't found the card, nor did she have any other leads to follow. And she had yet another mystery to solve, because she had no idea why there would be such a close copy of the one missing from her set.

'Perhaps the original was damaged,' she mused. 'If indeed these were the cards being used at the time of the murders in the seventeenth century, they wouldn't have been able to keep them as carefully as I can these days. As it is, some of the other cards are dirty as though they've been dropped in a puddle, and one of them has what looks like a bloodstain on it. Perhaps there was an accident and – without the opportunity to have a replacement one painted – whoever owned these at the time, my ancestor, might have just done the best they could. I mean, it's definitely a reproduction looking at the back, even though the artwork is detailed. It's only by comparing it to the real cards that we can see it's a copy.'

'Well, it fooled me,' Margot said. 'And Tristan's dad too. Although he was wily, even if he'd suspected it wasn't the real thing he wouldn't have told me, not when he knew I had the money to pay for it.'

'It is kind of the real thing,' Beatrice consoled her. 'You bought an antique tarot card because you liked it, and I'm guessing it's centuries old, as mine are. It just isn't part of this pack, although if this was made because the original was damaged, I might be looking for something which doesn't exist. Back to square one then,' she said. 'Thank you for letting me come and look.'

Margot kissed her on both cheeks. 'I'm just really sorry I don't have what you were hoping to find,' she said. 'Please keep me updated if you find any other clues, because now I too really want to know why someone made a copy. The fact that there's a story behind it makes me love my own card even more. And,' she grinned, 'now that it isn't the one you want, I don't feel obliged to sell it to you. I'm used to seeing it on the wall and I would have missed it.'

* * *

As the train sped back to London two hours later, tears welled in Beatrice's eyes and having realised she had no tissues in her bag, she kept rubbing her fingers across them and hoped nobody else in the carriage noticed.

She'd spent her outward journey with such excitement and high hopes that she was about to unite the pack. Somehow, she had it in her mind that by finding The Devil card, she was doing it for all the women in her family, her ancestors, all those who came before her. And whoever had owned them in London in 1644. But she'd failed, because whilst it had been nothing short of a miracle that Margot still had the card, it wasn't what she wanted it to be. And now there was another mystery – why was there a copy of it? – to go with the unanswered questions about the murdered women in London. No woman in her family, her ancestors, would be a part of such a thing, Beatrice knew this, even without a shred of proof – she could recognise it, feel it, in the cards.

It was twilight when she arrived home and let herself into the shop. The darkness falling outside filled the space with a gloom which matched her mood, as though the cards were empathising with her disappointment after her previous exuberance. Picking up her post from the mat, she went upstairs, her legs feeling tired and heavy, barely able to climb the steps.

A quick glance in the fridge confirmed her suspicion that there was nothing in there for dinner. 'Wine it is then, Bea,' she said out loud as she got a glass from the cupboard and poured a generous glass full. Taking her post, she flopped on the sofa and switched the television on, but every channel seemed to have a soap opera or game show on and in the end she found a radio station to listen to.

Flipping through several circulars and pamphlets advertising food delivery and fast food, she found an envelope at the bottom of the pile with her address handwritten in a sloping, loopy writing she didn't immediately recognise. Feeling her mood lift just slightly, hoping this may be something with another lead to her missing Devil card, she pushed her finger under the flap and opened it. Inside was something that could not be further from a light at the end of the tunnel.

Pulling out the thick cream vellum card, she didn't need to look at what it said, she could guess, but she started to read it anyway.

Mr Mark Riley and Ms Kerry Mortimer invite you to the occasion of their marriage.

She threw it on the coffee table. No wonder she didn't recognise the handwriting, it must be Kerry's. Why did her father think she'd want to attend, and be a witness to, him announcing to the world that he'd forgotten her mother and was in love with someone else? The tears which had been trickling out whilst she was on the train, now fell in a full flood and she bent forward, her hands on her face. She was failing her mother's memory at every turn. Unable to stop her father from moving on and forgetting their happy family, 'the three musketeers' as he used to call them, and unable to reunite the tarot pack. Perhaps it was destined to be forever torn apart, just like her family. Forever in pieces.

27

2025

It was a few days before Beatrice saw Jack again. He'd sent her a message late in the evening after she'd returned from Brighton, but she was still bitterly disappointed and couldn't face seeing him. She'd replied to his question about how her day had gone with a simple sad face emoji. Immediately he called to ask if she wanted him to come and give her a hug but she declined the offer. The double whammy of the end of her wild goose chase for the card together with the arrival of the wedding invitation made her want to pull up the drawbridge. She didn't want to see anyone, not whilst she was feeling so sorry for herself.

Despite her melancholy mood she had no option but to open the shop, and mid-morning on the day after her visit to Margot the bell rang as someone walked in. Looking up from her phone where she was mindlessly scrolling through social media and doing nothing productive, she saw a young girl, her eyes darting around the shop as though she was expecting something to jump out at her. She looked to be in her late teens, her long dark hair was wound into a thick plait resting over her shoulder. She was holding the end of it in her hand.

'Hi.' Beatrice mustered a welcoming brightness to her voice, despite not feeling it. She couldn't project her current disposition on paying customers. 'Can I help you with anything, or are you here to browse? You're welcome to have a look at the different cards I have in stock.'

'I was hoping for a reading.' The girl's voice was deep and husky. 'It says on your board at the end of the street that you do tarot readings. Do I have to make an appointment or can I just have one now, please?'

'Of course you can, I'm not exactly rushed off my feet with customers.' Beatrice smiled and looked around the empty space as though proving her point. She took the payment before switching on the lamps in the back room and locking the shop door, putting a sign in the window saying she was closed for the next hour.

They sat down at the table and Beatrice shuffled her cards. Silently she admonished herself for leaving them alone for the past couple of days whilst she'd been hunting for the elusive card to reunite the old pack. As she held them in her hands they emitted a familiar warmth and comfort. After Brighton the previous day, she hadn't wanted to think about tarot cards, but she should have had more faith in them and the good they could do. If she'd done a reading for herself, she might have found some solace.

'So how does this work, then?' the girl, who had introduced herself as Mia, interrupted her musing.

'The cards can help in different ways. Showing you how you might approach a problem or perhaps a life decision, or if you're just wondering about the future in general you can think of that as your cards are turned, and they will show you how your life is now, as well as options which might help you decide on a particular road to travel. An answer which will help you to make a decision. It's not science so nothing is cut and dried. It's an art, a way of being in rhythm with yourself. Do you still want to go ahead?' Beatrice said.

Mia paused for a moment, staring at the cards now in a pile on the table, then nodded. Her lips were moving as though she was silently praying.

Beatrice dealt out three cards as usual. 'Remember, you can think about what you need answers to if you wish, but either way the cards will be in tune with you.'

Mia's hands were now pressed together between her thighs and the silence in the room felt palpable. Reaching out, she turned over the first card, showing a warrior holding a sword and standing on a chariot drawn by two Sphinx.

'The Chariot,' Beatrice announced. Mia looked up at her, waiting for her to elucidate. 'This card speaks of a journey, often one towards a specific goal. That you have or need to set clear intentions even though you may need to navigate around difficulties on the road ahead.' Mia nodded slowly, obviously understanding what it meant to her. 'There have been difficulties I've overcome,' she said.

'The second card,' Beatrice carried on as she turned it over. 'Also from the Major Arcana, the picture cards, and this one is the Strength card.' It was another depiction of willpower and tenacity. 'This also denotes inner strength and resilience; you can use your courage inside to overcome any difficulty. Dig deep and you will find it.' In the silence, Beatrice turned the third card.

'The Six of Wands.' Now the previous two cards began to make sense. 'This speaks of success and achievement, the recognition of hard work and persistence.'

At this point Mia slumped back in her chair and nodded slowly. Her eyes were wet with tears even though a wide smile was stretching across her face. Beatrice grabbed the box of tissues on a nearby side table and passed them over. Customers being upset were all part of her job, sometimes having the truth spelled out was a jolt, even though they might have expected it when they asked for a reading.

'I've just been accepted onto a training scheme, an apprenticeship for a job I really, really wanted. I didn't get the right qualifications at school, too much messing about and not studying.' She gave a little laugh. 'So I went back to college and did the exams and even then I was rejected a second time when I went through the application process. So, just as the Strength card has shown, I returned and undertook yet more courses at college. I was determined to achieve my goal and yesterday I heard that I've done it. I suppose I was hoping the cards would tell me if I'm going to succeed in my chosen career. I've come so far already, and this last card,' she pointed to the Six of Wands, 'seems to say that I will.'

'You will, because you have the determination to do so. You have already demonstrated that, and you deserve to accomplish all that you wish to. Shall I write everything down?' Beatrice offered. 'And you can always contact me online. Let me write down my email address.'

They went back through the shop and Beatrice quickly wrote down which cards had been turned and what each of them meant, then added her email address. 'Message me if I can help with any further explanations,' she said. Mia left looking a lot happier than when she'd arrived, and Beatrice felt relieved. She wanted her customers to depart with more strength, a lightness as they saw a way forward in their life.

She walked back to the other room and gathered the cards up, looking at each of those she'd just turned. Mia had overcome so many difficulties, defied every obstacle in her way to accomplish what she had set her heart on. Without realising it, she had shown Beatrice that wallowing and telling herself that she had failed in her quest was not the answer. She too needed to harness her inner strength and get out there and carry on searching. The pursuit was not yet over.

* * *

Later that afternoon, the wind which had been blowing all morning began to increase and make itself known as a storm, which had been mentioned several times on the news over the past couple of days. Beatrice hurried to grab her sandwich board before it disappeared along the street, or worse, into the road where it might cause an accident.

She felt a warm flush of pleasure when she spotted Jack outside his shop looking up at the roof. Although she'd deliberately chosen to be on her own since arriving back from Brighton, the moment she saw him, she realised that perhaps she'd been wrong to do so. Seeing him made her heart lift and she smiled and waved.

'Hey, stranger,' he greeted her. Hurrying over, he took the board from her and walked with it towards her shop. As the first raindrops started to fall, they both ended up running the last few metres and diving in through the door.

'Thank you,' she said as she stored the board behind the counter. 'I hadn't realised how bad the weather was getting. You'd better get back to your shop before the wind gets any worse.'

'We shut a little early, I wanted to send Alex home in case the buses stop, so it's empty,' he said. 'I was just looking at my roof to see if I could spot any loose tiles although there isn't much I can do now even if there are any.'

Now he was inside with her, he didn't seem to be in a hurry to leave. Going to the door, he flipped the sign over to say it was closed and pulled the blind down before shooting the bolts across.

'Do you mind if I just check upstairs that your roof is okay? I can climb into the loft from the landing if you don't mind me having a root around,' Jack asked. 'I don't want any leaks to make themselves known.' Outside, a flash was followed a couple of seconds later by a long, low rumble of thunder making Beatrice jump. Already the rain had increased, the raindrops hitting the window and bouncing off the cobbles outside.

'Of course,' Beatrice said. 'I haven't put anything up there, I only came to London with the basics really.' She ran upstairs with Jack following, taking the steps two at a time.

'Tea? Coffee? Wine?' she asked, quickly checking in the fridge to make sure she had a bottle in there.

'Wine would be lovely, thank you,' Jack said. He collected a kitchen chair to stand on and stuck his head through the loft door. 'I can't see any daylight up here, so I reckon your tiles are okay.' Having reassured himself that her ceiling wasn't about to cave in, he settled on the sofa and picked up the book she was reading. 'This looks well read,' he said as he looked at the spine. '*The History of the Tarot*,' he read out. 'Don't you know all the history, given that it's your profession?'

'Not really.' Beatrice put two glasses of wine on the table with a bowl of tortilla chips, the only snack she could find. 'I did know some of the historical background and of course about my own association to my ancestral cards but there's still a lot I have yet to learn. I hadn't realised that tarot cards started as playing cards, not for reading as they are now. And as some of the designs on the cards in there are similar to mine, it makes me more certain that mine are from the same era. I'm only halfway through the book. It was on a shelf at home, so it must've been Mum's originally. I threw it in with my stuff when I left.'

Jack leant forward and took his glass and the bowl before sitting back and at the same time managing to shuffle himself along the sofa so he was sitting much closer to her. She could smell his warm skin and the spicy scent of his cologne, and she breathed in deeply. Whatever her head said about him just being friendly, her heart, in fact her whole body, wasn't listening. Instead of trying to move away – which would be impossible given that she was already sat close up against the arm of the sofa – she tentatively relaxed a little against him. She began to suspect her attraction to him was reciprocated as he lifted his arm and placed it along the back of the sofa.

'This looks posh, have you been invited to a garden party at the Palace?' Before she could stop him, Jack picked up the envelope containing the invitation to her father's wedding which Beatrice had forgotten she'd left on the table. It should have gone in the bin, but even though she had no intention of attending, she still needed to send a reply to tell them that.

'Ha, I don't think so.' Beatrice forced out a laugh, holding out her hand to take the envelope from him. She slipped it down the side of the cushion she was sitting on. 'It's a wedding invitation,' she explained, 'but I'm not going.'

'Not going?' Jack leant away from her so he could look her straight in the face. 'Is it because of the shop? Because I can find someone to mind it, if that's the reason. Alex's mum, Daisy, is looking for some part-time work. Sometimes she helps me out, but I can't offer her something regular. Why wouldn't you go? I love going to weddings, dressing up and everyone happy and in a good mood. Nice food, few drinks, dancing, it's great.'

Beatrice sighed. 'It's not just any wedding,' she admitted, 'it's my dad and his partner. As you know my mum died, but now he's forgotten about her and is busy making a new life with Kerry. Honestly, I can't believe he's done it. I thought he was as devastated about Mum dying as me, but no, he was straight on the dating apps and now he says it's time to move on. I haven't moved on and I don't want a stepmother. It's as though he's cutting Mum, and me, out of his new life.'

'I'm sure he isn't doing that,' Jack said. 'When you say he was online looking for someone else, do you mean immediately? Because surely your mum would have wanted you both to live your lives and be happy?'

'And so we were, or at least I thought we were, but it seems that Dad wasn't actually happy with it being just the two of us. It's been a couple of years now so no, he didn't go looking straight away for a replacement wife, that's true. But I can't forgive him for just casting the memories of Mum aside. He and Kerry are getting married just before Christmas, which makes it even worse. Mum loved Christmas and now Dad is ruining the whole celebration.'

'You can still enjoy it all, Christmas is a time for families.' Jack's arm slid off the top of the sofa so it was laid across her shoulders. He gave her a squeeze and Beatrice leant further into him.

'I'll celebrate here,' she answered. 'I can't go home. They're going away after the wedding and spending Christmas in Spain, so there won't be anyone about anyway. Nope,' she slapped her hands on her thighs, 'I'll put up a little tree here and go and buy lots of lovely festive food and wine, perhaps a couple of new books, and I'll be perfectly happy here.'

'Really? Happy?' Jack questioned. 'Or sad-but-putting-a-brave-face-on-it and drowning your sorrows?'

'Well, either way, that is what's happening.' Beatrice gave a shrug. She'd been trying very hard since she'd arrived in the

summer to build this new alternative life, and this was just
another brick in her wall of stoicism.

'Why don't you come with me and spend it in Cornwall
then? I only close the shop for a couple of days so it's a flying
visit, but my parents love having extra people around the table
for Christmas lunch. And,' he added, 'I'd really like it if you were
there. I think you'd like them, and they would definitely like you.
My family would all have you doing tarot readings.'

Beatrice thought for a moment. Despite what she'd just told
him, if she was truthful she wasn't looking forward to spending
Christmas on her own for the first time ever. Sadness piled on
sadness, no Mum, no Dad, none of the traditional celebrations at
home. It didn't take more than a few seconds to consider her
reply before she threw her arms around him, squeezing him
tightly.

'Thank you,' she said. 'I'd love to come and enjoy the festivi-
ties with you and your family.'

With both of her arms around him she felt his arm wrap
across her back and his other hand beneath her chin as he tilted
it up and his lips met hers. Smiling, she leant into him and
kissed him back.

* * *

It was several hours later by the time Jack left her flat. The
weather had worsened, and standing in the shelter of the shop
doorway, Beatrice watched him walking almost bent double
against the wind as the rain blew horizontally. She was getting
wet even standing where she was with just her head poking out,
but she was rewarded when he got to the end of the street and
turned around and blew a kiss to her.

Jumping back inside, she leant her shoulder on the door to

push it closed and locked it. Her hair, damp despite having barely been outside, was dripping cold droplets down her neck but nothing could wipe the smile from her face. She hugged her arms around herself as though trying to emulate how perfect it had felt when it was Jack's arms around her. Already she was missing his warmth.

Going back upstairs, she rinsed their glasses and the two plates they'd used when she'd cooked them egg and chips, which was all the food she'd had in the flat. They hadn't spent the whole evening kissing, although she could have quite happily done so, they'd also done a lot of talking. Filling each other in on their backgrounds and childhoods and Jack had spoken more about his parents.

It was past eleven o'clock and Beatrice was tired but she knew she was too happy and excited, her insides fizzing, to think about going to sleep. She realised she could no longer keep her feelings for Jack suppressed and instead would simply enjoy it whilst it lasted. Making a cup of tea, she flopped down on the sofa and picked up the book that they'd been discussing earlier.

She'd only been reading for five minutes, her tea still sitting steaming and untouched on the coffee table, when she sat forward and slowly went back through what she'd just read. The chapter was the one about the early tarot cards and how it was believed they had initially begun in Italy. Where her pack had originated from. But then the explanation went on to talk about the mystery of more than one almost identical copy of a Devil card which had surfaced over the centuries, how there had at one point been one in a gallery in Milan and another had appeared in Suffolk in the 2010s. There was a photo of that card, the one which Beatrice knew Margot now possessed.

Annoyingly there wasn't a photo of the one in Milan, so she had no idea if this was finally the actual one missing from her pack, or another copy, or in fact the one that had ended up in Suffolk. The book said there was definitely more than one replica and either way, it could be anywhere now. If it did transpire to still be there, and could actually be the card she was seeking, then how was she going to persuade the gallery to let her have it, to bring it back where it belonged? She reminded herself of her resolve to keep going, using her strength to carry on until she found the card to make her pack complete, and taking a photograph of the page, she sent Jack the images. There was no immediate reply and she went through to get into bed, still too motivated to sleep. Just when she thought she'd hit a dead end there was another trail to follow. All was not yet lost.

28

1644

'Please, sit yourself down.' Portia placed a stool at the table before fetching one for herself and collecting the cards from the cupboard. Holding out her hand, several pieces of gold fell into her palm and she quickly slipped them into her pocket. Offering her service for only that which a customer could afford to pay sometimes meant that she didn't earn a lot, so when a wealthier client arrived she was happy to accept more. She lay the shuffled pack down on the table.

'What do you wish to learn from the cards today?' she asked. The woman was dressed in a plain but neat fine wool gown with no darned patches, the hems not yet tatty and torn. Given the value of coins that had just changed hands and the constant state of high alert she was feeling, Portia needed to make sure that this was not some ruse by Niccolo.

'I have heard you can help women,' came the answer. Portia's fingertips touched the card she had just secreted in her sleeve as she'd shuffled the pack. It would be easy to replace were it not needed, but some intuition had told her this time it would, and she was right. Now it would be slipped in at the correct moment, swiftly and unseen.

'Help?' she asked. 'What do you need help with, goodwife?'

'It is not me, it is my sister. She is kept locked in the house by her husband, not allowed even go to the market. I must visit the shops for us both and take food to her. She is thin and pale and says she does not get enough to eat. I need to get her away from him, help her escape London so he can never find her. I am very fearful for her life.'

'And will she agree, if someone can do this for her? It would be extremely dangerous, and a woman who wishes to flee must be ready at a moment's notice.'

'She will, I promise. This morning, I delivered her provisions and I whispered that I was going to find a way to help her leave and she gave my hand a squeeze in acknowledgement. I know she will be ready if it can be arranged.'

Nodding slowly, Portia started the reading; as ever the tiniest of movements had placed The Devil card exactly where she needed it.

The first card showed a row of swords stood upright in the ground, and bound to one was a young woman, roped and blindfolded. 'The Eight of Swords, indicating someone being imprisoned,' she started, before turning the second card.

'The Five of Swords. See how the young man is collecting the weapons he is surrounded by? This denotes a situation where a person needs to move forward but must have belief in their abilities to do so. To be ready to fight.' Her customer gave a gruff laugh.

'That is exactly right,' she said grimly.

Portia turned the final one and watched as the usual consternation flitted across the woman's face.

'You must trust the cards,' she reassured her. 'The Devil,

what is the truth and what is an illusion. The illusion is that your sister lives in a house where her husband loves her so much he wants to keep her all to himself. The truth is that she is captive there and must be set free.' The other woman nodded, her eyes still transfixed to the card. Portia went on to explain what would happen when the time was right: taking the card and then slipping through the dark streets to the river. Emphasising that it was not for the faint-hearted, she worried that this customer's sister may not have the courage nor strength to go through with it. She explained what it would cost, the coins which had already changed hands wouldn't be enough for the danger of the task ahead.

Getting to their feet, Portia collated the cards again whilst the woman rummaged in the purse tied to her skirt and took out another, larger, handful of gold coins.

'How much do you need?' she asked. Her hands were shaking slightly. 'I will pay as much as you ask, if I can save my sister before he kills her.'

'That is payment enough,' Portia replied as the coins joined those already in her pocket. It would be a good addition to her coffers. 'Now, you must give her the card I shall give you now, a copy of The Devil card.' She went on to explain where and when the escape would take place. 'Tell your sister to keep away from her husband in any way she is able until the time comes,' she added. Unable to erase the fate of Nell and how she'd failed the young girl out of her mind, she didn't want history to repeat itself.

'I promise she will be at the river at ten o'clock as you have stated,' the woman assured her, wiping her fingers beneath her eyes. 'I will bid you goodbye now and thank you from my heart for that which you will do for us.' After she left, Portia put the money with the rest that she had accumulated. Now instead of it being kept for Vittoria's future it would be needed for them to abscond. And time was marching on.

*   *   *

Two days later, Portia waited to hear the calls of street hawkers with their pamphlets alerting the city folk that another woman had been taken and murdered, but all was quiet. Eventually, after they'd consumed some roasted pig's knuckle and salad vegetables for dinner she announced that she was going for a walk and left quickly before Vittoria decided to accompany her.

Pausing on the corner of Fenchurch Street and Gracechurch Street, she bought a news sheet in case the disappearance of the customer had been reported, but as she suspected, there was nothing. Folding it up and putting it in her pocket, she walked down to the river, her steps lengthening as she failed to over-come the feeling of panic until she was almost trotting.

As she reached the end of Rope Street, she almost bumped into someone coming the other way and as she stepped back-wards, she realised it was John. He put his hands on her shoulders to steady her.

'I was just coming to visit you,' he said, 'And I am guessing that you are on your way to see me for the same reason.'

Portia was trying to catch her breath, she couldn't decide if the rapid beating of her heart was a result of her hurrying, or the panic which was now racing through her body.

'Did the woman arrive with you last night?' she questioned, her voice coming in gasps. 'I expected to hear word of it on the streets as before, but there has been nothing.'

'That is why I was on my way to you. I would have come sooner but I had already agreed a job for this morning. You have guessed correctly, she did not appear.'

Portia felt herself break out in a cold sweat which swept over her, prickling her scalp and making her back burn. The vision of Nell's small, pinched face swam before her eyes. Was this another woman she had failed to save in time? Perhaps it was something as simple as there not being the opportunity. After all, she had only spoken with the sister, so the handing over of The Devil card and explanation of the process had to be done by someone else.

'I cannot do anything until, or if, the sister reappears,' she said. 'But I am very afraid of what may have happened. We both know there is always a risk that a husband discovers that his wife intends leaving. I do hope she is still safe.'

'Indeed,' John agreed, 'but you have done all that you can. Now you can only wait.' He gave her hands a squeeze and a chaste kiss on the cheek. 'I must return to my boat, there are a lot of people wishing to go places on the river today. I will try and call on you later in case you hear something.'

They said their goodbyes and Portia started to walk home, this time considerably slower. She hadn't said anything to John but now she was starting to recall the feeling she'd had when she had read the cards for this woman's sister. At the time she had fleetingly considered how she was now in even more danger, that Niccolo could send someone as a ruse to trick her, and perhaps this was indeed what had happened. She didn't even want to think of what he could do with the information if he knew what she was doing.

29

2025

Unable to sleep with the noise of the wind, Beatrice lay awake for hours and then when it finally blew over, slept in until eight o'clock. When she awoke, a quick check out of the window revealed there was no immediate evidence of damage to the mews.

Making some toast, she sat on the sofa to carry on reading her book whilst she ate. She hadn't received a reply to the message she'd sent Jack the previous night, nor was it displaying the two blue ticks to show that he'd read it. During her wakeful night she'd already googled the gallery in Milan and found an email address which, given her scant knowledge of Italian, she could only guess was the correct one. With some help from an app to translate her words into Italian and hoping she hadn't made any embarrassing mistakes, she sent a message enquiring about the card. At the back of her mind though was the niggling reminder that whoever she was innocently in a race with may had got there before her.

She wasn't sure they'd remember the card and it was even less likely that they still had it, so she took a photo of the page in her book and attached it together with a couple of photos of her cards. If by some miracle the owner still knew of it and more importantly its whereabouts, hopefully this proved she was legitimate and not someone planning to steal it.

There were no further mentions in the book of her card, but she did find some illustrations of ones from a similar era in a museum in Lewisham. Checking their webpage, she could see they were still being displayed, and she decided to go for a visit as soon as she was able.

It was already the end of October, and with people now starting to do their Christmas shopping in earnest, she was unsure if Jack would be able to accompany her as he'd done to the British Museum. She too had more customers in her shop and with an increasing number of online sales, Beatrice didn't think she'd be able to continue to stay closed two days a week. Perhaps, as Jack had suggested, it was time to advertise for an assistant.

Still with no response from him, she went downstairs at nine o'clock and opened the shop, taking her laptop with her. She was attempting to design a tarot reading gift voucher, after several requests from people asking to purchase them as Christmas gifts. Happy to oblige, knowing sales would be sparce in January, she needed to try and produce something quickly. The more money she could make at the moment, the better. Another reason, she admitted to herself, why the shop should be open seven days a week. Increasing footfall of customers wanting cards or readings would hopefully result in word of mouth creating extra business.

She was standing at the counter scrolling through the website of a designer she'd seen on social media, when Jack arrived. Unlike herself, unsure of how things would be between them after the previous evening, he was grinning from ear to ear.

'Good morning,' he said, leaning over the counter and kissing her on the lips. 'It looks like we all survived the storm, then. Apparently there's a fence down in the next street, but other than that it looks pretty normal out there.' Whilst he was talking, he'd moved around so he was standing next to her, his arms around her waist as he turned her to face him. The feeling of his body close to hers made her feel warm with pleasure and she grinned at him as she hugged him back.

'What are you looking at here?' he asked, bending in closer to her laptop screen. 'Are these some more old card designs you've found?'

'No, these are by an amazing artist, I saw her on Instagram and messaged to ask if she'd be interested in designing bespoke sets of cards to sell. They'd be very high-end, but there's an increasing interest in tarot cards and I think some people would pay for them. Similar to the antique sets I have in the display cabinets – the ones on the shelves are okay for people starting out, who want to do it as a hobby, but those who are serious might like a set that is personal to them. You have to bond with the cards, it's not as simple as opening the cellophane and cracking on.'

'What do you mean, bond? Like you have a connection with them?' Jack asked.

'Sort of. Mine are special to me, personal, as though I "know" them and they know me,' Beatrice said.

'And the old pack, the one with The Devil card missing, do you feel a relationship with those cards too?'

'Well, yes, but not in the same way. It's hard to describe. They aren't my cards and I don't know if I could do an adequate reading with them, even if I had the whole pack. Which I sincerely hope I will one day. But despite that, they do feel a part of me. As though they want me to tell their story and that there is something inherently moral and noble within them. I know it sounds daft, but it's the best way I can describe them. Anyway, Rachel is based in Streatham so I thought I'd set up a meeting. I've also discovered that the Horniman Museum in Lewisham, which isn't too far from there, has a couple of antique cards from about the right period. I could go and view those and then hopefully meet with Rachel, look at some of her designs in person. But the best thing is that I found a reference in that old book you were looking at last night about a single card, probably from the fifteenth century. A Devil card again. When the book was written it was in a gallery in Milan, there isn't a photograph of it but at least that sounds like a lead, if I can find out who owns it. I'm on the trail once again.'

'Any chance of a plus one coming with you to Lewisham? Not to the meeting with Rachel, that's business, but I would love to look around the museum. I've never been before, which is ridiculous as a Londoner. Depending on which day you are going, of course. As you no doubt also realise, it isn't easy to slide out of the shop on any day of the week now, it's beginning to get manic. Hurrah for Christmas shoppers who want to buy from a real bookshop.'

'Of course you can tag along.' Beatrice took his hand and squeezed it. 'I'd love you to. I think you are becoming almost as invested in finding my card as I am. I know it isn't at this museum, but it would be interesting to see cards of a similar era. It'll have to be next Monday now, as I don't think they're open on Sundays. I've decided to do as you suggested though, and take someone on to help me in here so the shop can stay open whilst I'm gallivanting about.'

They were interrupted by Alex popping his head around the shop door.

'Jack, there's a lady in to collect something she ordered

online, and I can't find it on the shelf. Can you come and assist, please?' he said.

'Yup, on my way,' Jack replied. The head disappeared again. 'I'd better go back. Let me know when you've organised your meeting and we can arrange a day out. As for a member of staff, what about Daisy? I mentioned her before – Alex's mum. I can vouch for her. She probably won't have any tarot expertise but she could learn, and I think she'd be quick too. Think about it. I can ask her to come and see you for a chat if you want. And in the meantime, how about going out for dinner tonight?'

Beatrice felt her heart skip a beat. She'd spent half the night worrying about whether he'd wake up in the morning regretting what had passed between them, but it seemed not. She'd buried her concerns in a small compartment in her brain and decided she would leave them there and just enjoy life for a while. If there were going to be regrets, they were for the future, she'd just deal with the present whilst she was living it.

30

1644

There was no further visit from the customer who hadn't arrived with John as arranged, and two days later as Portia was sitting at home preparing the vegetables for dinner a sudden loud knock at the door made her jump and drop the carrots she was holding so they rolled across the floor. She swore under her breath.

Opening it expecting to see one of her neighbours, she felt a flush of heat wash over her as she found Niccolo standing there. Having not seen him since the wedding she had truly begun to believe that he wasn't interested enough to find her. Or maybe he was now preparing to return to Italy, that was her most favoured assumption. Before she could bar the entrance with her body, he pushed past her and into their parlour.

'What are you doing here?' She put her hands on her hips, her chin jutting forward. Her heart was racing and her legs had turned to calves' foot jelly, but she wouldn't let him see that.

'We have some unfinished business,' he replied, pulling out a stool from beneath the table and sitting down on it. Bending down, he picked up one of her carrots and snapped it in half. Portia's hands went to her throat. She had no doubt that he could do the same to her neck with his giant hands, if he chose. He stretched his long legs out and crossed them at the ankle.

'And something else has come to my attention.' Reaching into the pocket of his jerkin, he produced a card and threw it on the table. Portia's eyes widened and she dragged a stool towards her and sank onto it before she fell to the floor. It was the copy of The Devil card that she'd given to the woman at the last reading, distinctive because it was the card with the tiny smudge Vittoria had made when she'd discovered it in the cupboard.

She cleared her throat. 'I have no idea what that even is.' Her voice was wavering. 'A tarot card, I assume?' She leant across to pick it up but he snatched it back and returned it to his pocket.

'You cannot think me so senseless?' he replied, his eyebrows low over his eyes, his forehead creased in a frown. 'This design is distinctive. One of the family of Collari, *your family*, cards. I have seen them before, when you lived with my brother and your sister in Milan. And you gave it to a visitor recently, a woman who came here asking for a reading but really asking for you to spirit away her sister.'

Now just as Portia had dreaded, the truth began to appear through the mists of her confusion. He had sent the other woman to trick her, although how did he know what she was doing? As though reading her mind, and full of his delight at tricking her, he laughed out loud at her confused face, pushing his so close to hers that she could smell the sour smell of rancid ale on his breath.

'You must be wondering how I realised what you have been organising, that you are a part of the murders in London. You think you are so clever and yet you are not. It only took the one discovery of a card dropped at the scene of a disappearance and for me to see a copy of that in a news sheet. Then when I saw you at Caterina's wedding I was reminded of your penchant for reading the cards in Milan and I started to add everything up until I very quickly realised you were involved. And, before I even came by this knowledge, I had already discovered your other secret, had I not?'

'I, I have no idea what you are talking about.' Portia shrugged her shoulders and tried to adopt the demeanour of someone who could not care less, who was innocent of all that she was being accused of. Even though her heart was beating so hard in her chest she imagined it might burst out at any moment.

'I saw Vittoria, I saw her eyes. At this very moment she is with my daughter, *her cousin*, enjoying a goblet of wine. The affliction she suffers from is exactly the same as your sister, Agnese.'

'Merely a coincidence,' Portia retorted. 'It is a condition known to the Collari women. I am a Collari.'

'Your sister's eyes, and the deep burnished auburn of her father's hair,' he continued, his eyes flicking to her own hair loose beneath her coif. Despite her Italian heritage, Portia's was only a mid-brown, paler than most of her contemporaries. 'I do not know how, or why you did it, but Vittoria is not your child, is she? Does she know that she is the child of my brother Lorenzo and his now dead wife Agnese.'

'You are talking such nonsense,' she said. She needed to keep denying it, even though just as she knew he would, he had worked out the truth. Lorenzo would have left both Vittoria and Agnese to their fate in the city, he cared so little for his wife. And even less for herself. But she knew there was no point in saying that to Niccolo, he wouldn't care what her motive had been.

'And this gives me a bit of a problem,' Niccolo said. He threw the pieces of carrot onto the table and leant forward, his head in his hands, shaking it slowly from side to side. 'As I told you, my brother, just like his wife, succumbed to the plague not twelve hours after we left the city.' He sat up again and looked at Portia who just stared blankly back at him. It was certainly no loss to her if Lorenzo was dead, the man had been a brute.

'I do not care what happened to him. As far as I am concerned the world is a better place without him in it. And Vittoria is no worse off.'

'She might not be, but I stand to be. Not knowing that Lorenzo had a child, an heir,' he spat the last two words, 'meant that his fortune came to me. But now I will lose it, and Caterina too as I have no sons to leave it to, because Vittoria is the one who should have actually inherited. The houses in Italy, the remains of the jewellery and the gold in his coffers, it is all, unbelievably, rightfully hers.'

Portia got to her feet and started to pace the floor, unable to keep still as she digested what she'd just been told. This put a very different perspective on Vittoria's life. She would want for nothing, they could return to Italy and live in comfort.

'So, as you can see, Vittoria is an obstacle I cannot ignore,' Niccolo said. 'Nor can I disregard you either. Because now you know the truth and I cannot have that being divulged anywhere.'

As his words dripped into her ears Portia felt a sickening fear crawl down her spine. She cleared her throat.

'And if I promise not to mention it?' she asked. 'Because at present, only myself – and you – know.'

'Indeed, and you have even bigger secrets you must keep hidden. That not only did you steal my brother's child, but also that you are involved in what is happening to the goodwives of London. There is a connection to them through your tarot cards. You are involved in the killings.'

'There are no murders, you have guessed that!' Portia was furious that he would even think her able to do such a thing. Before she could stop and consider what she was saying, she blurted out the truth. The truth which had applied to her and Vittoria fifteen years previously. 'Those women need to flee from a home life which would kill them. I merely assist in their escape. Just as my recent visitor, the one you sent, requested of me.'

'Emulating then what you yourself did. Except not only did you escape Milan, but you also stole a child. I assume Vittoria has not been told of your true relationship to her?'

'No,' Portia admitted. 'I have had no reason to tell her. It would break her heart, and mine.'

'Then perhaps I can be persuaded to keep my counsel, at least whilst it suits me to do so. Nor inform the constables of what you have been doing.' He patted the pocket containing the card. 'My insurance that you will agree to anything I ask of you. Because if you mention the truth about Vittoria's wealth to anyone, I will kill you both.'

Abruptly he got to his feet, knocking the stool he was sitting on backwards where it landed on the floor with a clatter. Now his eyes were narrowed in a way that she had witnessed many times before. He was behaving just as the Tabanelli men always did with threats. 'You were once a Tabanelli possession, and believe me, you still are. You can run but you are never hidden. Not you, nor my niece. We never give up what is ours.'

The door slammed as he walked out and Portia sank to her knees before they gave out altogether. She knew it didn't matter what deals Niccolo professed to make, because there was no denying what sort of man he was, his final words had reminded her of that. He was as much of a brute as his brother. He wouldn't just agree to a pact of silence, she and Vittoria were now in grave danger.

She must save Vittoria though, make her disappear, although now finally she'd have to admit what she did all those years ago. Whatever happened, when the girl discovered the truth it would be from her lips and nobody else's. She'd explain her deception and the reasons behind it. Even Maria didn't know for certain, although she must have guessed that Portia wasn't Vittoria's real mother, she didn't have the body of a woman who'd just given birth when just hours later she was searching out a wet nurse and explaining that she was leaving for Venice immediately. If she'd given birth, she would still be lying in. The secret was between the two of them, to never be spoken of.

She could only hope that Vittoria understood her motive. And why she was telling her now, because she couldn't divulge what she had just discovered about Lorenzo's fortune and the true owner of it.

31

2025

Late in the afternoon Jack sent a message suggesting dinner at the small Italian restaurant next-door-but-one to his shop. Beatrice, who had been checking her inbox feverishly hoping for a reply from Italy, sent back a thumbs up, whilst mentally checking through her wardrobe wondering what to wear.

With her father having driven her and all her worldly belongings to London she hadn't been able to fit much more in the car, along with her mother's collection of cards which filled several boxes, and the bare essentials. She'd only packed two small cases and a couple of large blue bags, the ones that didn't actually have some flat-packed furniture in them, and now she realised just how few clothes she'd brought with her. Enough jeans and T-shirts, but very little suitable for a date. And, whatever she'd told herself, this definitely felt like a date. Momentarily, her mind went to what decent underwear she'd brought as well.

At seven thirty she was already on her way downstairs when she heard the rapping of knuckles on the shop door. She could see his outline, the broad shoulders and blond hair shining beneath the street light, and she had to stop herself giving a tiny squeak of excitement.

Dinner, together with two bottles of Valpolicella, was a leisurely affair. Halfway through the meal she received a brief message from her father asking how she was, and she took a photo of her half-eaten dinner and glass of wine and sent it back. *I'll message later*', she quickly typed. Although she knew it had been the right decision to move away, that she couldn't stay knowing how he'd let her down and her mother too, she still missed him more than she had ever imagined she would. There was a hole in her life where he should be.

He was probably contacting her as a premise to ask if she'd received her wedding invitation. She hadn't yet replied to say she wouldn't be attending, putting it off because however hurt she was at the situation, in turn she knew her reply would upset him more. There was no right answer.

After a light-hearted disagreement about who was paying, which Beatrice won by saying she was going to the toilet and then stopping off at the bar to pay the bill without Jack even realising what she'd done, they walked back, hand in hand, towards the mews until they paused at the end outside Hampstead Books.

'Would you like to come up and see my flat?' Jack asked. 'It's nothing special, but I haven't shown you round yet. I have more wine, or you can have coffee; I buy the beans in a little shop on South End Road, which is so old it's probably been there as long as your cards have been around.'

'I don't know if they drank coffee in medieval times.' She laughed. 'But I'd love to come up for a drink, thank you.'

Unlike her own flat with just the one door and having to enter through the shop, his had a separate entrance around the corner, and he led her up a flight of stairs to another door at the top. Unlocking this, he stepped to one side, ushering her in.

'Come into the living room,' Jack said as he walked through a wide doorway and quickly switched on a couple of lamps.

Beatrice wasn't sure what she'd been expecting, something similar to her own perfunctory space, small but utilitarian, but this was quite different. It reminded her of Tristan's eccentric splendour, but this looked more well-ordered as though some thought had gone into ensuring items went together. Not Baroque meeting Art Deco with a splash of Post-Modernism.

The room was much larger than hers and painted in a deep midnight blue. There were two leather Chesterfield sofas, and a large square coffee table piled up with books. Along one wall, a fitted bookcase was also crammed with books, including some laid haphazardly on top of others where there was simply not enough space to hold them all. Two small occasional tables at each end of the larger of the sofas were also piled with books. In the middle of another wall stretched a wide, carved, wooden fireplace with a marble hearth. The two sash windows had thick, floor-length, mustard-yellow curtains, which Jack quickly pulled across. As he stretched up to grab them, his shirt tugged free of his jeans and Beatrice caught a tantalising glimpse of skin just above his waistband.

'Wow,' she said, dragging her eyes away from him and trying to ignore the feelings he was arousing and turning round in the middle of the room. 'This is amazing. All these books, it's like a library.'

'Ha, well, bookseller, son of booksellers, it kind of comes with the territory. A lot of these are ones that should be downstairs in the second-hand section of the shop, except I don't have enough space. They're all catalogued though, and I can find them if someone enquires. Believe me, I'm not the sort of person who would put their books on shelves alphabetically unless I had to, but if I didn't do it, I wouldn't be able to find anything and that might mean loss of a sale if a customer is waiting downstairs.'

Now that he'd mentioned it Beatrice started walking along the bookcases looking at the spines and realised he hadn't been joking, the books were indeed in alphabetical order. After ascertaining that she'd like to sample the highly commended coffee, Jack disappeared across the hall and into what she assumed was his kitchen as he carried on chatting, his louder voice carrying through.

She was sitting on one of the sofas flipping through a book she'd just picked up from the table beside her about the Impressionists when he arrived back with two mugs of coffee together with a Kilner jar filled with sugar, and a spoon. Jack passed her a mug and offered the sugar before placing it on the coffee table and sitting down beside her. He slid his arm around her and pulled her in close, kissing the top of her head as she laid it on his shoulder.

'This is a really lovely flat,' she said, blowing on her coffee and taking small sips. 'And also, really lovely coffee. I can understand why you go to a specialist shop for it.'

'There aren't many things that I'm particular about,' Jack said. 'Books, coffee and my friends. I only surround myself with things that are beautiful. Beautiful books, beautiful souls. Nothing else in this world matters as far as I'm concerned.'

Beatrice pushed herself back upright and looked at him to see if he was laughing at her, but he wasn't. He was looking into her eyes and taking her coffee and placing it with his on the table, he placed his hands either side of her face and started to kiss her. She slid her hands beneath his shirt until she felt them against his smooth skin which felt every bit as good as it had looked earlier and pulled him towards her so she could push her body against his.

'I haven't shown you my bedroom yet,' Jack whispered, his breath hot against her.

'Then I think you should,' Beatrice whispered back. She'd been unsure if he wanted to move their relationship on, in fact she hadn't been 100 per cent certain if she wanted to either. Carrying around so much hurt, she didn't think she could risk the potential for any more, but she couldn't deny the sexual attraction she was feeling, and she no longer wanted to. She was drawn to him in a way that she hadn't been to any man for a long while, and she'd had enough of dancing round on the periphery to her own life. Now she needed to dance right back into it.

Standing up, Jack took her hand and pulled her to her feet. He led her back through the entrance hall and into another room, as large and grand as the living room and dominated by an enormous wooden bateau bed. The walls in here were also lined with bookcases, but this time she ignored them, more intent on helping Jack divest himself of his clothes.

32

2025

Beatrice was standing at the counter in her shop. She was supposed to be updating her website, but in fact she was staring at the screen and not taking in any of the words on there. Instead, her mind was still in Jack's bedroom where they'd got very little sleep, but where she'd had the best night of her life. She'd finally returned home at 3.30 a.m. when Jack had reluctantly let her go, and after only a few hours' sleep she wasn't even sure she should be doing something as responsible as working on her website when she was so tired.

She took another sip of coffee from the cup beside her. It was almost tasteless compared to the drink Jack had made for her the night before and she resolved to buy a cafetière at the earliest opportunity and then visit the shop he'd recommended.

Her musing was interrupted by the notification of an email arriving, and she gave a little whoop of joy when she saw it was from the Arcardi Gallery, the one in Milan that had been mentioned in her book.

'Oh, yes, Bea,' she said as she clicked to open it, 'now we're on our way.'

Unfortunately, it wasn't as encouraging as she'd hoped, and her euphoria steadily dissipated as she quickly scanned the words.

They agreed they did at one time have the card. Indeed, they possibly still did, but it wasn't in a display cabinet any more, and it also didn't appear to be in the archives where, according to their records, it should be. They promised to do some further investigations and get back to her but couldn't guarantee it would be found. Beatrice gritted her teeth. How could a gallery lose an artefact and be so blasé about it? The email finished, '*We are very sorry and will be in contact again if we can locate the card you are searching for.*'

For one thing, she didn't even know if it was the card she was searching for, but more worryingly, if they didn't have it, had her adversary in this quest already got there before her? A despondency about trying to track down the card which she hadn't felt before descended on her, a cloak of disappointment.

'One step forward, two steps back,' she muttered to herself. Ignoring the work she'd been doing, she closed her laptop and put it on the shelf below the counter. She couldn't help the feeling that she was letting down her mother, her *nonna* and all those women who came before her if she was unable to reunite the cards.

Picking up her phone, she messaged Jack with the disappointing update, followed by a long line of sad emojis. His reply was almost instantaneous, some sad emojis mixed with some glass of wine emojis and now smiling again, she replied with a thumbs up. Somehow even when she was in despair about the whole search, he could still cheer her up.

* * *

The following Monday morning they were on a train heading towards Lewisham. Jack had been busy in the shop over the weekend, so it had been a few days since they'd seen each other, and she was surprised at how much she'd missed him. His unending cheerfulness, his ready smile and the sound of his deep voice, the way laughter would rumble in his chest. He'd greeted her with a lengthy kiss and she almost suggested they abandon the day's trip, but with the disappointing email from the gallery in Milan she needed to do something proactive.

'So, that seems to be a dead end,' Beatrice said as she explained in more detail how the Italian card had gone missing. 'They said they didn't sell it, they've been through their sales records and if it had been sold it would be entered there. Honestly, they didn't sound massively concerned, although I hope in reality, they're frantically running around looking for it. I keep telling myself that at least if they haven't sold it, the other person looking for it hasn't got there before me. But that is scant consolation if they've lost it.'

'So where do you go from here?' Jack asked. Beatrice merely shrugged her shoulders in answer to his question. They were both on their feet as the train pulled into the station, swaying with the movement. He wrapped his arm around her waist and held her close to him, the pair of them moving together. She wished they could stay on the train until the end of the line. After they'd been to the museum she was meeting Rachel but Jack would be going back to his shop. He'd had a delivery first thing that morning and it was all waiting for him.

'There's boxes and boxes of it.' He rolled his eyes as he said it. 'But hopefully stock that will all be shifted in the next few weeks. Alex messaged earlier to tell me that we can only reach the kitchen for much-needed coffee by going on an obstacle course.'

They found their destination easily and wandered around

the other exhibits, reading the descriptions. Beatrice was desperate to find the card she was looking for, but from their visit to the British Museum, she knew Jack didn't like to be hurried. He wanted to look in every cabinet. Secretly, she loved the fact that he took life at an unhurried, gentle pace, but there were times, like today, when she wanted them to move a bit quicker. Finally, they reached the right room and she scooted around, scouring everything for the display she'd come to see.

'Here, look,' she said, waving Jack over. She had to stop herself hopping from foot to foot in excitement. 'This has a similar look to my cards, doesn't it? Definitely the same era. It's The Hierophant and she does look quite similar to mine. The colours are more muted, but I suppose she's been exposed to more light over the centuries than mine have been.'

Whilst Beatrice was talking, her words spilling over each other, Jack was reading the explanation placed beside it.

'What did you say the gallery in Italy was called? Only this one is on loan from somewhere in Milan,' he said.

'Wait, what? Does it say where?' Beatrice paused in her chatter as she took in his words. Stepping over to where he was, she read the details. 'This is the same place,' she exclaimed. 'Maybe they haven't got my card because it's been loaned out? I wonder if they've thought of that. As soon as I get home later, I'll email them back and suggest it. This is at least a tiny glimmer of hope when I was beginning again to think I had none left.' She grinned up at Jack who, with a twinkle in his eyes, looked as though he might just be laughing at her exuberance. He leant down and kissed her, his lips soft against her own. She breathed in and caught the musky scent of his aftershave mixed with the warmth of his skin and she felt her blood pulse through her veins.

'You're so cute when you're excited,' he said. Now she was

certain he was teasing her, and she gave him a small push as she smiled. There was no disputing it, this search was more enjoyable with him alongside her. And to think she'd been so opposed to any sort of relationship when she'd first met him. Thank goodness she'd listened to her heart and not her head, just as that first tarot reading in her new London home had suggested when she'd turned the Page of Cups, and it told of a new relationship.

They said goodbye at the station as Jack caught the train back to the city and she carried on to Streatham where she'd arranged to meet Rachel in a cafe on the high street, rather than at her studio in a garden room behind her house which Rachel had mentioned in her social media posts. Beatrice could understand why she wouldn't want a stranger coming to her house or even knowing where she lived.

The coffee shop was almost empty; late morning on a Monday was obviously a good time to come. There was only one customer sitting at a table in the corner, a small espresso cup in front of her, a pile of folders to one side. With her waist-length, pink hair, Rachel was easily recognisable from her profile photo. She looked up and smiled at Beatrice as the cold draught from the opening door announced her arrival.

'Hi,' she said as she got to her feet and gave Beatrice a welcoming hug. Who said people in London were aloof and unfriendly? That wasn't the reality she'd experienced so far. Perhaps her cards were bringing her into the orbit of those she needed to be with. Divesting herself of her coat and ordering some more drinks, Beatrice sat down next to Rachel so she could properly see the pages being taken from various folders and spread out on the table. No wonder she'd sat at the largest table in the room, Rachel had brought plenty of examples of her illustrations.

'These are incredible,' Beatrice said in awe as she picked each one up, examining it close up. She turned them towards the light from the big cafe windows so she could fully appreciate the deep, rich colours together with tiny details, flecks and brush-strokes of gold. Each design, not cards but more like book graphics, was opulent and lavish. She really hoped the two of them could form a working relationship; there was a whole new branch to her business unfolding before her eyes. 'I absolutely love them, you're very talented,' she added with a wide smile. 'I do hope we can agree something so you can hand-paint tarot cards for me which we could then potentially make prints from. I haven't given a lot of thought to the finances but if you want to go ahead, we can discuss that. I've brought my own cards with me,' she patted her handbag, 'so you can see what's involved. I also have a really old pack and it would be wonderful if you could recreate those.'

Getting out her own cards, she flipped through some of the Major Arcana to show Rachel the decorative style.

'The designs on the backs of cards are always different,' she explained. 'There can be animals, flowers, stars, almost anything, although they should reflect the natural world in some way. Tarot cards came about centuries ago, around about the time of the ancient pack I have that once belonged to my ancestors, and it is reflected in the designs. Here, look, I have some photos of them on my phone.' Getting it out, she found the pictures to show Rachel.

Picking up The Magician card from the table, Rachel turned it from side to side. 'This is just a commercial pack, isn't it? I can see that this is a print.'

'Yes, these were bought for me for my eighteenth birthday. My mum took me to a specialist shop and we looked at many different ones. I needed some which spoke to me, which I could bond with; that is really important. And even so, it took several months before I felt properly attached to them. Now they're a part of me. And I'd like customers to be able to buy beautiful one-off designs and have the same sort of relationship with their cards. I have people come to the shop who would pay a decent amount of money for a set which are really a work of art. We would obviously work out a division of the profits which we are both happy with, given that they would be your original artwork.'

'And the old pack that you mentioned?' Rachel asked. 'Why do you want a copy made?'

'Two reasons,' Beatrice admitted. 'I can't use the pack because for one thing, they're too old and fragile. But also, there's one card missing. I can feel it when I hold them, they feel... I don't know, sad? There's a yearning for the one which completes them. I've been searching for the card, but I think I may have hit a brick wall now.' She decided not to mention the other supposed interested party. 'At one point I thought I had it, but unfortunately what I found was a copy. Not a proper replica, as I'd like you to do, if you don't mind recreating someone else's design. But one that up close I could see was more crudely drawn, and it was on much thinner parchment. So, although I am still on the hunt for the original, I would love to be able to use a pack which looks just like these.'

'I'm sure I could do that. How about I do some different samples of designs for packs, and bring them over to your shop and you could show me the old cards? We can talk money, and I can decide if I'm able to duplicate the others,' Rachel suggested.

'That would be wonderful.' Beatrice hugged her. 'How long will it take you? I'm so excited to see your ideas.'

'I'm just finishing a piece,' she said. 'I could probably get something done for you in the next couple of weeks. Just some mock-ups, and I can work out a timeframe too. It would take me a long time to create a whole pack, selling cards which are prints of my originals would be the most sensible option, I suspect. We can discuss it all before we agree anything formally though.'

'You're talking yourself out of a lot of work,' Beatrice warned her but laughing at the same time. 'Honestly, even though my shop has only been open a few months I truly believe that the customers I am thinking of will pay a four-figure sum for a set of hand-painted cards and there will be plenty of interest. People like to have something nobody else does. I'm certain the right customer will pay for a bespoke set.' They agreed to keep in touch by email and both packed away the cards and designs which were now spread out across the table. They'd been talking for so long their coffee had gone cold.

After saying goodbye, Beatrice made her way back to the train station. The weather had turned nasty whilst she'd been sitting inside, and she was shocked to see they'd been talking for ninety minutes. The cold wind of earlier was now blowing tiny flakes of snow sideways, cutting into her face and making it sting. Pulling the bag she was carrying across her body and in front of her, as though to use it as a shield against the weather, Bea put her head down and started to jog, keen to get onto a warm train.

33

1644

'Mama?' Vittoria looked over her shoulder to the backyard where Portia was collecting that morning's eggs. The chickens were laying well, helped no doubt by the long summer days, and the eggs were a welcome addition to their meagre diet. Every spare penny now needed to be saved towards what they would take with them to Winchester. When she'd originally started saving, Portia had never believed she would need to use it to escape, not again. But it was only a matter of time, and not much of it, before they would steal out in the middle of the night, bound for John and his boat. Another journey to freedom.

'What is it?' Portia put the basket of eggs on the table before shooing away the chickens which had followed her inside searching for crumbs on the floor, ones that had been missed by Maria's sweeping earlier.

'Elsebeth is here to see you.' Vittoria stepped to one side and indeed her friend was standing in the doorway as though unsure of whether she could enter. Her hands were tucked in front of her, gripping her purse. A nervous smile hovering on her lips broke wider as she saw Portia.

'Praise the Lord you are at home,' Elsebeth said. 'I would like to have my cards read, most urgently. Can you do that for a friend, please? Of course I have money to pay for it.'

'You do not need to pay.' Portia drew her further into the room. 'I will gladly do it for you. Take a seat here at the table. Maria is going to the market this morning and Vittoria shall accompany her.'

'Vittoria.' Maria's voice carried across the room. 'I have been thinking we should buy another two chickens, and I need you to help me choose them. You are far better with them than I am.' She had chosen something that would immediately appeal to the girl who enjoyed looking after the birds, treating their welfare and care as her own personal dominion. She often sat outside chatting to them as though they were her friends, so she wouldn't allow anyone else to choose which other ones should join the flock. Portia had to bite her tongue to stop herself from saying that it would be a waste of money. The chickens couldn't travel to their new life with them.

'Yes, I must make the decision,' Vittoria agreed. Full of her own importance, she pulled on her boots and collected her purse, tucking some stray hairs beneath her coif. Portia let out her breath in a steady stream, whilst silently thanking Maria for her quick thinking.

'Do you really need the cards read for you?' Portia asked the moment the front door had closed and the others were on their way. 'You look worried, scared in fact. What is the matter?'

'I should have confided in you when you came to me with your troubles, and for that I am a poor friend and I apologise,' Elsebeth said. 'But now I need to leave London, and quickly. I did something foolish, nay, worse than that, something that will shock you. I have been irresponsible and now my sins shall find me out. If my husband were to find out, he would throw me onto the streets, so I must be gone before he discovers my deception.'

Portia leant back in her chair and continued shuffling the cards whilst her mind raced. All of the escapes she had facilitated had been women fleeing from abusive men. That was why she did it and undertook such dangers. But Elsebeth was openly admitting she wanted to disappear because of something wrong she herself had done. Portia couldn't imagine that her sweet, gentle friend would ever undertake such a thing.

'Deception?' Portia asked as she finished with the pack and laid the cards on the table. The corner of The Devil card now secreted in an internal fold in her sleeve scratched her skin. Never would she have thought Elsebeth may require it, but now it seemed perhaps she did. She needed to decide, and quickly, whether she could help.

'I fell in love with a man who is not my husband. He came to our house on business, and I was attracted to him and he to me. When my husband travelled to Norwich on more than one occasion we had intimate relations with each other. It was very wrong of me, I admit. I have previously suspected that Peter is not the son of my husband, and now I am certain he is not. As you know we are both fair of hair and skin with blue eyes but as he grows, Peter has eyes of deepest brown. His hair remains as dark as the day he was born, and as time goes on his skin is becoming darker. My lover was a Moor, he travelled to England from Spain, so you can understand why I have these doubts. It will not be long before the truth will be obvious to all, already I can see questions in people's eyes. My husband does not visit the nursery often at the moment, but as Peter grows, he will want to see more of him and it will not be long before he realises. If I go now, I can take enough gold to start my life elsewhere.'

Portia picked up the cards from the table and started shuffling once again, giving herself some time as her mind turned over what she'd just been told. Elsebeth had told her that the truth would shock her, and she was correct. She had no knowledge of the man who'd visited nor that her friend had allowed him to lift her skirts, and it hadn't occurred to her that Peter's parentage was ever in question. All people held secrets, she knew that. And she knew what it was to run away with a baby who must be concealed, even though her circumstances had been different. How could she deny her best friend the chance that she had? What Elsebeth did was sinful and wrong, but hadn't she also sinned when she lied, when she didn't tell Lorenzo his baby daughter was born? Although she had not once regretted her decision.

'Please say that you can help me?' Elsebeth interrupted her musing. 'You previously hinted that you have helped women who need to disappear and start a new life somewhere else. And that you may also need to leave London. That is what I must do. Is it possible that you arrange it for me too?' She was openly crying now, her hands pressed together as though in prayer. In that moment Portia knew that she couldn't go before she'd helped this woman, her friend, to escape. It increased the danger of her own perilous position because during the time it would take for Elsebeth to be ready to flee, there was the risk of another visit from Niccolo. She'd just have to do whatever was necessary to prevent him from telling Vittoria her secrets. Whatever she had to. Then as soon as Elsebeth and Peter were gone, she, Vittoria and Maria would follow.

'I can do it.' Portia nodded. 'It will have to happen very soon though, because I am indeed also leaving. As I feared, I too am in danger, and I must depart this city under the cover of darkness.'

'Then please let me help you as you will help me,' Elsebeth

said. 'I have gold, a lot of gold. Whilst my husband does not know about my wrongdoings, I still have access to his coffers. If I steal away in the night and all the riches are taken it will just appear to be a robbery. I have more than enough for the both of us, enough that neither of us will have to worry about money for the rest of our lives.'

Portia thought about the few bits of jewellery remaining from what she'd brought from Italy. Hidden away in case of an emergency, and this was it. She was thankful that she had no need of anyone else's riches, she could support Vittoria and Maria herself.

'I have enough, thank you for your kind offer though. I will help you to leave and then I will follow immediately afterwards. We can be together, away from danger. John will row you to Teddington and from there you will be taken to Winchester where we can reunite and you can start a new life with Peter. It will be costly, the people who assist you need compensating, and they are paid well for what they do.'

'Of course, of course, thank you so much.' Now Elsebeth really was in tears as they ran down her cheeks and it took several minutes before Portia could explain what would happen.

'Will there be an opportunity soon, when your husband is away from home?' she asked. 'You must be on your own when it is time to go, and I have little time left before we must flee.'

'He leaves tomorrow for Kings Lynn where he has a warehouse. It is where he stores the merchandise which is brought from the Netherlands. If his previous visits are an indication, he will be gone for approximately a week.'

'That is fortuitous, for the days move quickly, and so must we.' Outside the door she heard the voices of Vittoria and Maria and quickly she and Elsebeth got to their feet.

'I will come to you soon,' she whispered. 'Be prepared for me.'

* * *

The more she mulled over what needed to be done, the more Portia began to realise that with the additional furore Elsebeth's disappearance would create, she, Maria and Vittoria would have to leave at the same time. It was the first time a woman together with her child would go missing, and her husband's servants would cause an uproar, that was certain. It would result in more constables, guards and vigilante groups prowling the streets, making it nigh on impossible for anyone to slip silently through the dark to the river and away.

She found it extremely difficult to behave as though everything was normal whilst she frantically planned both escapes. Arranging one was dangerous enough, even though she was now proficient at doing what she needed to. But this time, with two to organise, her own was going to be much more difficult. And she hadn't yet told John that she was going – how would he take it? Leaving him was something she just couldn't bear to think about. He meant more to her than she'd allowed herself – or him – to believe. And now she was sacrificing her own happiness, except it was she who'd created her current situation all those years ago, and now she was paying the price because she knew what Niccolo was planning. There was no denying she would be putting them all in grave danger, but no worse than they were already in, and she could only ask her cards to guide her so they got through it alive.

Beatrice stopped off at Hampstead Books on the way home from her meeting with Rachel and found Jack, just as he'd explained, in a back room full of boxes. Most of them were open, displaying the shining covers of new books. The air was full of the aroma of printer's ink and new paper.

'Best smell ever, new books,' she said.

'Definitely. It always reminds me of being here as a kid when my grandparents were still running the shop, alongside Mum and Dad. Well, not running it because they'd retired, but when they'd pop in to "help", except the visit was really to have a nose around and usually get on my parents' nerves. Because they opened it, this place was always their baby and even after it was signed over to Mum and Dad, they couldn't resist checking in from time to time. At least with my folks now in Cornwall, they can't do that as easily. Anyway, how did your meeting go?'

'Very well, thank you. More than that, it was excellent.' She wrapped her arms around herself and squeezed tight, trying to contain her excitement. 'Rachel could certainly do what I have in mind; a lot will depend on if we can work out the financial side. I may commission one pack if I can afford to, and subsequently have it reproduced. Then any others can be done as bespoke contracts. Those buyers can decide on the theme they want and work with Rachel on some samples. Once we know it's worth it for us both to go ahead, we can discuss the best way to move forward. Here, look.' She took the sample she'd brought back from the folder in her bag and handed it over. 'You can see why I'm so keen to get her on board.'

'Wow, that is amazing,' he agreed.

'I'll go home and let you get on,' Beatrice said, stepping backwards at the same time as climbing over an unopened box. 'Do you want to come round later? I'm going to go through all the information I've collated about my cards so far and see if I've missed anything, anywhere I could carry on searching. And I'm going to email the gallery in Milan again and ask about the card we saw earlier, because if that one is on loan, then perhaps my Devil card is too, and I might jog their memory.'

'That sounds great. See you at seven o'clock?'

They said their farewells, Jack blowing a kiss from across the room where he was effectively trapped behind the new stock. Beatrice blew one back and with a wide grin on her face and a cheery wave to Alex, she turned the corner and returned home. Since she'd arrived in London, so unsure at the time whether she'd made the right move and yet knowing she had no other alternative, she was feeling more content than ever. She was certain her mother was somewhere, watching her and somehow helping. If only she could reunite the family pack, whilst at the same time reuniting her own family once again. It felt as far away as ever, but was she also to blame? It was something she hadn't considered, and she didn't like how it made her feel. And still the wedding invitation sat on the mantelpiece.

* * *

'So, on this page is everything I've already found out.' Beatrice pointed towards one of the sheets of paper now spread over her dining table. They were enjoying a bottle of wine Jack had arrived with, as they looked at everything Beatrice had assembled during the afternoon. 'And this is what I'm still investigating. I'm no further on knowing why Margot has a copy of the exact card I'm searching for. So, at the moment my enquiries have gone cold, other than Milan, and I've heard nothing more from there. When I got home this afternoon, I emailed them again to ask about the card we saw at the museum, but I have little faith it will lead to anything. These here,' she picked up a written list, 'are all the people I've talked to. I can then see the line from one to the next. Not that it helps but sometimes by writing things down it makes me think in a different way and something suddenly becomes crystal clear. So far though, it's as murky as ever.'

'What's this at the bottom here?' Jack had picked up a list of all the information Beatrice had collated, which needed further enquiries if she knew where to look. 'Killing spree, does it say? Surely that isn't on your to-do list?'

'Not me, you idiot,' Beatrice replied, laughing. 'But you know, we've found more than one reference to The Devil card being responsible for women going missing and being murdered. That's the strangest part of this mystery. The women in my family are strong and supportive, I just cannot believe they would have been involved in hurting other women – far from it. And yet what is the likelihood there are two packs with a missing Devil card? And somehow, I get the feeling that the card's meaning, *"what is the truth and what is an illusion"* is telling us something. If only I could work out what it is.'

'How about using the old cards, the rest of the pack, to try and find the answer? Could they do that?'

'No, I've already thought of that. The other cards don't feel right with one of them missing. It is like they are aware they aren't whole, and I can't do a reading unless the pack is complete.'

'I'm sure something will come to you,' Jack reassured her. 'Why not leave all this paperwork here on the table? Sometimes looking at things and then moving them about triggers ideas. Like when you think about a crossword clue for a while, and suddenly a word comes to you.'

'Good idea,' Beatrice agreed, getting to her feet and going to the sofa. 'It's not going to jump out just sitting looking at it. It's so frustrating though. I feel as though the rest of the pack are urging me to find their missing piece.'

Jack joined her and sitting close, he wrapped his arm around her. 'When the time is right it will resolve itself,' he told her. She nodded and leant her head on his chest where she could feel his warm body and hear the comforting beat of his heart. Although she was exasperated at her investigations, she still felt calmer than she had for a very long time, and that was due to him.

'Do you have to go back to your flat tonight?' she asked him, her head still against his chest. There was a pause in the rising and falling as he held his breath.

'Are you saying what I think you're saying?' he asked. 'Because the answer is no, I have no reason to go home if there's the offer of a bed here.'

Sitting up a little so she could see his face, Beatrice could see he was grinning at her, his blue eyes blazing. 'There's definitely an offer,' she said.

* * *

Beatrice woke abruptly as Jack slid out of the bed and quietly picked up his clothes from where they were laid on the floor, slipping them on.

'Surely it isn't time to get up yet?' Beatrice raised her head from the pillow and looked at the alarm clock. 'No, I'm right, it's only six o'clock, way too early.'

'I don't want to go, believe me,' Jack said. Sitting on the edge of the bed, he bent down to kiss her. 'But I need to have showered and had breakfast before I open the shop. In addition, I have Alex's mum, Daisy, helping us today. Why don't I send her along to you for a chat? See if you think she'd be suitable as an assistant for you, if you're still thinking about hiring someone?'

'Thanks, if you can spare her, that would be great. I really do need a bit of help now and you can obviously vouch for her work ethic. But right now, it's too early to be out of bed.' Beatrice pulled the duvet over her head. 'It's still dark outside,' she added, her voice muffled.

Laughing, Jack pulled the covers down a little and kissed her. 'I'll see you later, sleepyhead,' he said, before returning them to where they were and going through to collect his shoes. She heard the receding sound of his footsteps as he ran downstairs, followed a couple of seconds later by the ring of the shop bell and a clunk as the door closed behind him.

Now awake though, Beatrice knew she wouldn't get back off to sleep and getting up, she wrapped herself in her dressing gown and went through to the kitchen to make some breakfast.

Her papers were still laid out on the table where they'd been abandoned the previous evening, so she took her bowl of yoghurt and fruit to the sofa. On the mantlepiece, as though condemning her for her lack of action, was the wedding invitation, still unanswered. She was certain her father already knew what her response would be, but it was only polite to let them know officially. Not that her dad would expect anything other than a carefully worded refusal. She doubted there was a card available that said, '*Thank you for the wedding invitation, but what about the woman you swore to love to your dying day and have now conveniently forgotten?*' A bit niche perhaps.

Putting her empty bowl on the coffee table, she went to a box file containing her stationery items and found a blank card and a pen. Quickly she wrote out an apology. It was respectful, succinct and didn't mention her mother. Addressing it to her father, she put it on the mantlepiece next to the invitation so she'd remember to post it when she next went out.

35

2025

Standing in the quiet of the shop, the bell on the door as it opened made Beatrice look up and to her delight, she recognised Heather walking in. Behind her was a tall, dark-haired man.

'How lovely to see you again,' Beatrice exclaimed. 'Are you back for another reading?'

'Not today.' Heather laughed. 'Although one day, definitely. No, today I'm here to introduce you to my son, Thomas.' Her face creased up as a wide smile spread across it. The man behind her stepped forward to shake Beatrice's hand.

'Goodness, how wonderful,' she exclaimed. 'I'm so pleased you found each other.'

'That's why I wanted to return and thank you,' Heather said. 'We were in the area so I insisted we did a small detour here. Your cards told me that it was the correct choice to go searching for my boy and they were right. If I hadn't come to see you, then my family wouldn't have ever been complete, because something was missing. I recognised what was the truth and what was an illusion and I used that knowledge to realise my dreams.'

'I am delighted to see you,' Beatrice told her. 'I don't often get to find out what has happened to my customers when they have a dilemma.'

Heather and Thomas said goodbye and left again, leaving Beatrice on her own. She was happy for the other woman, but what she couldn't get out of her mind was how Heather had held onto the hope that one day she would be reunited with Thomas, however long it took to find him. For him to find her. She needed to do the same with The Devil card, keep holding the belief that her pack and its missing card would one day be reunited.

Popping through to the kitchen to make a quick cup of tea whilst the shop was empty, she checked her phone. She left it in there whilst the shop was open because it felt safer, nobody could snatch it whilst her attention was taken elsewhere. These days, the first place she checked was her email, hoping for something back from the Arcardi Gallery in Milan and now, finally, to her delight there was a reply.

Her heart began to beat faster as she read what it said. They confirmed they did have a record of the card currently on loan to the Horniman, but in the meantime her email had triggered another line of enquiry for them and they'd researched in an alternative place for any record of the card she was searching for. And from there they'd found a handwritten note inside the front of a ledger stating the card was at the Museo Bagatti Valsecchi, also in Milan. They'd already been in contact with the curator to request its return, and they expected it back within the next twenty-four hours.

Beatrice was bouncing from foot to foot with excitement, and she quickly took a screenshot of the information and sent it to Jack with the caption 'BINGO!'

It was a full ten minutes, which felt like ten hours, before the shop door opened and he arrived.

'I've only just seen this. I was talking to Daisy about her

doing some hours here with you and she's really keen. This is amazing! How soon can you go and see if it's the actual card, or just another copy?'

Beatrice pulled the corners of her mouth down. 'Let's not even go there. I need to keep reminding myself it may not be the original,' she said. 'Because then I really will have reached the end of the line. In answer to your question, I don't know when I can get out there. But if, as I've been told, someone else is chasing the card, supposing they are hot on my heels and get there before me? We're fast approaching Christmas and I'm getting many more customers come in, I need to keep the shop open, I just can't skive off right now. And I doubt that I could get over there and back in two days.'

'Well, first of all, it's unlikely that your unseen adversary is discovering the information as quickly as you are, so hopefully you're worrying unnecessarily, at least in that respect,' Jack said. 'And secondly, if you fly out after you've closed on Saturday then you could return on Monday evening. And as I just explained, Daisy is really keen to come and work for you. She's very quick, she'd pick up the basics in a couple of hours. Of course, she can't do readings, but she can make appointments and sell cards for you. And sort out any online orders and package them up.'

'That does sound like an option. It would be good to have her here, a second pair of hands. She'd only need to do the Monday, I could have the shop closed on Sunday as normal. I'll send a reply and ask when I might be able to view it. Thank goodness I brought my passport to London with me.'

'Let me know if you hear anything more. And are you okay if I come with you? I'm almost as invested as much in your quest as you are now,' Jack said.

'Of course I'd love you to come,' Beatrice said. 'Milan will be beautiful with all the Christmas decorations up; it would be a fabulous getaway even without the added excitement of the card. I'll let you know as soon as I hear anything.'

The bell on the door gave a ring as a customer entered. Jack squeezed her and with a quick 'See you later' he was gone. They hadn't made any arrangements for that evening and Beatrice decided she'd leave it to him to make the next move. She knew how she now felt about the two of them, but she wasn't sure if that was reciprocated. If he was looking for a relationship.

Although she'd replied to the email the moment her customers left, by five o'clock there was still no answer. Jack had messaged simply a row of question marks and a playing card emoji, and she'd sent one back in a similar vein with a row of shrugging shoulders. He still hadn't mentioned them getting together later, and neither had she.

Closing the shop and going to her flat, she made a mug of soup to have with the remains of a sourdough loaf she'd bought from Jo the previous day. She'd just settled down on the sofa when a message from Jack pinged on her phone. Hoping it would be him suggesting they met up she opened it, only to feel a shaft of disappointment to read that he'd been going to pop round but had been invited to dinner by Daisy and Alex and he didn't feel he could say no. He added that Daisy would be coming to see Beatrice the following morning to have a conversation about the potential employment opportunity.

Although she understood why he couldn't come, Beatrice still felt disappointed despite telling herself she was being unreasonable. With no chance of seeing him that evening, she watched half of a James Bond film, which she found herself having difficulty understanding, and decided to have an early night. As she got to her feet, the card she'd written to her father stared at her accusingly from the mantelpiece, still unsent.

Out of the shower and about to climb into bed, Beatrice's

attention was caught by her phone lighting up momentarily with a notification. Hoping it was Jack saying goodnight, she opened it. It wasn't a message from him, however, but an email from Aldo Arcardi, the owner of the Milan gallery. She quickly scanned it, her eyes flying over the words so keen to see what news he had, and she hissed, 'Yes, yes, yes', as she read that he was now in possession of her card again. He included an invitation to visit whenever she could fly out, for a private viewing.

Forgetting her previous decision to let Jack make the next move, she messaged him immediately to tell him what the email said, before going online and booking a cheap flight for the following Saturday night. She'd just have to hope that Daisy would be suitable as an assistant as now, nothing would stop her going.

To her delight Jack knocked on the shop door at eight o'clock the following morning. She could hear him from her flat where she was writing a list of everything she needed to pack before Saturday. Running downstairs, she saw his face peering in, hands cupped against the glass and eyes screwed up. With the winter gloom, it was still quite dark inside.

Beatrice flicked the light switch, bathing the room in a soft glow. She didn't like it bright in the shop; in her opinion it spoiled the special ambience that the cards permeated, so she used soft white bulbs for a gentler atmosphere. Unlocking the door, she stood to one side to allow him in, almost losing her balance as he picked her up and holding her tight, spun her around in the small space.

'I saw your message late last night, but I didn't want to wake you up,' he said as he put her back on the floor and kissed her. 'This is great news, it *must* be your card. Have you booked a flight yet? And if so shall I book one too?'

'Well, yes, and yes,' Beatrice said. She was smiling widely, her arms wrapped tight around herself. 'As soon as I messaged you, I sorted travel for Saturday evening from Heathrow. I'm coming back on Monday evening.'

'Brilliant. And I asked Daisy to be here first thing this morning, I hope that's okay. She'll probably arrive shortly. Can you show me the flight details? I'll see if I can get on it with you.' Jack got his phone out and Beatrice pulled up the number on hers.

'I need to get this out.' She indicated her board, leaving him searching for her flight as she carried it to the end of the street. She already had one in-person tarot reading booked for that afternoon and two more online for later in the evening, but as always, she wanted to catch any shoppers passing by. And Rachel was coming to see her at lunchtime with some initial ideas, which she was really excited about. She'd decided that if the card in Milan wasn't the one belonging to her pack, or indeed if she wasn't able to buy it and reunite them, then she'd definitely ask Rachel to paint her a replica. Having taken a photograph of the card in Brighton, they knew what the front of it should look like.

By the time she arrived back, now carrying a bag containing two still warm croissants, Jack had booked a seat on the same plane. He followed her through to the kitchen to make them coffee.

'Sorry, no plates.' She offered him the bag and he took one out, immediately covering the counter and floor with flakes of buttery pastry as he bit into it. She took a cup from the worktop and pointed to the kettle, raising her eyebrows.

'Please.' Jack's voice was muffled as he tried to prevent any more crumbs falling from his impromptu breakfast. Beatrice made them both drinks.

He brushed his fingers together over the sink and washed them off before taking a sip of his coffee. 'What about a hotel in

Milan, have you booked that yet? And more importantly, did you book a double room?' He waggled his eyebrows at her and grinned. She felt her heart rate start to increase; she couldn't help how he made her feel. Perhaps she should stop wondering what or where this was going. Perhaps you couldn't help who you were attracted to and needed to grab life with both hands. For a moment, the thought made her stop what she was doing, a vision of her father and Kerry together, before she pushed it to the back of her mind to mull over later.

'No, I was going to do that today. Have you been there before?'

'Nope.' Jack shook his head. 'But you've got lots to think about, so let me sort it?'

Before Beatrice could answer she heard the shop door open. Putting her cup down on the counter, she hurried through to find a middle-aged woman with short, dark, spiky hair and wearing a pair of bright yellow dungarees grinning at her.

'Hi, Daisy.' Jack had followed Beatrice and seeing who it was, he made a quick introduction before saying goodbye.

'Yes, please, if you can arrange it,' Beatrice quickly said, and he gave her a thumbs up as he slipped out of the shop and she turned to invite Daisy into the back room where they could have a chat. Even by just being in the same space she could tell the other woman would be an asset to the shop, she exuded a calm ambience which would blend in well with how the shop needed to feel for her customers.

By mid-morning she'd arranged for Daisy to work three days a week to include every Sunday and Monday, and Jack had sent her a link for the hotel he'd booked. Her eyes had grown wide as she'd scrolled through the gallery of photographs. It was situated in a small lane close to the Duomo, in a building that in the seventeenth century had originally belonged to a wealthy merchant. The entrance looked like a church, with its lofty ceiling reaching up into a dome, painted as though the viewer were looking at a blue sky scattered with clouds. Although the floors and corridors appeared to be made of pale marble, the bedrooms were modern with glossy en suites, yet in contrast there were stone mullioned windows with gothic lancet tops reaching to the ceiling. She was desperate to find the card and couldn't wait to be there, where she hoped she would finally reunite the pack. And she couldn't deny that the fact she'd be there with Jack made it even better.

The day passed with a pleasing number of customers coming in, several of them making purchases. It seemed that a set of tarot cards was a popular choice for Christmas gifts and she wondered if she ought to make an emergency re-order of the cheaper sets.

Rachel called in with an envelope of initial artwork. Beatrice had a quick look and was delighted with what she saw, a mix of gothic and fantasy, dark rooms and dragons, and she promised to call when she had a moment. At four o'clock the door opened to admit a woman who announced herself as being the customer booked in for a reading.

'Come in,' Beatrice said. She liked in-person appointments to be towards the end of the day, so she could shut the shop and know it was unlikely anyone would arrive for a browse. Once she'd settled the woman in the back room, she quickly collected the sandwich board from the main pavement. Peeping through the window of Hampstead Books, she was disappointed not to spot Jack. Only Alex was visible and she hoped he wasn't too cross at the amount of time his boss was spending with her during opening hours, trips around London and now to Italy.

Returning to the back room of her shop, Beatrice switched on the lamps and offered her customer a glass of water whilst she collected her own. Doing a reading inevitably entailed a lot of talking and she knew from experience a drink was essential. Sitting down, she explained how the cards worked, and all the while she was talking, she couldn't help noticing the woman was fidgeting with her handbag, placed on her lap like some kind of shield. Protection.

Beatrice shuffled the cards. So familiar to her, like a best friend. Just touching them made her feel calm. How would her ancient family pack feel once it was complete? Laying three cards on the table she asked the woman to turn the first card.

'I'm hoping this will give me the answers I need,' came the woman's quiet reply as she laid the first card face up.

'As I explained when you booked, they might not tell you something obvious,' Beatrice reminded her. 'You may have to think at length about what I say, and you will then understand.

'The Nine of Swords,' she began. 'It speaks of worries, something which is causing a great anxiety. A problematic situation in which you must make a big decision. Possibly a life-changing one.' She searched the woman's face for clues as to whether she'd understood what the cards were saying, pleased to see her nodding slowly before turning the next card.

'The Eight of Cups. Now is the time to move on from a situation, to take control into your hands and make the right choice for yourself. A choice which only you can make.' The woman looked up and smiled.

'Yes, I do need to do that, and in reality, I know it.'

'Good, then let us turn the final card.' Beatrice flipped it over. The Devil. Her customer gasped.

'Why have I got that one?' she asked, her face reflecting the upset in her shaky voice.

'It doesn't mean something bad,' Beatrice reassured. 'It is

asking, what is real and what is an illusion. Consider what might not be as it appears in your life.'

'Well, that isn't difficult,' the woman admitted. 'I'm pregnant, you see.' She looked up from where she was staring at the cards and gave Beatrice a watery smile which didn't quite reach her eyes. She guessed that congratulations wasn't the correct response and kept quiet, waiting to see if anything else would be forthcoming.

'I had a stupid, drunken, one-night stand when I was away at a work conference,' the woman went on to explain. She put her bag, her barrier, on the floor. Perhaps, Beatrice considered, she was starting to feel safer. 'And now I'm pregnant. My husband and I have been trying for a baby for over a year, so he'll be made up if I tell him I'm expecting. But he will be broken, utterly bereft, if I tell him it might not be his, which is the truth. I just don't know what to do. I really want this baby because I'm so desperate to be a mum, but it would wreck my marriage, and I'll end up as a single mother, which I never imagined myself being. I can't get rid of it though, it's my baby. I totally believe every woman should have the choice, but that isn't for me.' She sank into a silence that stretched into ten seconds, twenty seconds, thirty seconds.

'What about the man you think may be the father?' Beatrice disturbed the hush. The woman rolled her eyes.

'My boss. What a classic, eh? I've been such an idiot. If I tell him he'll think of some way of engineering me out of my job. He's got a glamorous wife and a little boy about a year old. But I can't just keep quiet and let my husband think this baby is his, because my boss looks so different, I'm sure in time it would be obvious. Anyway, that would be morally wrong, to let my husband bond with a baby that isn't his. And I won't know which of them is the daddy unless I do a DNA test and if I did that I'd have to confess anyway. As the Eight of Swords says, I need to move on. This part of my life, my marriage, is over.'

'Occasionally the answer really is that clear,' Beatrice said. 'And the Devil tells you exactly that. Whether you tell your husband now or wait until he potentially realises it, the truth will come out. What is real, and the truth you already know, and what is an illusion. Which is what it will be if you say nothing, just an illusion, a deception.'

'I don't know what to say, or how to say it,' the woman repeated. 'I'm going to have to leave him and do it now before he even realises I'm pregnant. If I move away he won't see me and know the truth. I don't want him to know what I did. Which is selfish of me. I can't lie to him, I can't create an illusion.' She got to her feet. 'Thank you,' she said. 'Deep down I know what I must do. To leave. The Devil card has told me what my future must hold.'

'Perhaps you should first explain to your husband?' Beatrice suggested. She made a point of never advising what a client should do with the information the cards told them, but this time she felt compelled to. 'This is the twenty-first century, not the seventeenth century. His response may not be as decisive as you imagine, perhaps he would accept a child which isn't biologically his. And you won't know unless you ask him. If it is his, then you will be denying him the chance to be a father.'

Eventually, Beatrice let her out of the shop door and locked it behind her. Despite the sad state of her customer, she had a smile on her face. Sometimes the cards were a bit ambiguous at first, but not today. The Devil card had told the woman what she needed to do. As always, it brought Beatrice's thoughts back to the card she was seeking. Had that card too told someone, perhaps more than one person, what they must do?

36

1644

'John, I must speak with you immediately,' Portia gasped as she caught up with him sitting on a pile of stacked wood at Venours Wharf. She could hardly get the words out, exhausted after her exertions.

'What is the matter?' he asked. 'You look as though you have been running. Has someone exposed what you have been doing, what we have both been doing? Are we in danger?'

'No, at least not yet.' Portia paused and tried to catch her breath. 'But in two days' time, I must ask you to undertake the most difficult and important trip. The final one.'

John raised his eyebrows. 'The final one?' he repeated.

'Indeed, and there will be five of us so we will need two boats. Can you organise all of that?' she asked.

'I can hire a larger wherry to take you all,' he patted her hand, 'do not worry. But did I hear you right when you said "us"? Does this mean that you too are fleeing?'

'I must, and now before all my secrets are spilled and my life is torn apart like fine lawn. Before we are murdered in our beds. Myself with my daughter,' her voice caught slightly as she referred to Vittoria as such, 'and, I hope, Maria too. In addition, there will also be my friend Elsebeth and her infant son. I cannot tell you any more than that, but we will be here at close to ten o'clock. You will be paid handsomely for this final journey.' Portia finally gave way to the anguish she'd been carrying ever since Niccolo had visited her.

'My sweet, why are you crying. And what is this talk of murder?' John balanced the clay pipe he was smoking on the wood he'd previously been sitting on and wrapped his arms around her, his big hands rubbing her back, which just made her cry more. She'd never have guessed all those years ago when she'd run from Milan that her actions would end up breaking her heart. But at least she still had Vittoria, even though the thought of that couldn't console her at that moment. A precious gem to her, but at a high price.

'Sit down and tell me what has caused these tears,' John said, perching on his seat and pulling her down beside him, keeping his arm around her waist. She should have moved away, it was not seemly to be sitting so with a man to whom she was not wed, but she needed the comfort, especially from him.

'Tell me,' he prompted, wiping away the tears on her cheeks with the ball of his thumb. 'I do not understand what you are saying. The women you usually help, they are escaping violent men, bad situations they cannot remain in. But you are a widow. Why is someone now threatening you?'

'Because I have been lying all these years. I was never wed in Milan, that was a tale I told to explain why I had Vittoria, but the truth is she is not my child. She is my blood, but I did not give birth to her.'

'How can this be so? Surely she is your daughter if she is your blood, or why else has she always been with you?' He had his hands on her upper arms, holding her away so he could see her face, but Portia couldn't meet his eyes. This was the most difficult conversation she'd ever had.

'She is my sister's child. I lived with her and her husband,' Portia said. 'But he was not a good man. Milan in 1629 was a dangerous place, the plague was tearing through the city and he was preparing to leave to stay at his villa in Montevecchia. My dear sister Agnese caught the disease, as did many of our servants, and he left her for dead. The babe started coming but still his preparations to leave continued. In the moment Vittoria was born into the world, my sister's spirit left her body. My brother-in-law was too focussed on leaving, and I let him believe that the baby had not yet been born. He was gone within minutes and immediately I took Vittoria and ran. First, to Bergamo where I found Maria, a wet nurse, and from there to Venice where the three of us boarded a ship to London. I have lived a lie for fifteen years, although I am sure Maria knows the truth because no woman could have given birth and journeyed so soon afterwards. But I did it to save Vittoria. If her father knew about her, he would have taken her with him even though he did not care for her, just as he did not care for her mother. I loved her, nay, I *love* her as a mother would, as my sister would have done. I just did what she would have wanted me to.'

'You had a difficult decision, and you did what you needed to,' John said. 'Surely you could have told Vittoria the truth before now?'

'And have her reject me?' Portia shook her head. 'She has always called me Mama and I do not want her to stop, I never want her to know the truth. I love her like she is my daughter, and I cannot let her know what happened that day and risk her turning against me.'

'I understand why you did what you did,' John replied, 'but why must you now leave? What is this sudden danger? You are well settled, with friends in London. And me. You have me. I told you once before a little of how I feel about you, but the truth is you carry my heart in your hands. I will do anything for you, my life would not be complete without you in it.'

'I have the same feelings for you,' Portia whispered. 'But I feared if you had known the truth of what I did fifteen years ago, you might rescind your friendship,' Portia admitted. 'And now it is too late.'

'You have not told me why though,' he reminded her. 'Why can you stay no longer?'

'Because someone from Milan has found us. The man I asked you to follow before,' Portia said, going on to relay how Niccolo recognised Vittoria because she had the same eye condition as Agnese. 'Once he noticed that, he saw me. She looks a lot like her father, even though she has her mother's eyes. Have you never noticed she does not really resemble me? It did not take long for Niccolo to work out what I had done. And now it transpires that Lorenzo, Vittoria's father, died within half a day of leaving Milan, leaving her as his only heir. Niccolo believed that he had inherited it all, so as you can imagine he wants her gone. Permanently. That is why we must run, and run fast, so he can never find her. I must escape as I once did before, and soon. I am sorry I have lied to you for so long.'

'You do not need to apologise,' John chided. 'I understand why you wished for as few people as possible to know your secret. And of course I will help you. Will you go to Winchester as the other women have?'

'Yes, I have enough money saved to start a new life there.'

'And might there be a place for me in this new life?' John asked. 'I was not always a boatman, I can turn my hand to many skills. If you will consider it, we could be wed there and live as man and wife.'

'Oh, thank you, yes, yes, please. I would love you to accompany us, and I would love to be married to you.' Portia threw her arms around him, his suggestion the tiniest ray of sunshine in the deep, dark despair of her current situation. 'But first we have to get away from London. We will all be here the day after tomorrow at ten o'clock,' she reminded him. 'Nothing must go wrong. And when we have got away, I will finally tell Vittoria everything. How I saved her from danger not once, but twice in her life.'

Getting to her feet, she hugged John, remaining in his arms and trying to draw strength from the warmth of his broad chest for what lay ahead.

'Where are you going, Mama?' Vittoria asked as Portia picked up her basket. 'Are you going to the market? May I come with you?'

'Not this time,' she replied, her mind moving quickly to think of a reason the girl couldn't accompany her as she would usually do. 'I am going to visit John, and sometimes I like to visit him alone.'

That wasn't a lie, even though she then had to listen to Vittoria making coy comments and grinning at her. 'I know you are sweet on him,' she teased. Portia gave her a smile and didn't deny it. Soon she would see them married and despite the current heavy dread she was carrying around, Portia sincerely hoped that they could not only make their escape, but she and John would then be able to live their lives out as a married couple. Blowing Vittoria a kiss goodbye, she popped her purse in her pocket and left.

Ten minutes later she arrived at Elsebeth's house, knocking at the door. A maid showed her into a small parlour where she was joined by her friend moments later.

'You have come to tell me it is time to go?' Elsebeth asked as soon as they had greeted each other. Portia nodded.

'The boat will leave on the tide tomorrow night,' she said. 'I will come for you after dark, as I told you, and you must be ready to go. Will you be able to carry the gold you intend to take?'

Elsebeth nodded. 'I did think of the practicality of taking it all, so earlier today I visited a merchant at the London Exchange and purchased several pieces of valuable, very valuable, jewellery. They are far easier to hide upon my person. I have plenty enough to pay John handsomely. They can be sold wherever we both go and there is enough to last out our lifetimes and those of our children. Come and see.'

Holding her candle high, she led the way along dark, shadowed corridors until they reached a small room where she placed the candlestick on a side table.

'My husband's private chamber,' she explained. 'Here his safe is hidden. He never thought to conceal its whereabouts from me though, and as he is away from home, I have taken advantage and stored my jewellery inside.'

Taking a small gold key from her pocket, she held it up and Portia saw Elsebeth smile for the first time since she'd arrived. 'Nor did he keep from me where the keys are stowed. He always has one with him, but there is a spare kept here, in case our steward needs to access it. I hope I am far away before it is noticed what has been taken from inside.' Leaning into the safe, a space in the wall lined with lead which looked as heavy as the door Elsebeth had just opened, she drew out a large, intricately carved, wooden coffer. Carrying it carefully to the desk placed below an oriel window, she put it down and using a second, smaller key attached to the other one with a piece of red ribbon, she opened it, slowly lifting the lid.

Despite the scant light in the room, the gold and precious

stones in the box glowed as though they were lit from within, a
fire burning deep inside. Portia heard herself gasp before she
clamped her hand across her mouth and glanced towards the
door. She didn't want to alert anyone in the house. Tentatively
she lifted an item, unable to quite believe the scale of the riches
in front of her. Hanging from her fingers, a carcanet hung heavy.
A choker, a wide collar consisting of pearls interspersed with
rubies in gold filigree settings and falling at the centre a garnet
the size of a bantam's egg. This alone could raise enough
revenue to keep her family in comfort for the rest of their lives
and it was just one piece; shining from every corner of the coffer
were more gold and jewels. Her eyes caught the vibrant green of
emeralds the colour of spring leaves on a rowan tree, and clear
water-like droplets of diamonds sprinkled throughout
everything.

'This is so much more than I had envisaged,' Portia said as
she let her breath out slowly. She hadn't realised she was holding it.

'I do not intend to live in poverty,' Elsebeth asserted, her
hands on her hips. 'My husband is a cold, cruel man; he never
gave me the comfort and warmth my lover did. A lot of this was
my dowry from my father, so in truth I am merely taking back
what is rightfully mine. Yes, I now have additional pieces
purchased with some of the gold coin my husband kept in the
safe, but I must ensure I have enough to keep myself and my son
comfortably for the rest of our days. And you and your family
too. I always stand by my word, there is enough here for us both.
More than enough.' She lifted the heavy coffer again and
replaced it in the safe. 'No one can get it in here,' she reassured.
'I shall carry both keys with me until it is time to leave. Perhaps I
should make it appear as though a robbery has taken place?'

'That is a good idea,' Portia agreed. 'Usually when it is

discovered that a woman has gone, it is presumed thieves entered the house and they also took the wife and killed her, before disposing of her body in the river. It is important that this is what it appears to happen to you as well. Nobody will question when I disappear. I am sure they will not connect me with the so-called murders for I have no husband who would shout that Vittoria, Maria and I are gone.' Unless Niccolo then decided to go to the authorities when he discovered that she had left, she thought. It would be too late by then though – nobody would find them.

The two women left the room and returned to the main hall where they continued to talk, keeping their voices low.

'I completely understand your decision to leave,' Portia said. 'What mother wouldn't travel to the ends of the earth to protect their child?'

'As you too will do with Vittoria,' Elsebeth replied. 'Do you never hanker to return to Italy with her?'

Portia felt her heart jump in her chest. Such a thing was inconceivable.

'Never.' She shook her head. 'I cannot return. There are secrets in my homeland which must remain there. Perhaps one day I will explain to you.' Unbidden, the sneering face of Niccolo rose before her. Her secrets had now followed her here, and once again she was planning an escape, one on which both her life and Vittoria's depended.

38

2025

By Saturday evening, Beatrice had gone beyond her previous excitement and was now in full-on panic mode. Their flight wasn't until nine o'clock, landing two hours later, by which time it would be midnight in Milan. Jack had messaged ahead to let the hotel know their late arrival time. She'd only packed a small bag so it would fit beneath the seat in front, and they'd both checked in the previous night, managing to secure seats on the plane next to each other. She double-checked she had everything she needed, her passport and most importantly of all, the deck of cards which had started this whole search. She'd received encouraging emails from Tristan and Margot, who both said they were hoping as much as she was that this trip would culminate in a victorious end to her search.

'Are you ready to go?' Jack had arrived with a small black rucksack over his shoulder, and he was pointing at her own bag.

'Yes. I gave Daisy a key to the shop earlier. You were right, she's picked everything up really quickly. I've managed to squeeze in enough clothes for two days.' She indicated her bag. 'And the precious set of cards is in there of course. I'm so excited but also worried this is a wild goose chase to simply find another copy.' She didn't add that she was also very much looking forward to a short break in Italy, surely the most romantic place in the world, with him.

'Right, let's go then.' He picked up her bag and she followed him down through the shop.

* * *

Once they arrived at Heathrow, they went straight through security which was thankfully fairly quiet for a Saturday evening, before finding a bar where they ordered some food and a glass of wine.

'This is the way to begin a weekend away,' Jack said as he clinked his glass against hers. Beatrice grinned and nodded. She was certain she wasn't the only one thinking it was more than just another step in the search for her missing card, that there was the romantic element too.

The flight left on time and, exhausted after all the planning and anticipation, within minutes of take-off Beatrice felt her eyes growing heavy and she laid her head on Jack's shoulder. He took her hand and kissed the top of her head, and with a small smile, she nodded off.

It only felt like a minute later when she heard him say, 'Hey, sleepyhead,' as he moved his shoulder and squeezed her hand. Beatrice sat up, bewildered for a moment as to where she was. 'The signs are on for seatbelts, we'll be landing in five minutes,' he told her. 'You've managed to sleep for the whole flight.' He laughed at her horrified face as her mouth fell open.

'Oh no, I'm so sorry,' she said. 'How boring for you, sitting here whilst I drooled over your shoulder.' She pretended to dab at his shirt.

'It was fine, I brought a book.' He held up a paperback she hadn't previously noticed.

'I love her books,' she exclaimed as she saw which author it was. 'I haven't read this one though, may I borrow it when you've finished?'

'Of course. You've seen how many books I have. In fact, I've a whole shop you can borrow!'

Sitting upright and clipping her seatbelt into place, Beatrice smiled to herself. A boyfriend with a bookshop had to be the most perfect thing. She stopped for a moment. When had she started thinking of him as her boyfriend? They'd never had that conversation and only earlier that day she'd told herself that she was happy just going along for the ride for as long as it lasted. But the truth was, now she wanted more than that, and she wanted it with him. It was a sudden revelation but one she'd keep to herself until she was certain of his own feelings.

After finding a taxi in a rank at the airport, forty minutes later they were being dropped off at their hotel. In the dark, Beatrice couldn't see much of the city, but nevertheless she had an inexplicable sensation as though it was welcoming her back. She'd come home.

There were few street lamps so she couldn't really make out the exterior of the hotel as they pulled up outside but stepping into the lobby, she was immediately awed by the stone walls, the beautiful grey, marble-tiled floor and high above them the ornate, painted ceiling. All it needed, Portia thought, were some tiny cherubs.

A tired-looking night receptionist booked them in, handing over a key to their first-floor room and they climbed the wide stairs, the marble underfoot covered with a rich blue carpet. The bannisters were shining oak, blackened with age and smooth from the hundreds of hands holding them over the centuries. It felt as though they had walked into a historical drama set, but there was also a familiarity Beatrice couldn't understand.

Their room, which felt as big as Beatrice's entire flat, was as majestic as the reception area. A beautiful palace for a long-dead, rich, Milanese merchant, according to the website. A huge four-poster bed dominated the room, complete with embroidered tapestry drapes. Beatrice rubbed her fingers against them, feeling the raised bumps of hundreds of tiny hand-sewn stitches. All the furniture was carved from dark wood, the pale, sand-coloured stone walls covered with faded painted frescoes. An enormous fireplace stood opposite the bed. Going to the tall, narrow windows to pull the curtains closed, she looked out across the sleeping city and wondered if her card really was out there, waiting for her. Whether this was the end of her search, in the place where inexplicably, it felt like she'd returned home.

In the modern en suite with a state-of-the-art shower and double sinks, Beatrice quickly got ready for bed. Despite sleeping on the plane, she felt overcome with weariness, due, she guessed, to it already being past one o'clock. Jack was already in bed, his eyes closed and switching off the bedside lamp, Beatrice slid in, trying not to wake him. However, as she pulled the covers over herself she felt the warmth of his arm move across, as he scooped her towards him, and she pressed herself along his warm, smooth, muscular body. One that was now starting to feel familiar; its hard lines and broad chest, his long legs and the scar where he'd had his appendix removed, the tattoo on his shoulder. His body was a map, and one she was enjoying finding her way around. As he rolled on top of her in the dark, a wide smile curled across her face, as though it would illuminate the darkness.

* * *

The following morning Beatrice was up and ready for breakfast at seven o'clock, excited to get their day started. Jack still lay starfished on the bed looking peaceful, his long lashes resting on his cheeks, flushed with sleep. Today she hoped she'd finally find the missing card which would complete her pack. It was hard to quash the small voice inside her head which kept reminding her that this may still not be it. After all, it hadn't been in Brighton. And, even if it was indeed the actual one, then the owner might not want to part with it. Or it would be sold to whoever had also previously made enquiries if they discovered it was here and could afford more. She didn't even want to imagine that scenario.

She was finding it impossible to just sit around waiting patiently so, taking hold of Jack's foot, which was sticking out of the side of the duvet, she gave it a small shake. Wordlessly, with no alteration to the rhythm of his breathing, he pulled it back beneath the covers.

'Jack.' Beatrice tried to keep her voice gentle, but she heard it catch as it belied the strain, mixed in with excitement, she was feeling. 'We need to go to breakfast, so we're ready to go and find the gallery. I'm not sure where it is, and I don't want to be late.'

Opening one eye and then the other, he gave her a sleepy smile.

'It's still dark,' he said, pointing to the curtains which were showing no light around the edges, and to the various lamps lit around the room. 'What on earth time is it?'

'Just gone seven,' Beatrice admitted with a sheepish grin. 'But it's always good to be ready in plenty of time, and like I said, we need to find where we're going. And have breakfast first.' She wasn't sure she could eat anything, her stomach was churning so much, but she was certain Jack would.

'I'm positive Google Maps works just as well over here,' he

told her as he pushed himself into a sitting position. The sight of his bare chest made her face warm and she looked away. If he caught her looking at his naked body, he'd be dragging her back to bed and although that was a lovely thought, they didn't have enough time for that.

'Jump in the shower,' she told him. 'It's amazing, there are jets everywhere. I'll have a look and see if I can work out a route to the Arcardi Gallery.' Flopping down on an ornate, velvet-cushioned chair positioned at the desk which she'd already commandeered as a dressing table, she took her phone out of her handbag to start searching. In doing so her fingers grazed against the silk wrapping around the cards. She was certain she could feel a heat pulsating from them, that they knew they were home, although it was a ridiculous thought. Even so there was a tremor in the air, a silent vibration which was singing in her veins.

'Okay, shall we go and grab some breakfast?' Thirty minutes later Jack was showered, his damp hair curling into tendrils at the nape of his neck. He was dressed in smart, dark denim jeans with a plain, black, fine-knit jumper which stretched across his chest. Beatrice could see the definition of each taut muscle and her fingers twitched with the desire to run them across him.

Downstairs, the dining room was small, but as beautiful as the rest of the hotel. One wall was panelled in dark wood which might have made it gloomy except that there was a tall, wide window with numerous small panes of glass stretching across the back of the room and looking out onto a courtyard garden. In the centre window, a panel of stained glass depicted an ancient heraldic shield and Beatrice wondered if it had belonged to the original owner of the building. Despite the time of year, some flowers were still bravely blooming, adding a splash of bright colour against the dying foliage around them.

They sat down at a table and an old lady wearing a floor-length apron bustled over. Beatrice asked for two coffees before heading over to the buffet where she helped herself to a roll and some slices of cheese, together with some fruit and a yoghurt. There might not be many places open for lunch on a Sunday in winter, so she decided to eat whilst she had the opportunity. Jack followed suit.

After they'd finished, having both also drunk two espressos, Beatrice felt as ready as she ever would, to embark on what she hoped was the final part of the journey to reunite her cards.

'Did you work out how to get to the gallery?' Jack asked. He looked at his watch. 'We've got forty minutes.'

'I think so. It's about twenty minutes away, I reckon, if I've got the right place.' She opened her phone and showed where she'd entered the details in order to work out a route.

'That looks quite straightforward,' he said. 'Walk along to the Duomo and then down a couple of side streets. Shall we go and grab your bag and then set off?'

'Yes, please.' Beatrice smiled but she was conscious that her heart rate was now increasing, and she didn't think it was to do with the caffeine hit from the two coffees. This was potentially the final part of the puzzle – everything now depended on it. Following Jack upstairs, she quickly cleaned her teeth and double-checked the cards were in her handbag. She knew they were in there, she chided herself, she'd already looked a dozen times.

Outside, where it was now daylight, they could properly see the hotel and its surrounds, and Beatrice couldn't help grinning at everything. This felt like the real Italy, narrow streets with cobbles beneath her feet and tall buildings squashed together, not the tourist areas she'd seen on the internet. Pale stone walls, marble and narrow windows. Even the air smelled different.

Temperature-wise, it was slightly warmer than London but still cold enough to need her coat. She pulled the thick blue faux fur around herself. Jack was wearing his puffer jacket and he put his arm across her shoulder and pulled her in close so she could feel the warmth of his body.

'Excited?' he asked as he took her phone from her and looked up and down the street. 'Which way do we want to go?'

'Yes, I am, but very nervous too,' Beatrice admitted before pointing to where the street led its narrow way up a hill. 'I can just see the dome of the Duomo so it must be this way.' She pushed her phone into her pocket and they began to walk.

The street opened out onto a small square dominated by a church along one side and surrounded by terraced houses. There was a statue of Leonardo da Vinci in the middle of the piazza, and Beatrice paused to read the plaque.

Checking which way they needed to walk next, they continued their journey. She could feel her legs becoming increasingly wobbly the closer they got to their destination.

They turned a corner and were suddenly in the Piazza del Duomo, in front of the majestic cathedral, its marble façade glowing in the sunlight.

'Wow, that is impressive,' Jack said.

'Isn't it,' Beatrice agreed. 'Just amazing. We must go in and have a proper look round whilst we are here,' she said. 'Probably better tomorrow though, as there will be services today.' Jack nodded in agreement.

'Right.' She looked around for street names, wondering where they needed to go next.

'Down here, I think?' Jack pointed. He held her shoulders in his hands and bent down slightly so he could look into her eyes. 'Are you okay?' he asked.

'Yes, I'm fine, really. I'm excited, but at the same time I'm so frightened that we've come all this way and once again it won't be what I'm looking for.'

'There's only one way to find out,' he said and together, hand in hand, they walked towards the Via Stampa, on which was the Arcardi Gallery. Beatrice felt as though she was wading through deep snow; although her legs were moving and she was willing them to go faster, it appeared as though she was standing still. This time, would she find the truth and complete the circle?

39

1644

Portia paused as she folded the last pieces of laundry, already dry and stiff after being draped over the bushes around the edge of their small garden and under the baking sun. She had been sitting outside for a little while, but the brightness and heat had given her a headache and she'd come back inside. She was pleased she'd decided not to accompany Maria and Vittoria when they'd gone out earlier. Their old neighbour in St Pancras Lane had given birth days earlier to a little girl and Vittoria had been keen to visit and see the new arrival. Maria had made a caudle for the doubtless exhausted mother.

They'd been gone for almost three hours and the chiming of a church clock ringing one o'clock reminded Portia of how long they'd been out. She had expected them home a while ago and a ghost of a smile drifted across her face. Quite possibly, Vittoria would take the opportunity to pay a visit to her friends on the haberdashery stall whilst they were in the locale. Undoubtedly, she'd arrive home with more silk thread or ribbons.

Finally, thirty minutes later they were back, falling into the room in their haste to get inside. Portia was already eating her dinner, too hungry to wait any longer for them, and she lay down the piece of beef she was about to put in her mouth and looked enquiringly at the others.

'Do you have the Devil on your tail?' she asked, laughing. Their faces were flushed and sweaty. 'It is not a day to be hurrying, not in this heat.'

Maria had already poured two beakers of ale and she passed one to Vittoria who'd thrown herself in the seat beside the currently empty fireplace.

'Mama,' she said through gasps of air, 'something terrible happened at the market.'

At least Portia had been correct in her assumption of where they'd been. She turned to Maria, her eyebrows raised. To her surprise, the other woman was nodding vigorously in agreement.

'Vittoria was nearly a victim of the murderers taking women from their beds,' she said. 'They dared to try and snatch her in broad daylight. It was the most frightening thing I have ever known.'

Now Portia was on her feet, her dinner forgotten. 'What do you mean, someone tried to take her?' She knew, although she couldn't say, that it wasn't any night-time murderers, given that there was no such thing. Who then, was it? She had a very good idea who had ordered it, and her blood ran cold.

'After we had visited the new baby,' Vittoria explained, 'I thought we could pay a visit to our old friends on the ribbon stall. Whilst Maria was paying for some silks,' she produced them from her pocket and held them towards Portia to show her, 'I was just waiting to one side when someone caught hold of my arm. Before I realised what they were doing, another man took the other one and they began to pull me away. For a few moments I could not understand what was happening and I was trying to look for Maria but we were moving further away and I could no longer see her. I started to call out but one of them put his hand over my mouth and they dragged me faster.'

'Thankfully, I heard her just in time.' Maria took up the story. 'I suddenly realised she was no longer standing beside me, and then I spotted two rough-looking men trying to run with her gripped between them. I shouted at them to stop, and then gave chase.'

'I cannot believe what I am hearing,' Portia said as she looked between the pair of them in horror. 'How did you get away? And are you hurt?'

'I was screaming and struggling so much that two men who were packing their market stall away heard me, and they helped Maria to wrestle the two ruffians away from me. They then ran off. I do not understand why they chose me to abduct. Anyone can tell I am not rich and wasn't carrying money.'

'Because you were easy, that was why,' Maria pointed out. 'You were standing there waiting quietly as you always do, and they saw you and realised they could snatch you with little struggle. I wager that they had been watching us, perhaps even following us when we left St Pancras Lane.'

Watching them, following them. Suddenly it became obvious to Portia. With a mounting fear, she realised that these men must have had the house under surveillance, spying on them and following Maria and Vittoria when they left. Without a doubt sent by Niccolo to steal Vittoria away, to slit her throat or perhaps throw her in the river to make it look like another of the spate of supposed murders. It was clear that Maria and Vittoria already suspected that was who the culprits were. And Niccolo knew there was no such persons treading the streets of London.

Going to the window, she looked out at the street, pressing her forehead against the thick bubbly glass and trying to spot anyone who might still be out there watching their home. She couldn't see anyone, but she knew they'd be back to try again.

'London is no longer safe for three women living on their own,' she said to herself.

With her mind in turmoil, she was unable to work out what she needed to do first. Their escape was now even more critical. Putting her hands on her chest, she tried to still her racing heart and think pragmatically of what she needed to do, and in which order she needed to do it.

Telling the others not to leave the house for any reason and to bar the door behind her, she grabbed her shawl and stepped outside. Looking all around, she still couldn't see any sign of the men that the other two had described and lifting her skirt so she wouldn't trip, she hurried down the streets towards the river.

At first when she arrived at the wharf, John was nowhere to be seen. The combination of her anxiety and having run all the way meant her heart was now pounding, her brow damp with sweat. She could feel her shift sticking to her back. Perching on the edge of an old barrel, she leant her hands on her knees, her shoulders slumped forward as she tried to breathe in and out a little more calmly.

As her heart began to return to normal, she sat up again, shielding her eyes against the sun, watching the boats out on the river as she frantically scanned the view, looking for John. Despite all the boatmen having the same strong upper body lines from their years of pulling the oars, she knew she'd recognise him instantly when he came into sight. Assuming he did. They usually met here as it was close to his home and where he moored his boat, but there was no saying that he wasn't away upriver, perhaps waiting for another customer wanting a passage to Queenhithe. There were always plenty of men needing to visit the huge docks with their giant cranes lifting all the goods which came to London's quayside. All along the river ships waited, low in the water, weighed down by the wares they'd brought from aboard. Silks, spices, exotic foods. And she mused, sometimes bringing people fleeing a dangerous life, just as the *Sea Bird* had done fifteen years ago.

And now the safety she'd sought then, and that she had found, was being ripped away from her. Danger was now licking at her ankles like the flames depicted on her Devil card, the one which had saved so many and would do so for her this one final time. Because she couldn't live with the consequences if it didn't.

'Hoy!' From out on the river, she heard a loud call and squinting her eyes, she looked towards the noise, her body relaxing a little as she recognised John, his arm raised in a salute. She waved back, watching him as he swiftly rowed up to the jetty as though it were no effort at all. He was out of the boat and in front of her within seconds.

'My sweet.' He grabbed her hands and sat on the barrel she'd just vacated, pulling her down so she was perched on his lap. 'I did not expect to see you back again so soon. Is it not tomorrow that we flee? Have you changed your mind?'

'Not at all,' Portia said. 'But we are in even more danger than I had previously believed and we must go this very night. Niccolo is having us watched, his henchmen tried to abduct Vittoria from the market not one hour ago. We cannot tarry another day, there is no time to lose. Are you able to arrange what you need to with the women at Teddington?'

'Do not worry about that.' He patted her hands where they were clasped in her lap. 'I have friends there who can shelter us for a day if the onward horses are not yet ready. Do you need me to come with you now and help you prepare? I will do anything for you, you know that.'

'I think it best if you are not seen at my house. Let everything appear as normal as possible, given what is about to ensue. I will see you here tonight, a little after ten o'clock. I shall have to tell Vittoria what is going to happen, and she is not going to agree to go without a fight.' As she spoke, she was reminded of Agnese who, from being a small child, would push out her lower lip and stamp her feet if she wasn't happy with an instruction. Portia remembered that her little sister's first word had been 'no', and she had certainly carried on with her immovable attitude into adult life. She was adorable and loving, but if she didn't want to do something, she didn't do it. Right now, Portia wished Vittoria hadn't inherited the same trait, because they would be fleeing that night even if she had to carry the girl on her back.

Now she had to go home and start packing as many of their worldly belongings as she could, and on the way there she must quickly visit Elsebeth and warn her that they were to leave a day earlier than planned. She could only hope her friend could also be ready, because if she wasn't, they'd have to leave without her. Time was fast running out.

40

2025

Within a minute they were standing in front of the gallery window. The door and frame were both painted in a soft grey and a selection of old oil portraits filled the space.

'Well, here goes,' Beatrice said, wiping her hands down her jeans before pressing a buzzer located discreetly beside the door. She'd already been warned the shop was only open by appointment, so they'd need to ring to gain admittance. She shifted from foot to foot as she waited for some indication of activity inside.

Finally, after what was about two minutes but felt like ten, they heard the sound of a bolt being drawn back, and the door opened to reveal a man Beatrice guessed immediately was Aldo Arcardi. He looked exactly as she imagined him to be, probably mid-fifties and slim, smartly dressed in dark trousers and a navy-blue Ralph Lauren button-down shirt.

'Beatrice?' he asked, and she nodded, whilst he stepped forward to kiss both cheeks. He smelled of bergamot and sandalwood. Standing to one side, he ushered them in whilst shaking Jack's outstretched hand as they walked into the gallery.

The room inside was far larger than she'd have guessed from

the outside, like some sort of magic trick. She almost wanted to go back outside and walk in again. The expansive walls were hung with paintings similar to the ones in the window, fierce pan-faced people who lived centuries before and now looking displeased to be hanging on the wall and available for purchase. Several tables held carefully curated pieces: Murano glass which caught the light and threw out a myriad of coloured lights, small exquisitely carved marble busts that, to Beatrice's untrained eye, seemed to belong to the same era as those she'd previously seen in Florence – works by Michelangelo and his contemporaries.

'Absolutely lovely,' Beatrice said. '*Bellissimo*,' she added as she gestured to the items around the room.

'Yes, they command a very high price and people are happy to pay it,' Aldo replied. His English was excellent but his accent was heavy. Beatrice was relieved she could understand him.

'I can believe that,' she said, nodding. 'And you may also have the missing Devil from my pack of tarot cards too?' She couldn't engage in small talk, not when she was desperate to see what they'd come to view.

'I hope it is what you are searching for,' he replied. 'Do you have the other cards with you? I would be interested to see them.'

'Of course.' Beatrice took them out and laid the package on a desk placed to one side of the gallery space. Opening out the cloth, she took a few cards from the top of the pile and laid them out, before turning one over to display the back.

Aldo picked one up, holding it along the edge with his fingertips as he turned it back and forth.

'Stupendous,' he breathed. 'I have never seen a whole set of cards this old. *Fantastico*.' He placed it back down and taking a large white handkerchief from his pocket, he dabbed his eyes. Beatrice felt a swell of pride that he was as enamoured of her cards as she was. 'This is the same design as mine,' he said. 'There is also an elderly lady here in Milan, an acquaintance of mine, Francesca. She too is interested in these cards, although she has never told me why, and believe me, I have questioned her on several occasions. She has asked me more than once about the card I have because apparently she also has one, but I do not know how that can be so.'

Beatrice felt her heart sink. Margot had a copy, and now it sounded like Aldo must also have the same. And Francesca too. Why were there so many copies of this particular card? None of it was becoming any clearer.

Aldo retrieved a velvet-covered tray from a drawer set into the desk and laid it down. 'One moment,' he said before he disappeared behind a curtain obscuring the rest of the shop.

He returned less than a minute later, frowning. Already feeling worried, his expression did nothing for Beatrice's confidence. From a sheet of tissue paper he was carrying, he produced exactly what she was hoping. She could see the back of the card matched its comrades and as he held one corner and turned it over, the front looked as she imagined the Devil would. Similar to Margot's but more finely executed. Once it was laid on the tray, she bent down to take a closer look, taking a loupe she'd brought from her pocket.

'I fear it is not the actual card, merely a good copy,' Aldo said, slowly shaking his head. 'Feel the parchment, it is much thinner compared to yours.'

Beatrice didn't need to pick it up – as soon as he said the words she knew he was right. She could see that it was indeed another copy, albeit a very good one, just as Margot had. Her eyes welled up. They'd come all this way for no good reason. Why were there copies of this card, and would she ever find the original? Now she'd reached the end of the line with regards to her search. Rachel had already offered to paint a replacement and she was certain that it would be an excellent job, but it would never be the real one to complete the pack. Looking closer, she noticed she couldn't see a fingerprint smudge on this one.

'You're right,' she agreed. 'This is a hand-painted reproduction, just as I found in Brighton. What a shame. I do believe it to have also been of a similar era or thereabouts, just not the real thing. But thank you for letting me see it. And I'm sorry, because you have been duped as I have.'

'No,' Aldo protested, holding his hands up. 'This may only be a copy, but it's a seventeenth-century one, so still valuable in its own right. And if you ever discover why there are more than one, then it will lend provenance to mine. When do you fly home? I think Francesca would like to meet with you and see your cards, if you do not mind visiting her? Given that she has an interest in mine, perhaps she knows more of their history than she is telling me?'

'We aren't leaving until tomorrow afternoon,' Beatrice said. 'I'd love to meet her, especially if she too has another of the copies. And anyone who might have further information, however small, is worth talking with.'

'Wait here,' Aldo said. 'I will try and call her now, although she may be at Mass.' He glanced up at a large clock in a dark wooden case above the table. It was already ten o'clock. He disappeared once more behind the curtain and this time was gone for five minutes before reappearing with a big smile on his face, displaying his small, white, even teeth.

'She is most excited. I told her that you have an ancient pack of cards and are searching for the missing Devil card. She remonstrated that I did not tell her that you were coming.' He rolled his eyes. 'Can you go and visit her tomorrow morning?

She will be going to church soon and then out for dinner. I said you would, so I hope that's okay with you.'

'Yes, of course, we'd be delighted to,' Beatrice said. She looked at Jack and he nodded.

Aldo wrote out the address and drew a map showing where she was in relation to their hotel, and then with a lot of hugging and kissing of cheeks they left.

Beatrice walked up the street looking at her feet and not speaking. She'd walked down it just over an hour before with so much excitement and hope, and now once again she was disappointed. Perhaps she'd never find the card and make the pack whole again. Other than Francesca, she had nowhere else to go.

'Shall we find somewhere for a coffee?' Jack asked, taking hold of her hand. 'We might as well do some sightseeing today, as we now have somewhere to be tomorrow.'

'Yes, I suppose so,' Beatrice replied despondently.

'Hey.' Jack stopped and turned her to face him, tilting her face up to his. 'I know you didn't find what you hoped you would this morning, but you still have a new lead, don't you? And who knows what may turn up in years to come. You're such a determined person, I'm certain you will either find the card or discover what happened to it, however long it takes.'

'I know, you're right,' Beatrice admitted. 'I had pinned all my hopes on this being the one, although we know that there were several murders and that a card was found at one of the victim's homes so I suppose there was always the possibility that more than one copy was made. I know it sounds daft but I feel like I am letting my mum and my *nonna* down by not finding the real missing card. In fact, not just them, but all the women who came before them who read the cards. One of them must have known the truth.'

'Yes, it does sound daft,' he admonished. 'If it's right that you do so, then you'll solve the mystery. Have you done a reading and asked your own cards?'

'I haven't dared,' Beatrice admitted. 'I brought them here with me, but I thought it was better not to see what they say. Although now I've discovered that I'm no further on, perhaps when we go back to our room, I'll do a reading. Before, I was afraid, but now I have nothing to lose.'

They walked back to the cathedral and from there into the Galleria Vittorio Emanuele II where Beatrice stopped for a moment to admire the red and blue tiled floor before tilting her head back in awe at the glass-and-iron dome high above them.

After wandering along looking in the shop windows, even though they were mostly closed, they walked up to the Teatro alla Scala until they found a small coffee shop, where they bought cappuccinos and biscotti.

By the time they'd drunk their coffees and followed them with big bowls of seafood tagliatelle and a bottle of wine, it was mid-afternoon. The disappointment was still hanging over Beatrice like a cloud she couldn't shake off, and she admonished herself for getting her hopes up when she'd known in her heart that the probability of Aldo's card being the one she was seeking had been slim. They'd visit Francesca in the morning and see if she would tell them why she too was interested in the card, and then they'd go back to London and the new life she'd built for herself there and forget about this fruitless chase.

She'd spotted an email in her inbox from her dad and she knew it would be about the wedding invitation. Her RSVP was still unsent. She didn't want to face the disappointment she'd cause him, even though she'd made her thoughts on the subject very clear. Wasn't her moving to London enough of a clue?

'Shall we see if we can visit the cathedral?' Jack interrupted her musing. 'There will probably be an evening service but it's only three o'clock now, so we might be okay. After we've looked around and strolled back to the hotel, it will be dark. And I don't know about you, but after our late night yesterday, I could do with a snack this evening and then an early night.'

'A snack?' Beatrice made her eyes go wide and her mouth drop open. 'We've just eaten the biggest bowl of pasta I've ever had! I probably won't need to eat until Christmas Day.'

Leaning back in his chair, Jack caught the eye of the waiter and called out, '*Il conto, per favore.*'

'Have you been swotting up on your Italian?' Beatrice said. 'Please let me pay for this, you've been so kind coming with me, let me buy you lunch as a thank you?'

Holding his hands up, Jack smiled and nodded. 'Okay, thank you,' he said.

Once the bill was paid, Jack got to his feet and taking her coat from the back of her chair, he held it out for her to slide her arms in to. She followed him out of the restaurant and back into the piazza. A cold wind had blown up and was cutting through the narrow alleyways and streets as though playing a game of tag. Beatrice did up the buttons and pulled the furry collar up around her neck, whilst Jack put his arm around her and drew her in against him.

'It should be me thanking you,' he said. 'For letting me enjoy this stunning city with the most beautiful woman I've ever met. I know we haven't known each other long, but I feel more alive when I'm with you, which I haven't ever experienced with any of my previous girlfriends. I don't know where this – we – are going, but I hope it's a long way. A very long way.'

Tilting her face up, Beatrice kissed him. She couldn't stop her face splitting into the widest grin. Suddenly it didn't matter that she hadn't found the card in Milan, because she realised, she had found love there.

41

1644

Portia was frantically pushing as many of their belongings as she could possibly fit into a hessian bag. Rolling up shifts, night rails, coifs and underskirts as small as they'd go. Their aprons, hose and partlets went in together with Vittoria's ribbons and their bodkins and needles, until eventually she'd filled three bags with as much as she could. She tucked her cards just inside the topmost one.

Their kitchen items would have to be left behind, but she had enough money to replace them at their final destination. They'd need to wear or carry their shawls, and she'd also throw on the cloak she'd brought from Italy, despite the warmth of the evening, as there was no space left to pack it. The gold she'd saved and the jewels she still had were tucked into the top of a bag she would tie around her waist. All whilst she worked, her heart was beating so hard in her chest, she thought it would burst.

'Please, stop for just one moment and explain to me why you are packing all of our possessions?' Maria asked. 'Since you arrived back earlier, you have been like a whirlwind, frantically throwing everything we own into these sacks, but you will not tell us what is happening. What did you discover when you were out? Are we in danger as you suspected?'

'Yes, Mama, what is going on? You have been behaving so strangely recently,' Vittoria said.

Portia walked on unsteady legs to a chair and lowered herself down. She needed to think and think quickly.

'We are three vulnerable women, and I am now certain there are men watching our home.' At least that wasn't a lie. She'd told so many over the past fifteen years, it hardly mattered at this point, but what did matter was the absolute necessity to conceal her biggest deceit before it was laid bare and her life fell apart. 'And after what happened to you earlier, we now have no option other than to move again. I know that you do not wish it, Vittoria, but once the killers are caught then we can return here. See, I am leaving our furniture and kitchen items for when we come back.'

The girl looked dubious, but she nodded slowly. 'Where in London do you propose we go? Why don't we stay with Caterina and Filippo, as my uncle suggested? He is rich with many guards, and we will be safe there.'

Nowhere could be less safe, Portia thought. 'I have already arranged to go with Elsebeth to her house in Teddington where we will be protected. It is settled.' Portia would have to face more questions when they continued on by road to Winchester, but at present she just needed to ensure her plan was executed exactly as she intended.

'We will leave when the church bells ring nine tonight. And until then the door is barred to stop anyone entering.' Portia pointed to the heavy piece of wood wedged across the back of the door before going to the larder to plan what food she could cook to take with them.

* * *

The night was not as dark as Portia would have wished, but they could not wait any longer. She had told Elsebeth to be ready just before ten o'clock and in the twilight, Vittoria would take much longer to navigate the streets. They had to leave, and it had to be now.

Vittoria had suggested again that they threw themselves on the charity of Niccolo and Caterina, who would, she insisted, gladly take them in until the murderer who was stalking the streets was hanging from the gibbet at Tyburn Hill. There were several moments when Portia wanted to shout at her and tell her exactly what sort of person Niccolo was and that it was he they were fleeing from, but she managed to bite her lip and kept repeating the mantra that they were all in immediate danger. And also, that Elsebeth would be accompanying them because her husband was away and she too was fearful for her life and that of Peter's.

As night fell, the deepening shadows reflected in the scowl on Vittoria's face, it was time to leave. Maria had kept stoically quiet. Portia managed to find a moment to tell her that she understood if Maria wished to remain in their home, but the other woman shook her head.

'I do not understand why we are leaving like this, under the cover of darkness, but I am sure it has something to do with Master Tabanelli. I have seen the way your demeanour changes the moment he arrives. As though a wild animal caught in the eyes of the hunter. You knew him before, in Milan, and you chose to run then. If you say we must leave and we are in danger then I trust you, just as I did when you hired me and said you were leaving Italy because you were not safe. I will follow Vittoria across the seas, across the lands; wherever she goes, I go.

And I say the same to you, you are like a sister to me now. I have never questioned your decisions and come what may, I shall not question them now.'

Portia threw her arms around her, feeling her breath ragged in her chest. She had asked so much of this other woman over the years. Maria had nursed Vittoria at her breast, no wonder she considered herself a mother figure to the girl, and a sister to Portia. She'd been alongside, unquestioning, for fifteen years, and she would continue to be so.

'Then let us go.' She brushed her hands down her skirts and picked up one of the bags she'd packed earlier and passed a smaller sack containing the food to Vittoria. She and Maria had baked cake and bread with the remaining butter and flour they had, and she'd wrapped cheese and cold chicken. There were also a few apples, and two leather flasks containing ale.

In the corner, Maria shouldered the other two bags and Portia held her elbow out so Vittoria could link her arm through and be led through the streets. Now that they were about to leave she was quiet, for which Portia was secretly grateful; an obedient if angry girl was easier to deal with than one being loud and vocal as they crept along the quiet London lanes.

Portia had already planned out their route to avoid as many taverns as possible where men in their cups might fall out of the door and into the path of three vulnerable women. She also wanted to avoid the back alleys which slipped between tall dark buildings, only a glimmer of light from candles spilling out from behind shutters. It was in these places where cut-throats hid, waiting to slither out and steal from drunks who didn't have the wits to fight them off – drunks who would be left in a pool of blood to be found in the morning, stiff and cold. Three women without a male escort would be considered an easy target.

Thankfully, they met no one as they hurried through the

streets, and they reached Elsebeth's house without incident. At one point they spotted a night guard in the distance and, worried he would stop them and question their actions, they bent down and darted between the relative safety of one building and the next until they arrived at their first destination.

As planned, Elsebeth was waiting beside the stables. She had a bag at her feet and in her arms she held Peter, attached to her with a shawl tied across her chest. Without a word, Maria picked up the additional luggage.

'You have everything?' Portia asked. She wanted to ensure the jewels she'd been shown had been retrieved and was relieved when with the merest tilt of her head Elsebeth patted her stomach below where she held Peter. As she herself had done, the valuables were hidden beneath her clothing. As well as her money belt, Portia had stitched coins into her clothing too. She suspected Elsebeth had done the same; the small but valuable baubles were easy to secrete away.

Leading the way, Portia hurried towards the river. Every minute that had passed since she'd said goodbye to John, she grew increasingly desperate to be with him again. He was the only person that *she* could lean on in the way everyone depended on *her*, and right now she needed some support. Everything and everyone she carried on her shoulders weighed her down and now she felt as though she could barely put one foot in front of the next. As they walked down Thames Street, she could smell the river, hear it splashing against the wharf. She could just make out in the distance the dancing light of a lamp reflected in the swirling water. Portia stopped herself from breaking into a trot, knowing that Vittoria, still clinging to her, may possibly fall over.

Finally, as they arrived at the edge of the water, Portia disengaged herself and ran the last few steps to wrap her arms around

John. She breathed in the scent of his tobacco and the warmth of his skin as he held her to him.

'Everything has gone according to your plan?' he whispered in her ear, his breath hot against her throat.

'Yes,' she replied. 'All will be well now. We are safe, we are all safe.'

As the words she spoke dissipated in the night air, the quiet was broken by the sound of heavy boots echoing around the tall warehouses which surrounded them as a man stepped out from the dark shadows.

'You are going nowhere,' came the voice, its intonation revealing a now familiar heavy Italian accent. Niccolo stepped into the circle of the light thrown from John's lamp, and Portia gasped out loud.

'Vittoria, my precious.' He turned to the girl who was looking around wildly, barely able to see what was happening in the little light available. 'Come to your Uncle Niccolo.'

42

1644

Portia's arm shot out and grabbed Vittoria, pulling her around behind her. There was the rasp of a flint as Niccolo lit another lamp.

'Did you think I would let you disappear again?' he said. 'Once before, you stole your sister's child, and you shall not do it again.'

'Master Tabanelli?' Vittoria said. 'Why are you here? We must be away, there is a murderer about the streets of London tonight and he is coming for us.'

'There is no murderer,' Niccolo said, 'there never has been. I have brought Caterina with me now, if there were a murderer loose I assure you I would not have allowed her to be out after dark. Your mama, or rather your *aunt*, is responsible for the women who disappeared. They are now living elsewhere, although I do not yet know where, aided and paid for by this woman you believe to be your mother. Everything about her is a web of deceit and lies. And the biggest lie is who you are.'

'Mama?' Vittoria's voice sounded querulous, and Portia was pleased to see that Maria had slipped her hand firmly through the girl's arm, slowly making her step backwards, away from the two men. 'Why is Master Niccolo talking about a child that you stole? What child?'

'It is you,' Niccolo barked, the words snapping around Portia's head like a pack of rabid dogs biting at her. Everything she'd striven to keep secret was spilling out, the ugliness choking the air around them. Filling her lungs with its contamination so she couldn't breathe.

'It cannot be,' Vittoria replied. Portia could hear the obstinacy in her voice. 'This is my mama, she came to England with me because the plague was in Milan, and we were not safe. My father was a cruel man, he did not want me, so she took me and fled here. Our servant, Maria, came with us.'

'No, that is not the truth of what happened. Your father fell victim to the plague as did your real mother, Agnese. But her sister here, Portia, told your father, my brother, who was about to go to his villa in the hills, that you were not yet born. She was not telling the truth. You have the same affliction in your eyes as your mother did. It will only show itself in a child born to someone who also suffers and that is how I realised who you are, what she had done. This woman you have been calling Mama all these years did not give birth to you, she is just your aunt. And now I am here to claim you back, as a true Tabanelli. You will return to Italy with me on the next high tide.'

'Please come with us,' Caterina's voice from where she was still standing in the shadows rang out. 'My papa has told me everything and how much he wishes you to come back to our homeland and live with us all. You will be safe and we can be together forever.'

In the dim light, Portia could see the confusion on Vittoria's face as she turned her head from person to person. And John's brows were furrowed. He knew little of her past and now it was flooding out before him. Not only was Portia about to lose Vittoria, but also probably him as well.

'Mama, is what my uncle says true?' Vittoria asked. Her voice broke as she started to cry, and Maria wrapped her arms around her.

'It is, yes.' Portia couldn't see any reason to deny it now. All she could do was keep everyone together and to somehow leave as she had planned. She wasn't sure how she was going to achieve that now. 'But Niccolo does not tell you the whole truth. I had to take you and run because as I have told you, your father was a monster and he would have treated you, a mere girl, with no care or love. He was only interested in having sons. Already a baby girl, a sister to you and born the year before you, died because when she fell sick he would not allow the physician to visit, nor for someone to go to the apothecary. As you were being born, he was already preparing to leave us all in a house with the plague and run to his villa to save his own skin. He cared not for his wife or his child. Your mother breathed her last breath as you took your first, so I told him that you were not yet born. I knew he would think that you had sadly died within her. Minutes later, he abandoned us. He ran like a coward, leaving us in the plague-ridden house to be locked in there by the authorities. I never imagined we would be found here, but then you met Caterina, and inadvertently, she brought her father to our door. From that moment I knew we had to leave. But the truth, which Niccolo has failed to tell you, is that you are the rightful heir to your father's fortune, the one which Niccolo has claimed for his own. He does not wish to look after you, my precious, he wishes to kill you so he does not have to surrender the Tabanelli riches.'

'And the women who have been murdered in London,' Vittoria reminded her, 'you have been doing that also?' Her incredulous voice was stronger now.

'Of course not,' Portia exclaimed. 'Do you believe me capable of that? Why would I? The women came for tarot readings, and I used my cards to put in place a way for them to escape, just as I once did. To help them flee situations which may well have ended with them dead. Husbands who find their beds empty, and their wives gone, have assumed they have been taken and murdered in the night, but in fact those women are now living new lives elsewhere. Safe.'

'And is that why I found a copy of The Devil card?' Vittoria asked. 'Did that have something to do with what you have been orchestrating?'

'It did indeed,' Portia admitted. 'What is real and what is an illusion. Copies of the cards were given to those who came seeking assistance. They took them to John so he knew they'd been sent by me. Over the years I have saved many women from being killed by violent husbands, or fathers. Only once did I fail, and I will always carry that sadness in my heart. They escaped an existence that was an illusion, exchanging it for real, protected lives.'

'And is that why Elsebeth is also here? Her husband is cruel?'

'It is,' Elsebeth interrupted. 'Your mama, and truly that is who she is for she has protected you from the moment you drew your first breath, is saving myself and Peter from certain death. I, and many other women, owe our lives to what she has done. What she has achieved by reading people's fates in her cards. An angel, delivering The Devil card.'

'She is not your mama,' Niccolo hissed, taking two steps towards them. As they had all been speaking, Portia, John and Elsebeth had slowly moved towards Vittoria and Maria so they were now all standing in a group around the young girl. 'And now, you will come with me. Or I shall kill everyone here in front of your eyes and, as their blood pools at your feet, I will still have you.' He held his hand out as though expecting her to step forward and take it.

Vittoria's eyes flitted between Portia and Niccolo, and then to Maria as if waiting for someone to explain properly what she'd just been told. She couldn't see anyone's face properly in the dim flickering light of the lamps and Portia imagined that was adding to her confusion.

'Do not listen to him, do not do as he says.' Her voice came out sharply before Vittoria could make a move. 'Stay here, my darling, you are safe with me.'

'No,' Niccolo shouted. 'She has been twisting the truth for the whole of your life. But no longer. Now you will come and live the life, enjoy the riches that you should always have done. And you would like to come and live with Caterina, your cousin, would you not? We will all return to Italy together. Your homeland.'

As he was speaking, Maria had shuffled forward and put her arm around Vittoria, who now had her hands clapped over her ears, as though she did not want to listen to another word. She turned and buried her face in Maria's shoulder and the other woman wrapped both arms protectively around the girl.

'I have had enough of this time-wasting,' Niccolo spat. Bending down for a moment, he stood up again and Portia saw a flash of light at his hand as a stiletto knife, the long thin sharp blade favoured by the Italians, cut through the air. There was a collective gasp and Elsebeth screamed. She and Maria, still holding Vittoria, stepped backwards and melted into the darkness. John, who had been silent during the argument, instantly stepped forward so he was beside Portia. Although she was standing very still and watching what Niccolo's next move would be, she muttered to him to move away.

'Go and protect my girl, please, John,' she said.

'I cannot,' he said. 'At this moment you, my love, are the one who needs me.' In his hand he was holding a long piece of wood, and Portia realised it was one of the oars from his boat.

Before she could ask him a second time, Niccolo suddenly darted forward, lunging towards her with the knife. She felt a momentary sharp pain in her arm, but it only fuelled the anger which had been building in her until it now erupted in a boiling fury. Bending down as though she was badly injured, in one fluid movement she lifted her skirt a little and felt on her leg for that which she'd secreted there earlier. She was quite certain neither Maria nor Vittoria even knew she possessed it, but she'd brought it from Italy all those years before when she knew travelling a long way during the dark hours would carry an element of danger and she needed to be able to protect them all. From beneath the fabric, attached to her leg by a suspender used to hold up her hose, she pulled out a slim knife, similar in style to Niccolo's.

'You are not the only person to come armed,' she jeered. Now only the two of them stood in the circle of light, with John a little way to her right, his oar held in front of him as guards did with their pikes.

'You think I am afraid of a simple woman as yourself?' Niccolo taunted. 'I have told you what I want. Either you tell Vittoria to come with me tonight, or I will slit your throat right now in front of everyone.' He held his knife up, its blade horizontal and he swept it to one side, his arm outstretched as though he was doing as he'd just warned and slicing across her throat.

'Do not move an inch towards her,' John warned. He was now swaying the oar in a curve in front of him, stepping forward slowly as though to sweep Niccolo to one side. He was not quick enough though as Niccolo suddenly darted to his left and then he was behind John, stabbing with his knife. John shouted and fell to his knees, the oar clattering to the ground.

Portia felt sick as she watched him drop but she didn't have time to see how badly he was injured. Niccolo was now circling around her, the hand holding the knife – dripping with blood – making stabbing gestures towards her. With no option but to keep moving, she too was walking in a circle, her eyes constantly watching his blade. Her feet nudged John's abandoned oar and still keeping her eyes steady, in one swift movement, she bent her knees and picked it up. It was heavy, but she was holding the middle and it was well balanced.

'I grow tired of this dance,' Niccolo said through gritted teeth. 'Already you have caused the death of this man.' He waved his foot towards John, who was laid prone on the floor. 'Instruct Vittoria to come with me now, or you are next.' They had both paused walking. Portia could hear her blood pounding in her ears as the rage in her chest rose until it was roaring and as she opened her mouth the sound came out, an almighty outpouring of anger as though she were summoning the Devil himself. Her hands were tingling with the noise she was making and Niccolo, his face frozen in surprise, suddenly took two steps forward and leapt at her, his knife outstretched.

Portia stumbled, jumping over John who had rolled onto his back, his eyes opening and closing. She leant backwards as the blade swept past her chest, missing her by inches. Behind her, she could hear the splashing of the swirling river as it slapped against the wharf below and she knew she was close to the edge. If she took another step back, she'd be in the dark swirling waters racing past.

It seemed Niccolo had come to the same conclusion, and with a snarl he darted forward once more. As he did so, his foot slipped on the patch of blood slowly pooling around John and for a moment his arms flailed round in circles. Without stopping to consider what she was doing, Portia gripped the oar she was still holding in both hands and swung it in a wide arc, catching the side of his body as she continued to spin around until he was swept off the side of the quay. A long, carrying howl was followed by a splash, and then for a moment all was silent.

She momentarily looked quickly over her shoulder, but as she expected, already there was no sign of Niccolo who'd sunk below the water and would already be travelling downriver where he'd probably be washed up beneath London Bridge, or if not, on the Essex marshes.

Before she could check if John was badly injured, Vittoria broke free of where Maria was holding her and marched towards Portia still in the circle of lamplight.

'You've killed him!' she shouted. 'He's gone in the river, and he was my uncle, my family. And my best friend's father. And now you have taken him from us, just as you once took me from my father. Why did you not just let me talk with him? I could have told him I wished to stay with you, I would not have gone to Italy.'

'You saw him, you heard everything he said.' Portia was shaking her head so violently her coif slipped off the back of her hair. 'You would not have had a choice, he would have taken you whether or not you wished it. After killing me first. It mattered not what your relationship was to him, he would have found a way to get rid of you, he would not have given up his money for anyone.' At her feet John groaned and pushed himself up on his elbows. 'Dear God, I thought you were dead,' Portia exclaimed as she helped him to his feet. There was a patch of blood on his jerkin.

'Nay, I think he only slashed my arm,' he said. 'The blade did not penetrate, I am wearing a leather jerkin for that reason. You can never be sure who will be on the river. I think I hit my head though and lost consciousness.' His hand went to the back of his head and as he took it away blood dripped from his fingers.

'Come, we must leave.' Maria walked over carrying their luggage, followed by Elsebeth. Miraculously, Peter hadn't stirred throughout the noise. 'The guards will be alerted by the noise, let us return home.'

'We cannot, we must continue with our journey,' Portia said. 'There is nothing left in London, not for any of us.'

'So you can continue spiriting people away with your cards?' Vittoria hissed. 'Keeping people from their families, deciding the fates of others? Is that what your cards do?' Picking up the nearest bag, she started to pull the contents out and then, not finding what she was looking for, she started on the next one until the worn piece of silk wrapped around the tarot cards fell out. Snatching them up, Vittoria held the silk by one corner and with a flick of her wrist the cards cascaded out across the ground.

With a wail, Portia dropped to her knees and began to crawl around, gathering them up again. The beautiful painted designs still glowed despite the dim light as though drawing her to them. They were scattered over a large space and as she collected them up, holding them to her chest with one hand as she snatched up more with the other, she didn't notice Caterina step from the shadows and dip one knee as she scooped up The Devil card, slipping into her pocket. And then she was gone, an apparition stealing away into the night as though she was never there.

'Do you have them all?' John asked. His head was now swathed in a makeshift bandage which Maria was still tying the ends of. Portia slowly turned in a circle, searching all around.

'Yes, I think so. I cannot see any more and their coloured

illustrations are easily visible against the dark cobbles even with just the lamplight.'

'Then we must leave now,' he instructed her. 'We have been lucky to have not yet attracted the night watchmen. Caterina has disappeared and I am sure she will alert the constables. If the truth gets out about what happened here tonight, you will be hanged for murder.'

'Yes,' Portia agreed. The adrenalin was rapidly seeping out of her body, leaving her feeling exhausted and shaky. Turning to the others, she said sharply, 'Get in the boat now, John will help you all.' Without waiting for any protestation from Vittoria, she pushed her precious cards and the clothes back in the bags as Maria hurried the girl to the steps and led her down and into the boat where John was now standing to help each of them in. Portia was the last one, picking up the bags and the lamp Niccolo had been carrying.

From somewhere a few streets away she could hear shouting, the sound of heavy boots running and getting louder. It was time to leave. She'd escaped with Vittoria once, and she'd do it again. Just like all the women she'd helped over the years to start a new, safe life, the fate she'd uncovered in the cards predicting what would come to pass. No one ever truly knew what the truth was, nor what was an illusion.

43

2025

Returning their key to the receptionist and assuring her they'd leave a glowing review, which wouldn't be hard as they had already promised themselves they'd return in the summer for a longer visit, Beatrice and Jack walked to the street they'd been directed to by Aldo. It was close to where they'd been the previous afternoon and they found it without difficulty, a small, terraced stone house, which looked as though it had been there about the same length of time as the cathedral had. Beatrice knocked on the door at exactly ten o'clock.

Francesca must have been watching out of the window because it was opened almost immediately, revealing a tall, slender woman whose advancing years were only obvious because of the grey hair pulled tightly into a bun at the nape of her neck and the myriad of lines across her golden skin.

'*Buongiorno*,' Beatrice said, before introducing herself and Jack.

'Please, call me Francesca, and we do not have to speak Italian,' she said. 'I attended university at Oxford. My English is rusty, but hopefully adequate.'

She showed them into a small, yet elegant, living room. In the centre of the room was a small, low table with a carved wooden box sitting on it. It was inlaid with pale flowers.

'So, your family is Italian?' Francesca asked.

'Yes, on my mother's side,' Beatrice said. She caught a hint of a smile as the other woman gave a slight nod of her head, as though she'd been expecting that answer.

They were offered coffee, which they both declined, having already had several cups with their breakfast. Beatrice was starting to question whether her increased heart rate since they'd arrived was due to her emotions, or the overdose of caffeine she'd consumed.

Francesca sat down opposite Beatrice and placed her hands on the box in front of her.

'Aldo tells me that you have a pack of tarot cards but are missing The Devil card,' she said. 'And I have a Devil card, which is separate from its fellows. And a tale about this card and what it once did. Women who were lost to it.'

'I have seen Aldo's card, but it is not the one I am searching for,' Beatrice said. 'It's not the same quality of card and the artwork looks like it is a copy. I have also seen something similar in England. They aren't the right ones.'

'No. They are part of the story though, a very important part. Have you brought the pack with you?' Francesca was looking at Beatrice's handbag, which was resting on her knee. Jack had carried her overnight bag.

'Of course.' Opening her bag, she took out the cards and, as she'd done the previous day, she laid them out on the table, turning some over to display the illustrations.

'*Si. Si.* Yes, this is them, finally they have completed their journey and come home.' Francesca clasped her hands together, slowly shaking her head before she lifted the box lid and

removed a piece of heavy embroidered damask from which she
drew a card and laid it with the others.

Beatrice didn't even need to pick it up to know this was the
one she had been searching for. It was the one to complete the
pack. Lifting it carefully, she turned it over where she could see
the back, as beautifully decorated as hers were.

'This is it, the lost card,' she breathed. 'Finally.' Looking at
Francesca, she could see the old woman was in tears, and she
knew hers too were on the verge of spilling over. She couldn't
quite believe that she'd found it. And now she wondered if it had
been Francesca, the other person who'd been searching, except
she'd been trying to find the other copies because she already
owned the original. 'But I don't understand why there are copies
of it. Why this wasn't with the rest of the pack. And how do you
have it?'

'Let me tell you the story,' she said. 'And then you will understand. My full name is Francesca Caterina, and I was given this
card by my own mother, as she was given it by her mother. Just
as you were given the rest of them by your own mother, I expect.'
Beatrice didn't want to explain how she had found them after
her mother had died, so she just nodded.

'I was told this story, passed down the generations with the
card so that each custodian would know the truth when it was
time to reveal it. The original owner of your cards was a woman,
a very strong woman called Portia. She ran away from Milan in
the seventeenth century and took her sister's baby, Vittoria, who
was born moments before her mother, Agnese, died. They were
escaping both the plague and also the baby's father, Lorenzo,
who was a tyrant. Eventually they arrived in London and lived
there for many years. Portia read the cards and helped women to
escape dangerous lives, just as she had. When it was time for

each woman to leave, it's said they would take a copy she'd made of The Devil card. To show what was the truth of these women's lives and what was simply an illusion.'

'And that is why there are these replicas,' Beatrice said.

'Indeed, and perhaps somewhere there are others which have survived. I have been trying, not very successfully, to collate them and keep them with the one I had. Portia helped more and more women, and as their wives disappeared, the men of London started to believe they were being murdered. The illusion was allowed to continue.'

Beatrice nodded, now finally understanding the rumours and the news sheets they'd read in the British Library. 'What they believed was happening, and what was the truth,' she said, smiling.

'Yes,' Francesca said. 'But unluckily for Portia, Vittoria's uncle, Lorenzo's brother, Niccolo, arrived in London with his own daughter, Caterina, and he recognised his niece. The story goes that she had an anomaly in her eyes and immediately he knew who she was.'

'A coloboma,' Beatrice suggested. 'My *nonna* had one, a keyhole-shaped pupil. It affected her sight, but it was only in one eye.'

'Then quite possibly it was that condition, if it is genetic,' Francesca agreed. 'So Portia took Vittoria and ran but was apprehended at the river where there was supposedly a big fight. During the scuffle the cards, your cards, were scattered on the ground and although Portia collected them up, one had already been snatched up and hidden by Caterina. And there you have it. I am a descendant of hers, just as you are of Portia. Our two families have been intertwined through the centuries because of a deck of tarot cards and a woman who escaped her dangerous life so that later she was able to help many other women flee their own desperate lives. Now finally, the card is reunited as it should be. It has taken hundreds of years but the circle is complete once more. Your cards are precious because they are antique artefacts, but even more as part of your heritage.'

Beatrice looked across at Jack, who was looking as shocked as she felt. She didn't know what to say, the story was so incredible. Deep inside though, she had no doubts that it was true. Getting to her feet, Francesca asked if they would like a glass of grappa.

'Yes, please,' Jack answered for them both. 'I think we could both do with one.'

Half an hour and two glasses of grappa later, Beatrice was still asking questions and exclaiming over the account they'd just heard.

'All this time,' she said. 'I wish my mum was alive to hear it all. That our ancestor was so brave, and clever.'

'You come from a family of strong women,' Francesca said, 'who helped many others. Even though my own branch of the family does not come off well in the retelling, we women both still carry the Tabanelli blood through those two daughters, Vittoria and Caterina. And they had a strength that the men, Niccolo and Lorenzo, did not.'

'Yes, I believe that too.' Beatrice took hold of Francesca's hands, the skin thin and papery beneath her fingers. 'So, what happens to the card now?'

'Well, you must take it, of course,' Francesca said. 'I do not have any children to leave it to anyway, and it is the right ending to the story that it is reunited with its sisters. Perhaps if you have time before you leave, you could do a reading for me, with the cards?'

'Of course, I would love that. And it is only right that you are first. And thank you, I have no words to express my gratitude to you for gifting it to me.' Picking up the cards, Beatrice gently started to shuffle them before dealing three cards out, face down. Finally, for both of them this was a completion of the circle, one that was opened centuries before by a woman desperate to save a baby girl, to save her own life and then, to save many women's lives. 'Please turn the first card,' she instructed.

* * *

It was late at night by the time they arrived back in London, the queues for security at Heathrow snaking back from the self-scan machines for over a hundred metres. They'd agreed to order an Uber rather than waiting for a train, but it was still one o'clock in the morning when they were deposited outside Hampstead Books. Jack insisted on walking down the mews and waited whilst Beatrice opened the shop door. He pulled her in for a hug and a kiss which began slowly and gently but soon increased to something far deeper.

'I really don't want to let you go,' he whispered in her ear, 'but we should probably go to sleep in our own beds tonight and get some rest. It's been an exciting couple of days.'

'You are right.' Beatrice interspersed each word with a peck on his lips. 'And it has been a hell of a day today. My mind is all over the place, I don't know how I'm going to get to sleep. But I need to be in the shop first thing tomorrow, it's the last week before Christmas.'

They kissed one final time, and she went into the shop and locked it behind her before wearily climbing the stairs. In her bedroom, before she dropped her bags on the floor, she removed the cards, opening out the cloth so she could see the Devil sitting on top where it belonged. The sorrow she'd felt from the pack since she'd found them had gone. All was calm.

The following day the shop was constantly busy with people buying last-minute gifts. There had been a slew of internet orders which Daisy had run to the post office with at lunchtime and Portia hoped they'd get to their destinations in time.

All whilst she worked though, chatting with customers, doing a last-minute reading, writing out gift vouchers for readings in the new year, her phone was burning a hole in her pocket. Or rather, the still unanswered email from her father was. The wedding was in five days' time, and she couldn't put off replying, given that her invitation response was still upstairs. Too late to post it now, she felt guilty for not having spoken to him before. And she wasn't going to give him the reply he was expecting. Not now.

Since arriving home she'd read the cards – the ancient pack – twice, and each time she'd turned over the same ones that she had for Francesca. The Empress, representing a mother's love, nurturing. The Wheel of Fortune, telling of a circle now closed, and the Death card. The end of a cycle, time to let go and embrace this new beginning. The cards spoke of the cyclical nature of life. How all things were related, continuously shifting and transforming. Just as her own life had been transformed by her discovery of the cards and the journey they had taken her on. The women she'd met in London and their stories had all contributed to what she'd learned – that life wasn't easy, and people did whatever they could to smooth their path. Everyone deserved to live a happy and love-filled life, especially her father and Kerry.

Just like Portia, she, Beatrice, had also fled to London, scared of the changes around her. But she wasn't in danger, and she needed to confront her fears. The cards had shown the women she'd read for that they needed to move on with their lives and take a step on their onward journey. Finally, she understood, and she could do it too. It was time; taking her phone, she opened the email and hit reply.

44

1644

In the oak tree to her left, Portia could hear a blackbird singing and stepping away from the back door into her garden, she took a deep breath of the fresh, clear, country air. So different from the smells and noise in London. She could hear no one, not from in her own house nor from the large family who all shared the cottage a little further down the lane.

This was a new life. Finally, she could stop looking over her shoulder and waiting for the past, for what she did, to catch up with her. The heavy hand of retribution to fall upon her shoulder. Now, Vittoria knew it all.

Within a month of arriving in this quiet Hampshire village, Portia and John had married in a simple ceremony at the village church, and afterwards he moved into the cottage with them. He'd found work with a local stonemason, his strong upper body after years of rowing on the Thames making him ideal for carrying around large pieces of stone.

It had taken longer than a month, however, for Vittoria to forgive her for the terrible lies she'd told. Before the girl really understood why she'd done what she had in Milan. She'd seen how Niccolo had behaved when he showed his true colours, and that he would have killed Portia, and herself, in a moment. But now, six months later, she was once again calling Portia *Mama* and had stopped mentioning Caterina and her old London life. The blacksmith's son had started visiting, not put off by her visual impairment, attracted by her long auburn curls and sweet dimpled face. Portia suspected he would soon be asking for her hand in marriage, and she would gladly give it.

Elsebeth now lived quietly in a village just two miles away, and Vittoria loved to visit and play with Peter. As had been feared, the little boy didn't look remotely like the man who was meant to be his father and Elsebeth often said she knew she'd made the correct decision to leave. Her neighbours believed her tale that she was widowed and had moved away from London to be near her sister. If anyone wondered why Portia and Elsebeth didn't remotely resemble each other, or sound alike, they kept their counsel.

The only thing which still made Portia's heart heavy was her tarot cards. Once they arrived in Winchester, the journey having been thankfully uneventful, she'd unwrapped them. Although they had survived the turmoil on that final night they no longer looked as special as they once did, and that saddened her. Both her mother, her grandmother and who-knew-before-them had taken such care of the cards, understood how precious they were to the women in the family and how cherished they were. But now some of them were muddy and one of them had stains from where it had landed in John's blood.

Even worse though, one was missing. She didn't understand how it had happened because she'd held up the lamp and scoured the area to ensure she'd collected them all up, yet despite going through the pack numerous times, each time slower than the previous one, The Devil card had gone. Was it a sign, a punishment because she'd used her cards for more than just telling her customers what the future may hold? However it had happened, it now meant she couldn't use them. She tried creating a replacement, she could remember well what it looked like after making so many copies, but the pack felt wrong, it didn't like this imposter, and the cards seemed to rebel against her, the inverted King of Swords showing his anger and the Five of Cups telling of a period of mourning and of loss. Their message bold, and honest.

After Vittoria had calmed down, she asked Portia why she no longer read the cards.

'I have no need to earn money now,' Portia explained. Never would she need to save again. Vittoria would have a husband to look after her, and John earned enough to keep them comfortable. 'But there is another reason, too.' Although she had avoided saying anything and putting any blame on Vittoria, she went on to explain that somehow in the tumult at the quay The Devil card had disappeared. 'I can no longer read them; it is as though their sister is missing and they mourn her.'

'I am sorry, Mama, that I did that. I allowed my anger to overwhelm me when I did not understand why you had behaved as you did. And now your precious set is broken.'

'Perhaps it was meant to be,' Portia replied, shrugging her shoulders. 'When I am no longer here, the cards will be yours and I hope that one day you will have a daughter of your own. And who knows? Maybe when the cards are needed to help someone once again, then the lost card will return to unite them and fulfil their destiny once more.'

'Three, two, one.' Beatrice was counting down with the rest of the guests before – with a shout – everyone threw handfuls of dried flower petals up into the air, from where they drifted down like sweetly scented snow, to be trampled underfoot. She turned around to grin at Jack who, in a dark suit and his hair tied back, was looking so handsome he made her knees feel weak. It was Christmas Eve and they were both extremely lucky to have Alex and Daisy managing their shops, although they'd been instructed to close at lunchtime, as Beatrice and Jack would have done.

She glanced at her watch. It was almost three o'clock and would be dark within the hour. Already, deep grey clouds were gathering on the horizon heralding twilight approaching. Jack had added her to his car insurance and they would shortly leave to begin the long drive down to Newquay. They'd booked a hotel overnight in Bodmin, but he'd promised his mother they'd be with the family for Christmas breakfast, so it would mean an early start the next day.

'I'll just say goodbye to Dad and Kerry and we'd better make a move,' she said. Jack nodded and intertwined his fingers with hers as they walked inside to where the newlyweds were in the hotel reception pulling shards of confetti from their hair and laughing.

'Dad, I need to head off.' Beatrice tapped him on the arm. 'We've got a long drive.'

'Of course.' He nodded. 'Come here and give your old dad a hug and a kiss goodbye, eh?' He pulled her in so she was enveloped in his arms and pressed against his chest. He smelled as he always did, of security, and of love. For a while she'd lost that, but everything was right now; like her tarot cards had been reunited, so had her family. 'Thank you for coming,' he whispered in her ear so only she could hear him. 'I know how hard it must be for you, which is why I appreciate it all the more.'

'Don't, Dad.' Beatrice laughed shakily. 'You'll have me crying again. I'm pleased that we came, I'm glad I realised in time that Mum would have wanted me to be here. There's a time for running away, and a time to come home.' Turning to Kerry, she hugged the other woman, who held on to her tightly.

'Thank you,' she said. 'You being here has meant the world to your dad. And now, before you go, the most important part of the day.' Stepping backwards, she shouted, 'Gather round, ladies!'

The other female guests, five in total, wandered into the hall to find Kerry standing on the stairs with her back to the rest of them, her wedding bouquet of tight red rosebuds held aloft in her hands. Once again everyone counted down before the flowers flew through the air. Beatrice, who had no intention of attempting to catch them found them flying straight towards her, hitting her in the chest before she grabbed them. Everyone cheered and Kerry, still standing on the stairs, winked at her.

* * *

The drive to Bodmin was quiet and reasonably quick, the other holiday traffic now all at its destinations. Beatrice had laid the bouquet on the parcel rack where she kept looking at them and smiling.

'Don't worry, it's just a silly old custom,' she'd reassured Jack. 'My dad won't be expecting you to turn up requesting to see him.' But Jack had just given her a sideways smile and said nothing.

After leaving their hotel early on Christmas morning they continued their drive down into Cornwall. Ignoring the sat nav as they approached Jack's parents' home, he carried on driving until they arrived at the empty beach. Getting out of the car, they both stretched their legs, feeling cramped after so many hours in the car the previous day. Taking her hand, Jack led her down the steps and across the hard, damp sand to the edge of the sea where the tide was out. On the horizon the deep gold of the rising sun was starting to glow, like a lighthouse beacon illuminating the waves in front of it, gilding the tip of each one. Jack stood behind her and wrapped his arms around her.

'One journey ends, and another is just beginning,' he said.

'And no more running away,' Beatrice replied. 'Now I'm staying where I want to be.'

MORE FROM CLARE MARCHANT

Another book from Clare Marchant, *The House of the Witch*, is available to order now here:

https://mybook.to/HouseOfWitchBackAd

ACKNOWLEDGEMENTS

I can hardly believe that I'm writing the acknowledgements for my sixth book! Time, as they say, does indeed fly when you're enjoying yourself, and for me sitting in my little office and writing books is just the most wonderful thing to do.

Usually when I start writing my acknowledgements, I like to explain a little about how I arrived at the plot for the book and the historical nugget which attracted my attention, sending me off down rabbit holes of research. This book, however, has been rather different; this time the idea wasn't inspired by a person or an event in history, but rather my interest in tarot cards. Although, of course, I did find myself disappearing into the realms of research to learn more of their history, and whilst doing that I discovered that Milan was indeed ravaged by the plague in 1629.

Portia came to me as a mysterious Italian living in London, a woman with secrets and a past. I loved the idea of her reading tarot cards and being able to help other women through them. I also wanted Beatrice to have a small shop with dark corners which would be a perfect foil for her cards. Once I had those two strong women the rest of the story just flowed!

But writing a book – my piece of the process – is only one part of it being published. There are a lot of people who have worked very hard to ensure that this book is as good as it possibly can be, and this is my opportunity to give my heartfelt thanks to all of them. First of all, my thanks must go to my amazing editor, Isobel Akenhead, who always knows just the right way to fix things and never minds if I email with daft questions! You really are the best. And also thank you to the other fantastic people at Boldwood Books, Amanda Ridout, Wendy Neale, Claire Fenby, Isabelle Flynn, Hayley Russell, Grace Cooper and Ben Wilson. And also a huge thank you to Rachel Odendaal for all the brilliant marketing you do. Also many, many thanks to my amazing cover designer, Jane Dixon-Smith (another stunning cover!), my copy editor, Debra Newhouse and my proofreader Anna Paterson. And thanks as ever to my amazing agent, Ella Kahn; I really appreciate everything that you do for me, you are the best.

Writing is a very solitary occupation so I would be nowhere without my writing chums, especially those known to me as my fellow Fivers: Jenni Keer, Heidi Swain, Rosie Hendry and Ian Wilfred, and this book is for them. Endless support, endless love and endless laughs – October is now the highlight of my year. And a special thank you to my virtual office buddy, Jenni Keer, who is often on the receiving end of my gripes when I'm struggling with some part of the writing and is always available for brainstorming or with virtual coffee. Or virtual gin, depending on the size of the problem! A special mention must go to Kate Smith toiling away in the satellite office, thank you for some great office chat.

And gratitude, as ever, to my wonderful children, D, T, L, B, I and G. You're like my personal homegrown fan club! Thank you for always being there with your support and love. My final thanks and love go of course to my dearest husband, Des: golf widow-maker, supreme roadie and milky brew producer. What would I be without you?

If you've enjoyed reading *Daughter of the Tarot*, do please come and find me on Instagram and Facebook and say hello! It's always such a pleasure to hear from my lovely readers.

ABOUT THE AUTHOR

Clare Marchant is the author of dual timeline historical fiction. Her books have been translated into seven languages, and she is a USA Today bestseller. Clare spends her time writing and exploring local castles, or visiting the nearby coast.

Sign up to Clare Marchant's mailing list for news, competitions and updates on future books.

Follow Clare on social media here:

facebook.com/claremarchantauthor
x.com/claremarchant1
instagram.com/claremarchantauthor
tiktok.com/@claremarchantauthor

Letters from
the past

Discover page-turning
historical novels from
your favourite authors
and be transported
back in time

*Join our book club
Facebook group*

https://bit.ly/SixpenceGroup

*Sign up to our
newsletter*

https://bit.ly/LettersFrom
PastNews

Boldwood

Boldwood Books is an award-winning fiction publishing company seeking out the best stories from around the world.

Find out more at www.boldwoodbooks.com

Join our reader community for brilliant books, competitions and offers!

Follow us
@BoldwoodBooks
@TheBoldBookClub

Sign up to our weekly
deals newsletter
https://bit.ly/BoldwoodBNewsletter